**Mary Higgins Clark**'s books are world-wide bestsellers. She is the author of twenty-five suspense novels; three collections of short stories; a historical novel, *Mount Vernon Love Story*; and a memoir, *Kitchen Privileges*. She is co-author with her daughter Carol Higgins Clark of four suspense novels. She lives with her husband, John Conheeney, in Saddle River, New Jersey.

### PRAISE FOR MARY HIGGINS CLARK

'Clark plays out her story like the pro that she is . . . flawless'
*Daily Mirror*

'Mary Higgins Clark's awesome gift for storytelling has always been the secret of her strength as a suspense novelist. But let's credit her as well for something more subtle – her intuitive grasp of the anxieties of everyday life that can spiral into full-blown terror' Marilyn Stasio, *New York Times*

'There's something special about Clark's thrillers . . . the compassion she extends to her characters' *Publishers Weekly*

'The "Queen of Suspense" is renowned for her fast-moving prose and dazzling plot twists' *Good Book Guide*

'Should come with a warning: start in the evening and you'll be reading late into the night' *USA Today*

ALSO BY MARY HIGGINS CLARK, AVAILABLE FROM POCKET BOOKS UK

I Heard That Song Before
Two Little Girls in Blue
No Place Like Home
Night-time Is My Time
Second Time Around
Kitchen Privileges
Daddy's Little Girl
On the Street Where You Live
Before I Say Good-bye
We'll Meet Again
All Through the Night
You Belong to Me
Pretend You Don't See Her
My Gal Sunday
Moonlight Becomes You
Silent Night
Let Me Call You Sweetheart
Remember Me
Weep No More, My Lady
Stillwatch
A Cry in the Night
The Cradle Will Fall
A Stranger Is Watching
Where Are the Children?

BY MARY HIGGINS CLARK AND CAROL HIGGINS CLARK

Santa Cruise
The Christmas Thief
He Sees You When You're Sleeping
Deck The Halls

# MARY HIGGINS CLARK

## WEEP NO MORE, MY LADY

POCKET
BOOKS

LONDON • SYDNEY • NEW YORK • TORONTO

First published in Great Britain by William Collins Sons and Co. Ltd, 1987
First published by Pocket Books UK, 1996
This edition published by Pocket Books UK, 2007
An imprint of Simon & Schuster UK Ltd
A CBS COMPANY

3 5 7 9 10 8 6 4

Simon & Schuster UK Ltd
1st Floor
222 Gray's Inn Road
London WC1X 8HB

Simon & Schuster Australia
Sydney

www.simonandschuster.co.uk

A CIP catalogue record for this book is available from the British Library

ISBN: 978-1-84739-298-5

Printed and bound by
CPI Group (UK) Ltd, Croydon, CR0 4YY

*For my grandchildren . . .*
*Elizabeth Higgins Clark*
*and*
*Andrew Warren Clark*
*the two "Dirdrews"*
*With love, amusement and delight.*

# Acknowledgments

*Stillwatch*, my last novel, was set in Washington, D.C. Special thanks are in order for the good friends who assisted me in my attempt to give that book an authentic Washington flavor.

Mrs. Frances Humphrey Howard, sister of the late Vice-President Hubert H. Humphrey, generously shared her vast knowledge of life in the nation's capital with me. She and her network of friends were always readily available to answer my questions about everything from protocol to the inner workings of Congress.

John and Catherine Keeley assisted me in creating the Cable Network background and planning the crucial travel times and routes. William Jackman, vice-president of the Air Transport Association of America, lent his expertise to guide me in the technical aspects of a vital airline investigation.

Abiding thanks to my editor, Michael V. Korda, whose perception and understanding make it a challenge and a pleasure to embark on the long road between story concept and completed novel.

Finally, my love and gratitude to my agent, Pat Myrer, who before her retirement helped me to plan this new book and christened it with the title *Weep No More, My Lady*.

# Prologue
## July, 1969

*The Kentucky sun was blazing hot. Eight-year-old Elizabeth huddled in a corner of the narrow porch, trying to tuck herself into the thin band of shade from the overhang. Her hair was heavy on her neck even though she had tied it back with a ribbon. The street was deserted; almost everyone was taking a Sunday-afternoon nap or had gone to the local pool. She wanted to go swimming too, but she knew better than to ask. Her mother and Matt had been drinking all day, and they'd begun to quarrel. She hated it when they fought, especially in summer, when the windows were open. All the kids would stop playing and listen. Today's fight had been really loud. Her mother had screamed bad words at Matt until he hit her again. Now they were both asleep, sprawled on the bed with no cover on them, the empty glasses on the floor beside them.*

*She wished her sister, Leila, didn't work every Saturday and Sunday. Before she took the Sunday job, Leila used to call it their day, and she'd taken*

*Elizabeth around with her. Most of the nineteen-year-old girls like Leila were hanging around with boys, but Leila never did. She was going to go to New York to be an actress, not get stuck in Lumber Creek, Kentucky. "The trouble with these hick towns, Sparrow, is that everybody marries right out of high school and ends up with whiny little kids and Pablum all over their cheerleader sweaters. That won't be me."*

*Elizabeth liked to hear Leila talk about how it would be when she was a star, but it was scary too. She couldn't imagine living in this house with Mama and Matt without Leila.*

*It was too hot to play. Quietly she stood up and smoothed her T-shirt under the waistband of her shorts. She was a thin child with long legs and a spray of freckles across her nose. Her eyes were wide-set and mature—"Queen Solemn Face" Leila called her. Leila was always making up names for people—sometimes funny names; sometimes, if she didn't like the people, pretty mean ones.*

*If anything, the inside of the house was hotter than the porch. The glaring four-o'clock sun shone through the dingy windows, onto the couch with its sagging springs and the stuffing that was beginning to come out at the seams, and the linoleum floor, so old that you couldn't even tell what color it had been, cracked and buckled under the sink. They'd lived here for four years now. Elizabeth could vaguely remember the other house, in Milwaukee. It was a little bit bigger, with a real kitchen and two bathrooms and a big yard. Elizabeth was tempted to straighten up the living room, but she knew that as soon as Matt got up the room would be a mess again, with beer bottles and cigar ashes and his clothes dropped where he shed them. But maybe it would be worth a try.*

*Snores, unpleasant and gruff, came from behind the open door of Mama's bedroom. She peeked in. Mama and Matt must have made up their fight. They were all wrapped up in each other, his right leg thrown over her left, his face buried in her hair. She hoped they'd wake up before Leila got home. Leila hated to see them like that. "You must bring your friends to visit Mama and her fiancé," she'd whisper to Elizabeth in her actressy voice. "Show off your elegant background."*

*Leila must be working overtime. The drive-in was near the beach, and sometimes on hot days a couple of the waitresses didn't show up. "I've got my period," they'd whine to the manager on the phone. "Real bad cramps."*

*Leila had told her about that and explained what it meant. "You're only eight and that's young, but Mama never got around to telling me, and when it happened I could hardly walk home, my back hurt so much, and I thought I was dying. I won't let that happen to you, and I don't want other kids hinting around like it's something crazy."*

*Elizabeth did the best she could to make the living room look better. She pulled down the shades three-quarters of the way, so that the sun didn't glare so much. She emptied the ashtrays and washed the tops of the tables and threw away the beer bottles that Matt and Mama had emptied before their fight. Then she went into her room. It was just big enough to hold a cot, a bureau and a chair with a broken cane seat. Leila had given her a white chenille bedspread for her birthday and bought a secondhand bookcase which she'd painted red and hung on the wall.*

*At least half the books in the bookcase were plays. Elizabeth selected one of her favorites,* Our Town. *Leila had played Emily last year in high school, and she'd rehearsed her part with Elizabeth so often that Elizabeth knew the part too. Sometimes in arithmetic class she'd read a favorite play in her mind. She liked it a lot more than chanting times tables.*

*She must have dozed off, because when she opened her eyes, Matt was bending over her. His breath smelled of tobacco and beer, and when he smiled he breathed heavier and that made it worse. Elizabeth pulled back, but there was no way to escape him. He patted her leg. "Must be a pretty dull book, Liz."*

*He knew that she liked to be called by her whole name.*

*"Is Mama awake? I can start to fix supper."*

*"Your mama is going to be sleeping for a while. Why don't I just have me a little lie-down and maybe you and I can read together?" In an instant, Elizabeth was pushed against the wall and Matt*

*was taking up all the room on the cot. She began to squirm. "I guess I'll get up and start to make hamburgers," she said, trying not to sound scared.*

*His grip was tight on her arms. "Give Daddy a nice big squeeze first, honey."*

*"You're not my daddy." Suddenly she felt trapped. She wanted to call Mama, to try to wake her up, but now Matt was kissing her.*

*"You're a pretty little girl," he said. "You're going to be a real beauty when you grow up." His hand was moving up her leg now.*

*"I don't like that," she said.*

*"Like what, baby?"*

*And then over Matt's shoulder she could see Leila in the doorway. Her green eyes were dark with anger. In a second, she was across the room, pulling Matt's hair so hard his head yanked back, shouting words at him that Elizabeth didn't understand. And then she screamed, "Bad enough what those other bastards did to me, but I'll kill you before you start on her!"*

*Matt's feet hit the floor with a thud. He pulled to one side, trying to get away from Leila. But she kept twisting his long hair, so that every move he made hurt. He began to yell back at Leila and try to hit her.*

*Mama must have heard the noise, because her snoring stopped. She came into the room, a sheet wrapped around her, her eyes circled and bleary, her pretty red hair disheveled. "What's going on* here?" she mumbled in a sleepy, angry voice, and Elizabeth saw the bruise on her forehead.

"You better tell this crazy kid of yours that when I'm just being nice and reading to her sister, she better not act like there's something wrong with it." Matt sounded mad, but Elizabeth could tell he was scared.

"And you'd better tell this filthy child molester to get out of here or I'll call the police." With a final tug, Leila released Matt's hair, stepped around him and sat on the cot with Elizabeth, hugging her tight.

Mama started to yell at Matt; then Leila started to yell at Mama, and in the end, Mama and Matt went to their room and kept on fighting; then there were long silences. When they came out of the room, they were dressed and said everything was a misunderstanding and as long as the girls were together, they'd just go out for a while.

After they left, Leila said, "Want to open a can of soup and maybe fix us a hamburger? I've got to do some thinking." Obediently Elizabeth went into the kitchen and prepared the meal. They ate in silence, and Elizabeth realized how glad she was that Mama and Matt were gone. When they were home, they were either drinking and kissing or fighting and kissing. Either way it was awful.

Finally, Leila said, "She'll never change."

"Who?"

"Mama. She's a boozer, and if it isn't one guy it

*will be another, until she just runs out of all the men left alive. But I can't leave you with Matt."*

*Leave! Leila couldn't be leaving. . . .*

*"So get packed," Leila said. "If that creep is starting to paw you, you're not safe here. We're going to take the late bus to New York." Then she reached over and tousled Elizabeth's hair. "God alone knows how I'll manage when we get there, Sparrow, but I promise I'll take care of you."*

*Later, Elizabeth was to remember that moment so clearly. Leila's eyes, emerald green again, the anger gone, but with a steely look in them; Leila's slim, taut body and catlike grace; Leila's brilliant red hair brightened even more by the light from the overhead fixture; Leila's rich, throaty voice saying, "Don't be scared, Sparrow. It's time to shake the dust of our old Kentucky home off our feet!"*

*Then with a defiant laugh, Leila began to sing, "Weep no more, my lady. . . ."*

# Saturday,
## August 29, 1987

# 1

Pan American flight 111 from Rome began to circle on its final approach to Kennedy Airport. Elizabeth pressed her forehead against the glass, drinking in the brilliance of the sun gleaming on the ocean, the distant outline of the Manhattan skyscrapers. This was the moment she had once loved at the end of a trip, the sense of coming home. But today she passionately wanted to be able to stay on the plane, to go wherever its next destination might be.

"It's a lovely sight, isn't it?" When she'd boarded the plane, the grandmotherly-looking woman next to her had smiled pleasantly and opened her book. Elizabeth had been relieved; the last thing she'd wanted was a seven-hour conversation with a stranger. But now it was all right. They'd be landing in a few minutes. She agreed that it was a lovely sight.

"This was my third trip to Italy," her seatmate continued. "But it's the last time I'll go in August. Tourists all over the place. And so terribly hot. What countries did you visit?"

The plane banked and began its descent. Elizabeth decided it was just as easy to give a direct answer as to be noncommittal. "I'm an actress. I was working on a film in Venice."

"How exciting. My first impression was that you reminded me a little of Candy Bergen. You're just about as tall as she is and have the same lovely blond hair and blue-gray eyes. Should I know your name?"

"Not at all."

There was a faint bump as the plane landed on the runway and began taxiing. To deter any more questions, Elizabeth made a business of pulling her carry-on bag from under the seat and checking its contents. If Leila were here, she thought, there wouldn't be any question about identifying *her*. Everyone recognized Leila LaSalle. But Leila would have been in first class, not coach.

*Would have been.* After all these months, it was time the reality of her death set in.

A newsstand just beyond the Customs enclosure had stacks of the early-afternoon edition of the *Globe*. She couldn't help seeing the headline: TRIAL BEGINS SEPTEMBER 8. The lead read: "A visibly angry Judge Michael Harris scathingly denied further postponements in the murder trial of multimillionaire Ted Winters." The rest of the front page was filled with a blowup of Ted's face. There was a stunned bitterness in his eyes, a rigid set to his mouth. It was a picture snapped after he'd learned that the grand jury had indicted him for the murder of his fiancée, Leila LaSalle.

* * *

As the cab sped toward the city, Elizabeth read the story—a rehash of the details of Leila's death and the evidence against Ted. Pictures of Leila were splashed over the next three pages of the paper: Leila at a premiere, with her first husband; Leila on safari, with her second husband; Leila with Ted; Leila accepting her Oscar—stock publicity shots. One of them caught Elizabeth's eye. In it, Leila had a hint of softness in her smile, a suggestion of vulnerability that contrasted with the arrogant tilt of her chin, the mocking expression in her eyes. Half the young girls in America had imitated that expression, copied Leila's way of tossing her hair back, of smiling over her shoulder. . . .

"Here we are, lady."

Startled, Elizabeth looked up. The cab had stopped in front of the Hamilton Arms, at Fifty-seventh Street and Park Avenue. The paper slid off her lap. She forced herself to try to sound calm. "I'm so sorry. I gave you the wrong address. I want to go to Eleventh and Fifth."

"I already turned off the meter."

"Then start a new fare." Her hands shook as she fumbled for her wallet. She sensed the doorman was approaching and did not raise her eyes. She did not want to be recognized. Unthinkingly she had given Leila's address. This was the building where Ted had murdered Leila. Here, in a drunken rage, he had pushed her off the terrace of her apartment.

Elizabeth began to shiver uncontrollably at the

image she could not banish from her mind: Leila's beautiful body, wrapped in the white satin pajamas, her long red hair cascading behind her, plummeting forty stories to the concrete courtyard.

And always the questions. . . . Was she conscious? How much did she realize?

How awful those last seconds must have been for her!

If I had stayed with her, Elizabeth thought, it never would have happened. . . .

# 2

After a two-month absence, the apartment felt close and stuffy. But as soon as she opened the windows, a breeze blew in, carrying the peculiarly satisfying combination of scents that was so specially New York: the pungent aura of the small Indian restaurant around the corner, a hint of the flowers from the terrace across the street, the acrid smell of fumes from the Fifth Avenue buses, a suggestion of sea air from the Hudson River. For a few minutes Elizabeth breathed deeply and felt herself begin to unwind. Now that she was here, it was good to be home. The job in Italy had been another escape, another temporary respite. But never out of her mind was the realization that eventually she would have to go to court, as a prosecution witness against Ted.

She unpacked quickly and placed her plants in the sink. It was clear that the superintendent's wife had not honored her promise to water them regularly. After plucking away the dead leaves, she turned to the mail that was stacked on the dining-room table. Rapidly she skimmed through it, tossing out ads and coupons, separating personal letters from bills. She smiled eagerly at the beautiful handwriting on one envelope and the precise return address in the upper corner: *Miss Dora Samuels, Cypress Point Spa, Pebble Beach, California.* Sammy. But before she read that one, Elizabeth reluctantly opened the business-size envelope with the return address OFFICE OF THE DISTRICT ATTORNEY.

The letter was brief. It was a confirmation that she would phone Assistant District Attorney William Murphy upon her return on August 29 and make an appointment to review her testimony.

Even reading the newspaper and giving Leila's address to the cabbie had not prepared her for the shock of this official notice. Her mouth went dry. The walls seemed to close in around her. The hours she had testified at the grand jury hearings flashed through her mind. The time she had fainted on the stand after being shown the pictures of Leila's body. Oh, God, she thought, it was starting all over again. . . .

The phone rang. Her "Hello" was barely audible.

*Mary Higgins Clark*

"Elizabeth," a voice boomed. "How are you? You're on my mind."

It was Min von Schreiber! Of all people! Elizabeth instantly felt wearier. Min had given Leila her first modeling job, and now she was married to an Austrian baron and owned the glamorous Cypress Point Spa in Pebble Beach, California. She was an old and dear friend; but Elizabeth didn't feel up to her today. Still, Min was one of the people Elizabeth could never say no to.

Elizabeth tried to sound cheerful. "I'm fine, Min. A little tired, maybe. I just got home a few minutes ago."

"Don't unpack. You're coming to the Spa tomorrow morning. There's a ticket waiting at the American Airlines counter. The usual flight. Jason will pick you up at the airport in San Francisco."

"Min, I can't."

*"As my guest."*

Elizabeth almost laughed. Leila had always said those were the three hardest words for Min to utter. "But, Min—"

"No 'buts.' When I saw you in Venice you looked too thin. That damn trial will be hell. So come. You need rest. You need pampering."

Elizabeth could see Min, her raven-black hair coiled around her head, always assuming in her imperious way that what she wanted was automatically granted. After more futile protests in which she listed all the reasons why she should not come, could not, she heard herself agreeing to Min's plans.

"Tomorrow, then. It will be good to see you, Min."
She was smiling when she put the receiver down.

Three thousand miles away, Minna von Schreiber
waited for the connection to break, then immediately began to dial another number. When she
reached her party, she whispered, "You were right.
It was easy. She agreed to come. *Don't forget to act
surprised when you see her.*"

Her husband entered the room as she was talking.
He waited until the call was completed, then burst
out, "You did invite her, then?"

Min looked up, defiantly. "Yes, I did."

Helmut von Schreiber frowned. His china-blue
eyes darkened. "After all my warnings? Minna,
Elizabeth could pull this house of cards down
around our ears. By the end of the week, you will
regret that invitation as you have never regretted
anything in your life."

Elizabeth decided to get her call to the district
attorney over with immediately. William Murphy
was obviously glad to hear from her. "Miss Lange, I
just started to sweat you out."

"I told you I'd be back today. I wouldn't have
expected to find you in on Saturday."

"There's a lot of work. We definitely go to trial on
September eighth."

"I read that."

"I'll need to review your testimony with you so it
will be fresh in your mind."

"It's never *not* been in my mind," Elizabeth said.

"I understand. But I have to discuss the kind of questions the defense attorney will ask you. I suggest you come in on Monday for several hours and then let's plan to have long sessions next weekend. You *will* be around?"

"I'm leaving tomorrow morning," she told him. "Can't we talk about everything on Friday?"

She was dismayed at the answer. "I'd rather have one preliminary meeting. It's only three o'clock. You could be down here in a cab in fifteen minutes."

Reluctantly she agreed. Glancing at Sammy's letter, she decided to wait until she came back to read it. At least it would be something to look forward to. Showering quickly, she twisted her hair into a topknot and put on a blue cotton jumpsuit and sandals.

Half an hour later, she was sitting across from the assistant district attorney in his crowded office. The furniture consisted of his desk, three chairs and a row of battleship-gray steel files. There were expandable cardboard files piled on his desk, on the floor and on top of the metal cabinets. William Murphy seemed unaware of the messiness of his work space—or else, Elizabeth thought, he had finally come to terms with what could not be changed.

A balding, chubby-faced man in his late thirties with a strong New York accent, Murphy conveyed an impression of keen intelligence and driving energy. After the grand jury hearings, he had told her that her testimony was the main reason Ted had been indicted. She knew he considered that high praise.

Now he opened a thick file: *The People of the State of New York* v. *Andrew Edward Winters III*. "I know how hard this is for you," he said. "You're going to be forced to relive your sister's death, and with that all the pain you experienced. And you're going to testify against a man you liked and trusted."

"Ted killed Leila; the man I knew doesn't exist."

"There are no 'ifs' in this case. He deprived your sister of her life; it's my job—with your help—to see that he's deprived of his freedom. The trial will be a terrible ordeal for you, but I promise that once it's over it will be easier to get on with your own life. After you are sworn, you will be asked to state your name. I know 'Lange' is your stage name. Be sure to tell the jury your legal name is LaSalle. Let's review your testimony again.

"You will be asked if you lived with your sister."

"No, when I left college I got my own apartment."

"Are your parents living?"

"No, my mother died three years after Leila and I came to New York, and I never knew my father."

"Now let's review again your testimony, starting with the day before the murder."

"I had been out of town for three months with a stock company. . . . I got in on Friday night, March twenty-eighth, just in time to catch the last preview of Leila's play."

"How did you find your sister?"

"She was obviously under a terrible strain; she kept forgetting her lines. Her performance was a shambles. Between acts I went to her dressing room. She never drank anything but a little wine, and yet she was drinking straight Scotch. I took it from her and poured it down the sink."

"How did she respond?"

"She was furious. She was a totally different person. She had never been a big drinker, but she was suddenly drinking a lot. . . . Ted came into the dressing room. She shouted at both of us to get out."

"Were you surprised by her behavior?"

"I think it would be more accurate to say that I was shocked."

"Did you discuss it with Winters?"

"He seemed bewildered. He'd been away a lot too."

"On business?"

"Yes. I suppose so. . . ."

"The play went badly?"

"It was a disaster. Leila refused to come out for a curtain call. When it was over we went on to Elaine's."

"Who do you mean by 'we'?"

"Leila . . . Ted and Craig . . . myself . . . Syd and Cheryl . . . Baron and Baroness von Schreiber. We were all close friends."

"You will be asked to identify these people for the jury."

"Syd Melnick was Leila's agent. Cheryl Manning

is a well-known actress. Baron and Baroness von Schreiber own Cypress Point Spa in California. Min —the Baroness—used to have a model agency in New York. She gave Leila her first job. Ted Winters —everyone knows who he is, and he was Leila's fiancé. Craig Babcock is Ted's assistant. He's executive vice-president of Winters Enterprises."

"What happened at Elaine's?"

"There was a dreadful scene. Someone yelled to Leila that he'd heard her play was a turkey. She went wild. She shouted, 'You bet it's a turkey, but I'm wringing its neck. You hear that, everybody? I *quit*!' Then she fired Syd Melnick. She told him he had only stuck her in the play because he wanted his percentage—that for the last couple of years he'd been putting her in anything he could because he needed the money." Elizabeth bit her lip. "You have to understand this wasn't the real Leila. Oh, sure, she could get uptight when she was in a new play. She was a star. A perfectionist. But she never behaved like that."

"What did you do?"

"We all tried to calm her down. But it only made her worse. When Ted tried to reason with her, she took off her engagement ring and threw it across the room."

"How did he respond?"

"He was furious, but he tried not to show it. A waiter brought the ring back and Ted slipped it into his pocket. He tried to make a joke of it. He said something like 'I'll hold it till tomorrow when she's in better shape.' Then we got her to the car and brought her home. Ted helped me to put her to bed. I told him I'd have her call him in the morning, when she woke up."

"Now on the stand I'll ask you what their living arrangements were."

"He had his own apartment on the second floor in the same building. I spent the night with Leila. She slept past noon. When she woke up, she felt rotten. I gave her aspirin and she went back to bed. I phoned Ted for her. He was in his office. He asked me to tell her he'd come up about seven o'clock that evening."

Elizabeth felt her voice quaver.

"I'm sorry to have to keep going, but try to think of this as a rehearsal. The more prepared you are, the easier it will be for you when you are actually on the stand."

"It's all right."

"Did you and your sister discuss the previous night?"

"No. It was obvious she didn't want to talk about it. She was very quiet. She told me to go to my place and get settled. I had literally dropped my bags home and rushed to her play. She asked me to call her around eight and we'd have dinner together. I assumed she meant she and Ted and I would have dinner together. But then she said she wasn't going to take his ring back. She was through with him."

"Miss Lange, this is very important. Your sister

told you she was planning to break her engagement to Ted Winters?"

"Yes." Elizabeth stared down at her hands. She remembered how she had put those hands on Leila's shoulders, then run them across Leila's forehead. *Oh, stop it, Leila. You don't mean that.*

*But I do, Sparrow.*

*No, you don't.*

*Have it your way, Sparrow. But call me around eight, okay?*

The last moment of being with Leila, of putting the cold compress on her forehead, of tucking the blankets around her and thinking that in a few hours she'd be herself again, laughing and amused and ready to tell the story. "So I fired Syd and threw Ted's ring, and quit the play. How's that for a fast two minutes in Elaine's?" And then she'd throw back her head and laugh, and in retrospect it would suddenly become funny—a star having a public tantrum.

"I let myself believe it, because I wanted to believe it," Elizabeth heard herself telling William Murphy.

In a rush she began the rest of her testimony. "I phoned at eight. . . . Leila and Ted were arguing. She sounded as if she'd been drinking again. She asked me to call back in an hour. I did. She was crying. They were still quarreling. She had told Ted to get out. She kept saying she couldn't trust any man; she didn't want any man; she wanted me to go away with her."

"How did you respond?"

"I tried everything. I tried to calm her. I reminded her that she always got uptight when she was in a new show. I told her the play was really a good vehicle for her. I told her Ted was crazy about her and she knew it. Then I tried acting angry. I told her . . ." Elizabeth's voice faltered. Her face paled. "I told her she sounded just like Mama in one of her drunks."

"What did she say?"

"It was as if she hadn't heard me. She just kept saying, 'I'm finished with Ted. You're the only one I can ever trust. Sparrow, promise you'll go away with me.' "

Elizabeth no longer tried to check the tears that welled in her eyes. "She was crying and sobbing. . . ."

"And then . . ."

"Ted came back. He began shouting at her."

William Murphy leaned forward. The warmth disappeared from his voice. "Now, Miss Lange, this will be a crucial point in your testimony. On the stand, before you can say whose voice you heard, I have to lay a foundation so that the judge is satisfied that you truly recognized that voice. So this is how we'll do it. . . ." He paused dramatically.

"Question: You heard a voice?"

"Yes," Elizabeth said tonelessly.

"How loud was that voice?"

"Shouting."

"What was the tone of that voice?"

"Angry."

"How many words did you hear that voice say?"

In her mind, Elizabeth counted them. "Eleven words. Two sentences."

"Now, Miss Lange, had you ever heard that voice before?"

"Hundreds of times." Ted's voice was filling her ears. Ted, laughing, calling to Leila: *"Hey, Star, hurry up, I'm hungry"*; Ted deftly protecting Leila from an overly enthusiastic admirer: *"Get in the car, honey, quick"*; Ted coming to her own opening performance last year Off Broadway: *"I'm to memorize every detail to tell Leila. I can wrap it all up in three words: You were sensational. . . ."*

What was Mr. Murphy asking her? . . . "Miss Lange, did you *recognize* whose voice shouted at your sister?"

"Absolutely!"

"Miss Lange. *Whose* voice was that shouting in the background?"

"It was Ted's . . . Ted Winters'."

"What did he shout?"

Unconsciously she raised her own voice. " 'Put that phone down! I *told* you, put that phone down.' "

"Did your sister respond?"

"Yes." Elizabeth stirred restlessly. "Do we have to go through this?"

"It will be easier for you if you get used to talking about it before the trial. Now, what did Leila say?"

"She was still sobbing . . . she said, 'Get out of

here. You're *not* a falcon. . . .' And then the phone slammed down."

"She slammed the phone down?"

"I don't know which one of them did it."

"Miss Lange, does the word 'falcon' mean anything to you?"

"Yes." Leila's face filled Elizabeth's mind: the tenderness in Leila's eyes when she looked at Ted, the way she would go up and kiss him. "God, Falcon, I love you."

"Why?"

"It was Ted's nickname . . . my sister's pet name for him. She did that, you see. The people close to her—she gave them special names."

"Did she ever call anyone else by that name—the name *Falcon*?"

"No . . . never." Abruptly, Elizabeth got up and walked to the window. It was grimy with dust. The faint breeze was hot and muggy. She thought longingly of getting away from here.

"Only a few minutes more, I promise. Miss Lange, do you know what time the phone was slammed down?"

"Precisely nine thirty."

"Are you absolutely sure?"

"Yes. There must have been a power failure when I was away. I reset my clock that afternoon. I'm sure it was right."

"What did you do then?"

"I was terribly upset. I had to see Leila. I ran out.

It took me at least fifteen minutes to get a cab. It was after ten when I got to Leila's apartment."

"And there was no one there."

"No. I tried to phone Ted. There was no answer at his place. I just waited." Waited all night, not knowing what to think, half-worried, half-relieved; hoping that Leila and Ted had made up and were out somewhere, not knowing that Leila's broken body was lying in the courtyard.

"The next morning, when the body was discovered, you thought she must have *fallen* from the terrace? It was a rainy March night. Why would she have gone out there?"

"She loved to go out and stand and just look at the city. In any weather. I used to tell her to be careful . . . that railing wasn't very high. I thought she must have leaned over; she had been drinking; she fell. . . ."

She remembered: Together she and Ted had grieved. Hands entwined, they had wept at the memorial service. Later, he had held her when she could no longer control her racking sobs. "I know, Sparrow. I know," he said, comforting her. On Ted's yacht they had sailed ten miles out to sea to scatter Leila's ashes.

And then, two weeks later, an eyewitness had come forth and sworn she had seen Ted push Leila off the terrace at nine thirty-one.

"Without your testimony, that witness, Sally Ross, could be destroyed by the defense," she heard William Murphy saying. "As you know, she has a history of severe psychiatric problems. It's not good that she waited that length of time before coming forward with her story. The fact that her psychiatrist was out of town and she wanted to tell him first at least explains it somewhat."

"Without my testimony it's her word against Ted's, and he denies going back up to Leila's apartment." When she had heard about the eyewitness, she had been outraged. She had totally trusted Ted until this man, William Murphy, told her that Ted denied going back to Leila's apartment.

"You can swear that he was there, that they were quarreling, that the phone was slammed down at nine thirty. Sally Ross saw Leila pushed off the terrace at nine thirty-one. Ted's story that he left Leila's apartment at about ten after nine, went to his own apartment, made a phone call, then took a cab to Connecticut doesn't hold up. In addition to what you and that other woman testify, we also have a strong circumstantial case. The scratches on his face. His skin tissue under Leila's fingernails. The testimony of the cabbie that he was white as a sheet and trembling—he could hardly give directions to his place. And why the hell didn't he send for his own chauffeur to take him to Connecticut? Because he was in a panic, that's why! He can't come forward with proof of anyone he reached on the phone. He has a motive—Leila rejected him. But one thing you have to realize: the defense will harp on the fact that you and Ted Winters were so close after her death."

"We were the two people who loved her best," Elizabeth said quietly. "Or at least, I thought we were. Please, can I go now?"

"We'll leave it at that. You do look pretty beat. This is going to be a long trial, and it won't be pleasant. Try to relax next week. Have you decided where you'll be staying these next few days?"

"Yes. Baroness von Schreiber has invited me to be her guest at Cypress Point Spa."

"I hope you're joking."

Elizabeth stared at him. "Why would I joke about that?"

Murphy's eyes narrowed. His face flushed and his cheekbones suddenly became prominent. He seemed to be struggling not to raise his voice. "Miss Lange, I don't think you appreciate the seriousness of your position. Without you, the other witness would be annihilated by the defense. That means that your testimony is about to put one of the richest and most influential men in this country in prison for at least twenty years, and thirty if I can make Murder Two stick. If this were a Mafia case I'd have you hidden away in a hotel under an assumed name and with a police guard until this trial is over. Baron and Baroness von Schreiber may be friends of yours, but they're also friends of Ted Winters' and are coming to New York to testify for him. *And you seriously propose to stay with them at this time?*"

"I know that Min and the Baron are testifying as character witnesses for Ted," Elizabeth said. "They don't think he's capable of murder. If I hadn't heard him with my own ears I wouldn't have believed it either. They're following their conscience. I'm following mine. We all do what we have to do."

She was not prepared for the tirade Murphy let loose at her. His urgent, sometimes sarcastic words pounded in her ears. "There's something fishy about that invitation. You should see that for yourself. You claim the Von Schreibers loved your sister? Then ask yourself why the hell they're going to bat for her murderer. I insist you keep away from them, if not for my sake or your own neck then because you want justice for Leila."

In the end, embarrassed at his obvious contempt for her naïveté, Elizabeth agreed to call off the trip, promised that instead she'd go to East Hampton and there either visit friends or stay in a hotel.

"Whether you're alone or with someone, *be careful*," Murphy told her. Now that he had gotten his way, he attempted a smile; but it froze on his face, and the expression in his eyes was both grim and worried. "Never forget that without you as a witness, Ted Winters walks."

Even with the oppressive mugginess, Elizabeth decided to walk home. She felt like one of those punching bags that were weighted with sand and flopped from side to side, unable to avoid the blows rained on them. She knew the district attorney was right. She should have refused Min's invitation. She decided she wouldn't contact anyone in the Hamp-

tons. She'd check into a hotel and just lie on the
beach quietly for the next few days.

Leila had always joked, "Sparrow, you'll never
need a shrink. Put you in a bikini, dunk you in the
briny and you're in heaven." It was true. She remembered her delight in showing Leila her blue
ribbons for swimming. Eight years ago, she'd been a
runner-up for the Olympic team. For four summers
she'd taught water aerobics at Cypress Point Spa.

Along the way she stopped to pick up groceries—
just enough to have a salad for dinner and a quick
breakfast. As she walked the last two blocks home
she thought of how remote everything seemed—as
if she were seeing her whole life before Leila's
death through the far lens of a telescope.

Sammy's letter was on top of the mail on the
dinette table. Elizabeth reached for the envelope
and smiled at the exquisite handwriting. It so viv-
idly brought Sammy to mind—the frail, birdlike figure; the wise eyes, owlish behind rimless glasses; the
lace-edged blouses and sensible cardigans. Sammy
had answered Leila's ad for a part-time secretary
ten years ago and within a week had become indispensable. After Leila's death, Min had hired her as a
receptionist-secretary at the Spa.

Elizabeth decided to read the letter over dinner.
It took only a few minutes to change into a light
caftan, fix a salad and pour a glass of chilled chablis.
Okay, Sammy, time for our visit, she thought as she
slit the envelope.

The first page of the letter was predictable:

Dear Elizabeth,

I hope this finds you well and as content as possible. Each day I seem to miss Leila more and can only imagine how you feel. I do think that after the trial is behind you, it will get better.

Working for Min has been good for me, although I think I will be giving it up soon. I really have never recovered from that operation.

Elizabeth turned the page, read a few lines; then, as her throat closed, pushed aside the salad.

As you know, I've continued to answer the letters from Leila's fans. There are still three large bags to finish. The reason I am writing is I have just found a very troubling anonymous letter. It is vicious and apparently was one in a series. Leila had not opened this one, but she must have seen its predecessors. Perhaps they would explain why she was so distraught those last weeks.

What is so terrible is that the letter I found was clearly written by someone who knew her well.

I had thought to enclose it in this envelope, but am not sure who is collecting your mail while you are away and would not want this seen by a stranger's eyes. Will you call me as soon as you return to New York?

My love to you.

Sammy

With a growing sense of horror, Elizabeth read and reread Sammy's letter. Leila had been receiving unsigned *very troubling, vicious* letters from someone who knew her well. Sammy, who never exaggerated, thought they might explain Leila's emotional collapse. For all these months, Elizabeth had lain awake trying to understand what had driven Leila into hysteria. Poison-pen letters from someone who knew her well. *Who? Why?* Did Sammy have any inkling?

She grabbed the phone and dialed the office at the Spa. Let Sammy answer, she prayed. But it was Min who picked up the receiver. Sammy was away, she told Elizabeth. She was visiting her cousin somewhere near San Francisco and would be back Monday night. "You'll see her then." Min's tone became curious. "You sound upset, Elizabeth. Is it something about Sammy that can't wait?"

It was the moment to tell Min that she was not coming. Elizabeth started to say, "Min, the district attorney . . ." Then she glanced down at Sammy's letter. The overwhelming need to see Sammy swept over her. It was the same kind of compulsion that had sent her rushing to Leila that last fateful night. She changed the sentence. "No hurry at all, Min. I'll see you tomorrow."

Before she went to bed, she wrote a note to William Murphy with the address and phone number of the Spa. Then she tore it up. To hell with his warning. She wasn't a Mafia witness; she was going to visit old friends—people she loved and trusted, people who loved and cared about her. Let him think she was in East Hampton.

*He had known for months that it would be necessary to kill Elizabeth. He had lived with the ever-present knowledge of the danger that she represented, and had planned to eliminate her in New York.*

*With the trial coming, her mind must be constantly reliving every moment of those last days. Inevitably, she would realize what she already knew—the fact that would seal his fate.*

*There were ways to get rid of her at the Spa and make it seem to be an accident. Her death would cause less official suspicion in California than in New York. He thought about her and her habits, looking for a way.*

*He consulted his watch. It was midnight in New York. Sweet dreams, Elizabeth, he thought.*

*Your time is running out.*

# Sunday,
## August 30

QUOTE FOR THE DAY:
*Where is the love, beauty and truth we seek?*
—Shelley

Good morning, dear guest!

Welcome to another day of luxury at Cypress Point Spa.

Besides your personalized program, we are happy to tell you that there will be special makeup classes in the women's spa between 10 A.M. and 4 P.M. Why not fill in one of your free hours learning the enchanting secrets of the world's most beautiful women, as taught by Madame Renford of Beverly Hills?

Today's guest expert in the men's spa is famous bodybuilder Jack Richard, who will share his personal workout schedule at 4 P.M.

The musical program after dinner is a very special one. Cellist Fione Navaralla, one of the most acclaimed new artists in England, will play selections by Ludwig van Beethoven.

We hope all our guests will have a pleasant and pampered day. Remember, to be really beautiful we must keep our minds tranquil and free of distressing or troubling thoughts.

Baron and Baroness Helmut von Schreiber

# 1

Min's longtime chauffeur, Jason, was waiting at the passenger gate, his silver-gray uniform gleaming in the sunny terminal. He was a small man with a trim, neat build, who had been a jockey in his youth. An accident had ended his racing career, and he had been working as a stable hand when Min hired him. Elizabeth knew that, like all of Min's people, he was intensely loyal to her. Now his leathery face broke into welcoming furrows as he saw her approach. "Miss Lange, it's good to have you back," he said. She wondered if, like her, he was remembering that the last time she came to the Spa she had been with Leila.

She bent over to kiss him on the cheek. "Jason, will you cut that 'Miss Lange' number? You'd think I was a paying guest or something." She noticed the discreet card in his hand with the name Alvirah Meehan on it. "You're picking up someone else?"

"Just one. I thought she'd be out by now. First-class passengers usually are."

Elizabeth reflected that few people economized

on air fare when they could afford to pay a minimum of three thousand dollars a week at Cypress Point Spa. With Jason she studied the disembarking passengers. Jason held the card up prominently as several elegantly dressed women passed, but they ignored it. "Hope she didn't miss the flight," he was murmuring as one final straggler came from the passageway. She was a bulky woman of about fifty-five with a large, sharp-featured face and thinning reddish-brown hair. The purple-and-pink print she was wearing was obviously expensive, but absolutely wrong for her. It bulged at the waist and thighs and hiked unevenly over her knees. Intuitively Elizabeth sensed that this lady was Mrs. Alvirah Meehan.

She spotted her name on the card and approached them eagerly, her smile delighted and relieved. Reaching out, she pumped Jason's hand vigorously. "Well, here I am," she announced. "And boy, am I glad to see you! I was so afraid there'd be a foul-up and no one would meet me."

"Oh, we never fail a guest."

Elizabeth felt her lips twitch at Jason's bewildered expression. Clearly Mrs. Meehan was not the usual Cypress Point guest. "Ma'am, may I have your claim checks?"

"Oh, that's nice. I hate to wait for luggage. Sort of a pain in the neck at the end of a trip. Course, Willy and I usually go Greyhound, and the bags are right there, but even so . . . I don't have too much stuff. I was going to buy a lot, but my friend, May, said,

'Alvirah, wait and see what other people are wearing. All these fancy places have shops. . . . You'll
pay through the nose,' she said, 'but at least you'll
get the right thing, you know what I mean.' " She
thrust her ticket envelope with the baggage stubs at
Jason and turned to Elizabeth. "I'm Alvirah
Meehan. Are you going to the Spa too? You sure
don't look like you need to, honey!"

Fifteen minutes later, they were settled in the
sleek silver limousine. Alvirah settled back against
the brocaded upholstery with a gusty sigh. "Now,
*that* feels good," she announced.

Elizabeth studied the other woman's hands. They
were the hands of a working person, thick-knuckled
and callused. The brightly colored fingernails were
short and stubby, even though the manicure looked
expensive. Her curiosity about Alvirah Meehan was
a welcome respite from thinking about Leila. Instinctively she liked the woman—there was something remarkably candid and appealing about her—
but who *was* she? What was bringing her to the Spa?

"I still can't get used to it," Alvirah continued
happily. "I mean, one minute, I'm sitting in my
living room soaking my feet. Let me tell you, cleaning five different houses a week is no joke, and the
Friday one was the killer—six kids and they're all
slobs and the mother's worse. Then we hit the lottery. We had all the winning numbers. Willy and I
couldn't believe it. 'Willy,' I said, 'we're rich.' And
he yelled, 'You bet we are!' You must have read
about it last month? Forty million dollars, and a

minute before, we didn't have two quarters to rub together."

"You won *forty million* dollars in the lottery?"

"I'm surprised you didn't see it. We're the biggest single winners in the history of the New York State lottery. How about that?"

"I think it's wonderful," Elizabeth said sincerely.

"Well, I knew what I wanted to do right away, and that was to get to Cypress Point Spa. I've been reading about it for ten years now. I used to dream about how it would be to spend time there and hobnob with the celebrities. Usually you have to wait months for a reservation, but I got one just like that!" She snapped her fingers.

Because Min undoubtedly recognized the publicity value of Alvirah Meehan's telling the world about her lifelong ambition to go to the Spa, Elizabeth thought. Min never missed a trick.

They were on the Coastal Highway. "I thought this was supposed to be a beautiful drive," Alvirah said. "It don't look so hot to me."

"A little farther on it becomes breathtaking," Elizabeth murmured.

Alvirah Meehan straightened up in the seat and turned to Elizabeth, studying her intently. "By the way, I've been talking so much I missed your name."

"Elizabeth Lange."

Large brown eyes, already magnified by thick-rimmed glasses, widened perceptibly. "I know who you are. You're Leila LaSalle's sister. She was my favorite actress in the whole world. I know all about Leila and you. I think the story of the two of you coming to New York when you were just a little girl is so beautiful. Two nights before she died, I saw a preview of her last play. Oh, I'm sorry—I didn't mean to upset you. . . ."

"It's all right. I just have a terrible headache. Maybe if I just rest a bit . . ."

Elizabeth turned her head toward the window and dabbed at her eyes. To understand Leila, you had to have lived that childhood, that trip to New York, the fear and the disappointments. . . . And you had to know that however good it sounded in *People* magazine, it wasn't a beautiful story at all. . . .

*It was a fourteen-hour bus ride from Lexington to New York. Elizabeth slept curled up in her seat, her head on Leila's lap. She was a little scared, and it made her sad to think of Mama coming home to find them gone, but she knew Matt would say, "Have a drink, honey" and pull Mama into the bedroom, and in a little while they'd be laughing and squealing and the springs of the bed would creak and groan. . . .*

*Leila told her which states they were going through: Maryland, Delaware, New Jersey. Then the fields were replaced with ugly tanks and the road got more and more crowded. At the Lincoln Tunnel, the bus kept stopping and starting. Elizabeth's stomach began to feel kind of funny. Leila* noticed. "Good God, Sparrow, don't get sick now. It's just another few minutes."

She couldn't wait to get off the bus. She just wanted to smell cool, clean air. But the air was heavy, and it was so hot—hotter even than at home. Elizabeth felt fretful and tired. She was about to complain, but then she saw how tired Leila looked.

They had just left the platform when a man came over to Leila. He was thin, and his dark hair was curly but started pretty far back. He had long sideburns and small brown eyes that got squinty when he smiled. "I'm Lon Pedsell," he said. "Are you the model the Arbitron Agency from Maryland sent?"

Of course Leila wasn't the model, but Elizabeth could tell she didn't want to just say no. "There wasn't anyone else my age on this bus" was the way she answered him.

"And obviously you are a model."

"I'm an actress."

The man brightened up as though Leila had given him a present. "This is a break for me, and I hope for you. If you can use a modeling job, you'd be perfect. The pay is one hundred dollars for the sitting."

Leila put down her bags and squeezed Elizabeth's shoulder. It was her way of saying, "Let me do the talking."

"I can tell that you're agreeable," Lon Pedsell said. "Come on. I've got my car outside."

*  *  *

*Elizabeth was surprised at his studio. When Leila talked about New York, she'd thought that every place Leila worked would be beautiful. But Lon Pedsell took them to a dirty street about six blocks from the bus terminal. Lots of people were sitting on stoops, and garbage was spilled all over the sidewalk. "I have to apologize for my temporary situation," he said. "I lost the lease on my place across town, and the new one is still being equipped."*

*The apartment he brought them to was on the fourth floor and as messy as Mama's house. Lon was breathing hard because he insisted on carrying the two big suitcases. "Why don't I get a Coke for your sister, and she can watch television while you pose?" he said to Leila.*

*Elizabeth could tell that Leila just wasn't sure what to do. "What kind of model am I supposed to be?" she asked.*

*"It's for a new swimsuit line. Actually, I'm doing the test shots for the agency. The girl they choose will do a whole series of ads. You're pretty lucky you ran into me today. I have a hunch you're just the type they have in mind."*

*He brought them into the kitchen. It was a tiny, dingy room with a small television set on a ledge over the sink. He poured a Coke for Elizabeth and wine for Leila and himself. "I'll have a Coke," Leila said.*

*"Suit yourself." He turned on the television set. "Now, Elizabeth, I'm going to close the door so I can*

*concentrate. You just stay here and keep yourself amused."*

Elizabeth watched three programs. Sometimes she could hear Leila saying in a loud voice, *"I don't like that idea,"* but she didn't sound scared, just kind of worried. After a while she came out. *"I'm finished, Sparrow. Let's get our bags."* Then she turned to Lon. *"Do you know where we can get a furnished room?"*

*"Would you like to stay here?"*

*"No. Just give me my hundred dollars."*

*"If you'll sign this release . . ."*

When Leila signed, he smiled over at Elizabeth. *"You must be proud of your big sister. She's on her way to becoming a famous model."*

Leila handed him the paper. *"Give me the hundred dollars."*

*"Oh, the agency will pay you. Here's their card. Just go over in the morning and they'll issue a check."*

*"But you said—"*

*"Leila, you really are going to have to learn the business. Photographers don't pay models. The agency pays when it gets the release."*

He didn't offer to help them carry down their bags.

A hamburger and milk shake at a restaurant called Chock Full o' Nuts made both of them feel better. Leila had bought a street map of New York

*City and a newspaper. She began to read the real
estate section. "Here's an apartment that sounds
about right: 'Penthouse; fourteen rooms, spectacu-
lar view, wraparound terrace.' Someday, Sparrow. I
promise."*

*They found an ad for an apartment to share.
Leila looked at the street map. "It doesn't look too
bad," she said. "Ninety-fifth Street and West End
Avenue isn't that far, and we can get a bus."*

*The apartment turned out to be okay, but the
woman's nice smile disappeared when she learned
that Elizabeth was part of the deal. "No kids," she
said flatly.*

*It was the same everywhere they went. Finally, at
seven o'clock, Leila asked a cabdriver if he knew of
any cheap but decent place to stay where she could
bring Elizabeth. He suggested a rooming house in
Greenwich Village.*

*The next morning they went to the model agency
on Madison Avenue to collect Leila's money. The
door of the agency was locked, and a sign read,
"PUT YOUR COMPOSITE IN THE MAILBOX." The
mailbox had a half-dozen manila envelopes in it
already. Leila pressed her finger on the bell. A voice
came over the intercom. "Do you have an appointment?"*

*"We're here to pick up my money," Leila said.*

*She and the woman began to argue. Finally the
woman shouted, "Get lost." Leila pressed the bell
again and didn't stop until someone yanked the*

*door open. Elizabeth shrank back. The woman had heavy dark hair all done up in braids on her head. Her eyes were coal black, and her whole face was terribly angry. The woman wasn't young, but she was beautiful. Her white silk suit made Elizabeth realize that the blue shorts she was wearing were faded and the dye on her polo shirt had run around the pocket. She had thought Leila looked so pretty when they started out, but next to this woman Leila seemed overdressed and shabby.*

*"Listen," the woman said, "if you want to leave your picture you can. You try barging in here again and I'll have you arrested."*

*Leila thrust out the paper in her hand. "You owe me one hundred dollars and I'm not leaving without it."*

*The woman took the paper, read it and began to laugh so hard she had to lean against the door. "You really* are *dumb! Those jokers pull that stuff on all you hicks. Where'd he pick you up? In the bus terminal? Did you end up in the sack with him?"*

*"No, I did not." Leila grabbed the paper, tore it up and ground the pieces under her heel. "Come on, Sparrow. That guy made a fool of me, but we don't have to give this bitch a good laugh about it."*

*Elizabeth could see that Leila was so upset she was about to cry and didn't want the woman to see it. She shook Leila's arm off her shoulder and stood in front of the woman. "I think you're mean," she said. "That man acted nice, and if he made my sister work for nothing you should feel sorry about it, not make fun of us."* She spun around and tugged Leila's hands. *"Let's go."*

They started for the elevator, and the woman called after them, "Come on back, you two." They ignored her. Then she yelled, "I said come back!"

Two minutes later they were in her private office.

"You've got possibilities," the woman told Leila. "But those clothes . . . You don't know a thing about makeup; you'll need a good haircut; you'll need composites. Did you pose in the raw for that creep?"

"Yes."

"Terrific. If you're any good, I'll submit you for an Ivory Soap commercial, and right then is when your picture will show up in a girlie magazine. He didn't take any movies of you, did he?"

"No. At least, I don't think so."

"That's something. From now on, I do the booking for you."

They left in a daze. Leila had a list of appointments at a beauty salon for the next day. Then she would meet the woman from the model agency at the photographer's. "Call me Min," the woman had said. "And don't worry about clothes. I'll bring everything you need."

Elizabeth was so happy her feet could hardly touch the ground, but Leila was very quiet. They walked down Madison Avenue. Well-dressed people hurried by; the sun was shining brightly; hot dog carts and pretzel stands seemed to be on every corner; buses and cars honked at each other; nearly *everyone ignored the red lights and sauntered through the heavy traffic. Elizabeth had a wonderful sense of being home. "I like it here," she said.*

*"So do I, Sparrow. And you saved the day for me. I swear, I don't know who's taking care of who. And Min is good people. But, Sparrow, there's something I've found out from that stinking father of mine, and from Mama's lousy boyfriends, and now from that bastard yesterday.*

*"Sparrow—I'm never going to trust a man again."*

# 2

Elizabeth opened her eyes. The car was sliding noiselessly past Pebble Beach Lodge, along the tree-lined road where glimpses of estate homes could be seen through hedges of bougainvillea and azaleas. It slowed down as it rounded a bend and the tree that gave Cypress Point Spa its name came into view.

Disoriented for a moment, she brushed the hair back from her forehead and looked around. Alvirah Meehan was beside her, a blissful smile on her face. "You must be worn out, poor thing," Alvirah said. "You've been asleep practically since we left the airport." She shook her head as she gazed out the window. "Now, this is really something!" The car passed through the ornate iron gates and wound its way up toward the main house, a rambling three-story ivory stucco mansion with pale blue shutters. Several swimming pools were dotted through the grounds near the clusters of bungalows. At the north end of the property there was a patio, with umbrella tables scattered around both sides of the Olympic-size pool. Identical adobe buildings were on either side of the pool. "These are the men's and women's spas," Elizabeth explained.

The clinic, a smaller edition of the main house, was at its right. A series of paths lined by high flowering hedges led to individual doorways. The treatment rooms were entered through these doors, and treatments were spaced far enough apart so that guests avoided encountering each other.

Then, as the limousine followed the curve of the driveway, Elizabeth gasped and leaned forward. Between the main house and the clinic, but placed well behind them, a huge new structure had come into view, its black marble exterior, accentuated by massive columns, making it loom like an ominous volcano about to erupt. Or like a mausoleum, Elizabeth thought.

"What's *that*?" Alvirah Meehan asked.

"It's a replica of a Roman bath. They had just broken ground for it when I was here two years ago. Jason, is it open yet?"

"Not finished, Miss Lange. The construction just goes on and on."

Leila had openly mocked the plans for the bath-house. "Another of Helmut's grand schemes for separating Min from her money," she said. "He won't be happy until Min is officially declared a shopping-bag lady."

The car stopped at the steps of the main house. Jason leaped out and rushed to open the door. Alvirah Meehan struggled back into her shoes and, stooping awkwardly, hoisted herself from the seat. "It's like sitting on the floor," she commented. "Oh, look, here comes Mrs. von Schreiber. I know her from her pictures. Or should I call her Baroness?"

Elizabeth did not answer. She stretched out her arms as Min descended the steps from the veranda, her gait rapid but stately. Leila had always compared Min in motion to the *Q.E. 2* steaming into harbor. Min was wearing a deceptively simple Adolfo print. Her luxurious dark hair was piled on her head in a swirling French knot. She pounced on Elizabeth and hugged her fiercely. "You're much too thin," she hissed. "In a swimsuit I bet you look scrawny." Another bear hug and Min turned her attention to Alvirah. "Mrs. Meehan. 'The world's luckiest woman.' We are *enchanted* to have you!" She eyed Alvirah up and down. "In two weeks, the world will think you were born with a forty-million-dollar spoon in your mouth."

Alvirah Meehan beamed. "That's the way I feel right now."

"Elizabeth, you go up to the office. Helmut is

waiting to see you. I'll escort Mrs. Meehan to her
bungalow, then join you."

Obediently Elizabeth went into the main house
and walked through the cool marble-floored foyer,
past the salon, the music room, the formal dining
rooms and up the sweeping staircase that led to the
private rooms. Min and her husband shared a suite
of offices that overlooked the front and both sides of
the property. From there Min could observe the
movements of guests and staff as they went back
and forth between the areas of activity. At dinner
she was frequently known to admonish a guest.
"You should have been in aerobics when I saw you
reading in the garden!" She also had an uncanny
knack of noticing when an employee kept a guest
waiting.

Elizabeth knocked softly on the door of the private office suite. When there was no answer she
opened it. Like every room in Cypress Point Spa,
the offices were furnished exquisitely. An abstract
watercolor by Will Moses hung on the wall over the
oyster-colored couch. An Aubusson rug shimmered
on the dark tile. The reception desk was authentic
Louis XV, but there was no one seated there. She
felt an immediate sense of sharp disappointment,
but reminded herself that Sammy would be back
tomorrow night.

Tentatively, she walked to the partially open door
of the office Min and the Baron shared, then gasped
in surprise. Baron Helmut von Schreiber was standing at the far wall, where pictures of Min's most

famous clients were hung. Elizabeth's eyes followed him, and she bit her lip to keep from crying out.

It was Leila's portrait Helmut was studying, the one Leila had posed for the last time she was here. The vivid green of Leila's dress was unmistakable, the brilliant red hair that floated around her face, the way she was holding up a champagne glass as though offering a toast.

Helmut's hands were clasped tightly behind his back. Everything about his stance suggested tension.

Elizabeth did not want him to know that he had been observed. Swiftly she retraced her steps to the reception room, opened and closed the door with a loud thud, then called, "Anyone home?"

An instant later he rushed from the inner office. The change in his demeanor was dramatic. This was the gracious, urbane European she had always known, with the warm smile, the kiss on both cheeks, the murmured compliment. "Elizabeth, you grow more beautiful every day. So young, so fair, so divinely tall."

"Tall, anyhow." Elizabeth stepped back. "Let me look at you, Helmut." She studied him carefully, observing that no trace of tension showed in his baby-blue eyes. His smile was relaxed and natural. His parted lips showed perfect white teeth. How had Leila described him? *"I swear, Sparrow, that guy makes me think of a toy soldier. Do you suppose Min winds him up in the morning? He may have decent ancestry, but I bet he never had more than a nickel behind him till he latched on to Min."*

*Elizabeth had protested, "He's a plastic surgeon, and certainly he's knowledgeable about spas. The place is famous."*

*"It may be famous," Leila had retorted, "but it costs a bundle to run, and I'd bet my last dollar even those prices can't carry that overhead. Listen, Sparrow, I should know. I've married two free-loaders so far, right? Sure he treats Min like a queen, but he's putting that tinted head on two-hundred-dollar pillowcases every night, and besides what she's spent on the Spa, Min's dumped a pile of dough into that broken-down castle of his in Austria."*

Like everyone else, Helmut had seemed grief-stricken at Leila's death, but now Elizabeth wondered if that had only been an act.

"Well, tell me. Am I all right? You look so troubled. Perhaps you have found some wrinkles?" His laugh was low, well bred, amused.

She made herself smile up at him. "I think you look splendid," she said. "Perhaps I'm just shocked to realize how long it's been since I've seen you."

"Come." He took her hand and led her to the grouping of Art Deco wicker furniture near the front windows. He grimaced as he sat down. "I keep trying to convince Minna that these objects were meant to be seen, not used. So tell me, how has it been for you?"

"Busy. Of course, that's the way I want it to be."

"Why haven't you come to see us before this?"

*Because in this place I knew I'd be seeing Leila everywhere I turned.* "I did see Min in Venice three months ago."

"And also, the Spa holds too many memories for you, yes?"

"It holds memories. But I've missed you two. And I'm looking forward to seeing Sammy. How do you think she's feeling?"

"You know Sammy. She never complains. But my guess would be—not well. I don't think she's ever recovered, either from the surgery or from the shock of Leila's death. And she is past seventy now. No great age physiologically, but still . . ."

The outer door closed with a decided thump, and Min's voice preceded her entrance. "Helmut, wait until you see the lottery winner. You have your work cut out for you. We'll need to arrange interviews for her. She'll make this place sound like seventh heaven."

She rushed across the room and embraced Elizabeth fiercely. "If you knew the nights I've lain awake worrying about you! How long can you stay?"

"Not very long. Just until Friday."

"That's only five days!"

"I know, but the district attorney's office has to review my testimony." Elizabeth realized how good it felt to have loving arms around her.

"What do they have to review?"

"The questions they'll be asking me at the trial.

The questions Ted's lawyer will be asking me. I thought telling the simple truth would be enough, but apparently the defense will try to prove I'm mistaken about the time of the phone call."

"Do *you* think you might be mistaken?" Min's lips were grazing her ear, her voice a suggestive stage whisper. Startled, Elizabeth pulled back from the embrace in time to see the warning frown on Helmut's face.

"Min, do you think if I had the slightest doubt—"

"All right," Min said hastily. "We shouldn't talk about that now. So you have five days. You're going to be pampered; you're going to rest. I made out your schedule myself. You start with a facial and massage this afternoon."

Elizabeth left them a few minutes later. The slanting rays of the sun danced on the beds of wild-flowers along the path to the bungalow Min had assigned her. Somewhere in her subconscious she experienced a sense of calm observing the brilliant checkerblooms, the wood roses, the flowering currant hedges. But the momentary tranquillity could not mask the fact that behind the warm welcome and seeming concern, Min and Helmut were different.

They were angry and worried and hostile. And that hostility was directed at *her*.

# 3

Syd Melnick did not find the drive from Beverly Hills to Pebble Beach enjoyable. For the entire four hours, Cheryl Manning sat like a stone, rigid and uncommunicative, in the seat beside him. For the first three hours she had not allowed him to put the top down on the convertible. She wasn't going to risk drying out her face and hair. It was only when they approached Carmel and she wanted to be recognized going through town that she'd permitted the change.

Occasionally during the long ride, Syd glanced over at her. There was no question she looked good. The blue-black hair exploding in a mass of tendrils around her face was sexy and exciting. She was thirty-six now, and what had once been a *gamin* quality had evolved into a sultry sophistication that became her well. *Dynasty* and *Dallas* were getting long in the tooth. Audiences eventually got restless. There was a definite move to say "Enough" to the steamy love affairs of women in their fifties. And in Amanda, Cheryl had finally found the role that could make her a superstar.

When that happened, Syd in turn would be a big-time agent again. An author was as good as his last book. An actor as bankable as his last picture. An agent needed megabucks deals to be considered topflight. It was again within his grasp to become a legend, the next Swifty Lazar. And *this* time, he told himself, he wouldn't screw it up at the casinos, or blow it on the horses.

He would know in a few days if Cheryl had the part. Just before they left, at Cheryl's insistence, he had phoned Bob Koenig at home. Twenty-five years ago, Bob, fresh out of college, and Syd, a studio gofer, had met on a Hollywood set and become friends. Now Bob was president of World Motion Pictures. He even *looked* the part of the new breed of studio head, with his rugged features and broad shoulders. Syd knew that he himself could be typecast for the stereotypical Brooklynite, with his long, slightly mournful face, receding curly hair and slight paunch that even rigorous exercise didn't help. It was another thing he envied Bob Koenig for.

Today Bob had let his irritation show. "Look, Syd, don't call me at home on a Sunday to talk business again! Cheryl did a damn good test. We're still seeing other people. You'll hear one way or another in the next few days. And let me give you a tip. Sticking her in that play last year when Leila LaSalle died was a lousy judgment call, and it's a big part of the problem with choosing her. Calling me at home on Sunday is a lousy judgment call too."

Syd's palms began to sweat at the memory of the conversation. Oblivious of the scenery, he pondered the fact that he had made the mistake of abusing a friendship. If he wasn't more careful, everyone he knew would be "in conference" when he phoned.

And Bob was right. He *had* made a terrible mistake, talking Cheryl into going into the play with only a few days' rehearsal. The critics had slaughtered her.

Cheryl had been standing next to him when he called Bob. She'd heard what Bob said about the play's being the reason she might not get the part. And of course, *that* triggered an explosion. Not the first one, nor the last.

That goddamn play! He'd believed in it enough to beg and borrow until he had a million dollars to invest in it! It could have been a smash hit. And then Leila had started boozing and trying to act as if the play were the problem. . . .

Anger parched Syd's throat. All he had done for that bitch, and she'd fired him in Elaine's in front of a roomful of show-business people, cursing him out at the top of her voice! And she knew how much he'd sunk into the play! He only hoped she'd been conscious enough to know what was happening before she hit the concrete!

They were driving through Carmel: crowds of tourists on the streets; the sun bright; everybody looking relaxed and happy. He took the long way and threaded along the busiest streets. He could hear people comment when they started to recognize Cheryl. Now, of course, she was smiling, little Miss Gracious! She needed an audience the way other people needed air and water.

They reached the gate to Pebble Beach. He paid the toll. They drove past Pebble Beach Lodge, the Crocker Woodland, to the gates of the Spa.

"Drop me off at my bungalow," Cheryl snapped. "I don't want to bump into anybody until I get myself together."

She turned to him and pulled off her sunglasses. Her extraordinary eyes blazed. "Syd, what are my chances of becoming Amanda?"

He answered the question as he had answered it a dozen times in the last week. "The best, baby," he said sincerely. "The best."

They'd better be, he told himself, or it was all over.

# 4

The *Westwind* banked, turned and began its descent into Monterey airport. With methodical care, Ted checked the instrument panel. It had been a good flight from Hawaii—smooth air every foot of the way, the cloud banks lazy and floating like cotton candy at a circus. Funny; he liked the clouds, liked to fly over them and through them, but even as a kid he had despised cotton candy. One more contradiction in his life . . .

In the copilot's seat John Moore stirred, a quiet

reminder that he was there if Ted elected to turn over the controls to him. Moore had been the chief pilot for Winters Enterprises for ten years. But Ted wanted to make this landing, to see how smoothly he could bring the plane in. Set the wheels down. Land on his feet. It was all one, wasn't it?

Craig had come forward an hour ago and urged him to let John take over.

"Cocktails are ready at your fahvoreet tahbl' in the cornaire, Monsieur Wintairs."

He'd done his flawless imitation of the captain at the Four Seasons.

"For Christ's sake," Ted had snapped, "no more of your impersonations today. I don't need that now."

Craig had known enough not to argue when Ted decided to stay at the controls.

The runway was rushing toward them. Ted eased the nose of the plane up slightly. How much longer would he be free to fly planes, to travel, to have a drink or not have a drink, to function as a human being? The trial would begin next week. He didn't like his new lawyer. Henry Bartlett was too pompous, too conscious of his own image. Ted could imagine Bartlett in a *New Yorker* ad, holding up a bottle of Scotch, the caption reading, "This is the only brand I ever serve my guests."

The main wheels touched the ground. The impact inside the plane was almost unnoticeable. Ted threw the engines into reverse. "Nice landing, sir," John said quietly.

Wearily, Ted brushed his hand over his forehead. He wished he could get John over the habit of calling him "sir." He also wished he could get Henry Bartlett over the habit of calling him "Teddy." Did all criminal lawyers think that because you need their services, they have the right to be condescending? An interesting question. Had circumstances been different, he wouldn't have had anything to do with a man like Bartlett. But firing the man who was supposed to be the best defense lawyer in the country at a time when you're facing a long prison sentence wouldn't be smart. He had always thought of himself as smart. He wasn't so sure anymore.

A few minutes later, they were in a limousine heading for the Spa. "I've heard a lot about the Monterey Peninsula," Bartlett commented as they turned onto Highway 68. "I still don't see why we couldn't have worked on the case at your place in Connecticut or your New York apartment; but you're paying the bills."

"We're here because Ted needs the kind of relaxation he gets at Cypress Point," Craig said. He did not bother to hide the edge in his voice.

Ted was sitting on the right side of the roomy back seat, Henry beside him. Craig had taken the seat facing them, next to the bar. Craig raised the lid of the bar and mixed a martini. With a half-smile he handed it to Ted. "You know Min's rules about booze. You'd better drink up fast."

Ted shook his head. "I seem to remember another time when I drank up fast. Have you got a cold beer in there?"

"Teddy, I absolutely have to insist that you stop referring to that night in a way that suggests you don't have complete recall."

Ted turned to look directly at Henry Bartlett, absorbing the man's silver hair, his urbane manner, the faint hint of an English accent in his voice. "Let's get something straight," he said. "You are not, I repeat *not* to call me Teddy again. My name, in case you don't remember it from that very sizable retainer, is Andrew Edward Winters. I have always been called Ted. If you find that too difficult to remember, you may call me Andrew. My grandmother always did. Nod if you understand what I just said."

"Take it easy, Ted," Craig said quietly.

"I'll take it a lot easier if Henry and I establish a few ground rules."

He felt his hand grip the glass. He was unraveling. He could feel it. These months since the indictment, he'd managed to keep his sanity by staying at his place in Maui, doing his own analysis of urban expansion and population trends, designing hotels and stadiums and shopping centers he would build when all this was over. Somehow he'd managed to make himself believe that something would happen, that Elizabeth would realize she was wrong about the time of the phone call, that the so-called eyewitness would be declared mentally incompetent . . .

But Elizabeth was sticking to her story, the eye-witness was adamant about her testimony and the trial was looming. Ted had been shocked when he realized his first lawyer was virtually conceding a guilty verdict. That was when he had hired Henry Bartlett.

"All right, let's put this aside until later," Henry Bartlett said stiffly. He turned to Craig. "If Ted doesn't want a drink, I do."

Ted accepted the beer Craig held out to him and stared out the window. Was Bartlett right? Was it crazy to come here instead of just working from Connecticut or New York? But somehow whenever he was at the Spa, he had a sense of calm, of well-being. It came from all the summers he'd spent on the Monterey Peninsula when he was a kid.

The car stopped at the gate to Pebble Beach onto the Seventeen Mile Drive, and the chauffeur paid the toll. The estate homes overlooking the ocean came into view. Once he had planned to buy a house here. He and Kathy had agreed it would be a good vacation place for Teddy. And then Teddy and Kathy were gone.

On the left side, the Pacific sparkled, clear and beautiful in the bright afternoon sun. It wasn't safe for swimming here—the undertow was too strong—but how good it would feel to dive in and let the salty water wash over him! He wondered if he would ever feel clean again, ever stop seeing those pictures of Leila's broken body. In his thoughts they were always there, gigantically enlarged, like billboards on a highway. And in these last few months, the doubts had begun.

"Quit thinking whatever you're thinking, Ted," Craig said mildly.

"And stop trying to read my thoughts," Ted snapped. Then he managed a weak smile. "Sorry."

"No problem." Craig's tone was hearty and genial.

Craig had always had a knack for defusing situations, Ted thought. They'd met at Dartmouth as freshmen. Craig had been chunky then. At seventeen, he'd looked like a big blond Swede. At thirty-four he was trim, the chunkiness hardened into solid muscle. The strong, heavy features were more becoming to a mature man than to a kid. Craig had had a partial scholarship to college but had worked his backside off at every job he could get—as a dishwasher in the kitchen, as a room clerk in the Hanover Inn, as an orderly in the local hospital.

And still he's always been around for me, Ted reminded himself. After college, he'd been surprised to bump into Craig in the washroom at the executive office of Winters Enterprises. "Why didn't you ask *me* if you wanted a job here?" He hadn't been sure he was pleased.

"Because if I'm any good, I'll make it on my own."

You couldn't argue with that. And he'd made it, clear up to executive vice-president. If I go to prison, Ted thought, he gets to run the show. I wonder how often he thinks about that. A sense of disgust at his own mental processes washed over him. I think like a cornered rat. I *am* a cornered rat!

They drove past the Pebble Beach Lodge, the golf course, the Crocker Woodland, and the grounds of Cypress Point Spa came into view. "Pretty soon you'll understand why we wanted to come here," Craig told Henry. He looked directly at Ted. "We're going to put together an airtight defense. You know this place has always been lucky for you." Then, as he glanced out the side window, he stiffened. "Oh, my God, I don't believe it. The convertible—Cheryl and Syd are here!"

Grimly he turned to Henry Bartlett. "I'm beginning to think you're right. We should have gone to Connecticut."

# 5

Min had assigned Elizabeth the bungalow where Leila had always stayed. It was one of the most expensive units, but Elizabeth was not sure that she was flattered. Everything in these rooms shouted Leila's name: the slipcovers in the shade of emerald green Leila loved, the deep armchair with the matching ottoman. Leila used to sprawl on that after a strenuous exercise class—"My God, Sparrow, if I keep this up they can measure me for a thin shroud"; the exquisite inlaid writing desk—"Sparrow, remember the furniture in poor Mama's place? Early Garage Sale."

In the short time Elizabeth had been with Min and Helmut, a maid had unpacked her bags. A blue tank suit and ivory terry-cloth robe were lying on the bed. Pinned to the robe was the schedule of her afternoon appointments: four o'clock, massage; five o'clock, facial.

The building housing the women's spa facilities was at one end of the Olympic pool—a rambling, self-contained one-story structure built to resemble a Spanish adobe. Placid from the outside, it was usually a whirlwind of activity within as women of all ages and shapes hurried along the tiled floors in terry-cloth robes, rushing to their next appointments.

Elizabeth braced herself to see familiar faces—some of the regulars who came to the Spa every three months or so and whom she had gotten to know well during her summers working here. She knew that inevitably condolences would be offered, heads shaken: "I never would have believed Ted Winters capable . . ."

But she did not see one single familiar face in the array of women padding from exercise classes to beauty treatments. Nor did the spa seem as busy as usual. At peak it accommodated about sixty women; the men's spa held about the same number. There were nothing like that many.

She reminded herself of the color coding of the

doors: pink for facial rooms; yellow for massage; orchid for herbal wraps; white for steam cabinets; blue for sloofing. The exercise rooms were beyond the indoor pool and seemed to have been enlarged. There were more individual Jacuzzis in the central solarium. With a touch of disappointment, Elizabeth realized it was too late to soak in one of them for even a few minutes.

Tonight, she promised herself, she'd go for a long swim.

The masseuse who had been assigned to her was one of the old-timers. Small of frame but with powerful arms and hands, Gina was clearly delighted to see her. "You're coming back to work here, I hope? Of course not. No such luck."

The massage rooms had obviously been done over. Did Min never stop spending money on this place? But the new tables were luxuriously padded, and under the expert hands of Gina she could feel herself begin to relax.

Gina was kneading her shoulder muscles. "You're in knots."

"I guess I am."

"You have plenty of reason."

Elizabeth knew that that was Gina's way of expressing her sympathy. She knew too that unless she began a conversation, Gina would be silent. One of Min's firm rules to her help was that if guests wanted to talk, it was all right to converse with them. "But don't you be yakking about your own problems," Min would say at the weekly staff meetings. "Nobody wants to hear them."

It would be helpful to get Gina's impressions on how the Spa was doing. "It doesn't seem to be too busy today," she suggested. "Is everybody on the golf course?"

"I wish. Listen, this place hasn't been busy in nearly two years. Relax, Elizabeth, your arm feels like a board."

"Two years! What's happened?"

"What can I say? It started with that stupid mausoleum. People don't pay these prices to look at mounds of dirt or listen to hammering. And that place still isn't finished. Will you tell me why they needed a Roman bath here?"

Elizabeth thought of Leila's remarks about the Roman bath. "That's what Leila used to say."

"She was right. I'll need to have you turn over now." Expertly the masseuse re-draped the sheet. "And listen, you brought up her name. Do you realize how much glamour Leila gave this place? People wanted to be around her. They'd come here hoping to see her. She was a one-woman ad for the Spa. And she always talked about meeting Ted Winters here. Now—I don't know. There's something so different. The Baron spends money like a maniac— you saw the new Jacuzzis. The interior work on that bathhouse goes on and on. And Min is trying to cut corners. It's a joke. He puts in a Roman bath, and she tells us not to waste towels!"

The facialist was new, a Japanese woman. The

unwinding that had begun with the massage was completed by the warm mask she applied after the cleansing and steaming. Elizabeth drifted off to sleep. She was awakened by the woman's soft voice. "Have you had a nice nap? I left you an extra forty minutes. You looked so peaceful, and I had plenty of time."

# 6

While the maid unpacked her bags, Alvirah Meehan investigated her new quarters. She went from room to room, her eyes darting about, missing nothing. In her mind she was composing what she would dictate into her brand-new recording machine.

"Will that be all, madame?"

The maid was at the door of the sitting room. "Yes, thank you." Alvirah tried to imitate the tone of her Tuesday job, Mrs. Stevens. A little hoity-toity, but still friendly.

The minute the door closed behind the maid, she raced to get her recorder out of her voluminous pocketbook. The reporter from the *New York Globe* had taught her how to use it. She settled herself on the couch in the living room and began:

"Well, here I am at Cypress Point Spa and buhlieve me it's the cat's meow. This is my first recording and I want to start by thanking Mr. Evans for his confidence in me. When he interviewed me and Willy about winning the lottery and I told him about my lifelong ambition to come to Cypress Point Spa, he said that I clearly have a sense of the dramatic and the *Globe* readers would love to know all about the goings-on in a classy spa from my point of view.

"He said that the kind of people I'll be meeting would never think of me as a writer and so I might hear a lot of interesting stuff. Then when I explained I'd been a real fan of movie stars all my life, and know lots about the private lives of the stars, he said he had a hunch I could write a good series of articles and who knows, maybe even a book."

Alvirah smiled blissfully and smoothed the skirt of her purple-and-pink traveling dress. The skirt tended to hike up.

"A book," she continued, being careful to speak directly into the microphone. "Me, Alvirah Meehan. But when you think of all the celebrities who write books and how many of them really stink, I believe I just might be able to do that.

"To get to what's happened so far, I rode in a limousine to the Spa with Elizabeth Lange. She is a lovely young woman and I feel so sorry for her. Her eyes are very sad, and you can tell she's under a big strain. She slept practically the whole way from San Francisco. Elizabeth is Leila LaSalle's sister, but very different in looks. Leila was a redhead with green eyes. She could look sexy and queenly at the same time—kind of like a cross between Dolly Parton and Greer Garson. I think a good way to describe Elizabeth is 'wholesome.'

"She's a little too thin; her shoulders are broad; she has wide blue eyes with dark lashes, and honey-colored hair that falls around her shoulders. She has strong, beautiful teeth, and the one time she smiled she gave off just the warmest glow. She's pretty tall —about five foot nine, I guess. I bet she sings. Her speaking voice is so pleasant, but not that exaggerated actressy voice you hear from so many of these young starlets. I guess you don't call them starlets anymore. Maybe if I get friendly with her, she'll tell me some interesting things about her sister and Ted Winters. I wonder if the *Globe* will want me to cover the trial."

Alvirah paused, pushed the rewind button and then the replay. It was all right. The machine was working. She thought she ought to say something about her surroundings.

"Mrs. von Schreiber escorted me to my bungalow. I almost laughed out loud when she called it a bungalow. We used to rent a bungalow in Rockaway Beach on Ninety-ninth Street right near the amusement park. The place used to shake every time the roller coaster went down the last steep drop, which was every five minutes during the summer.

"This bungalow has a sitting room all done in light blue chintz and Oriental scatter rugs . . . they're handmade—I checked . . . a bedroom with a canopy bed, a small desk, a slipper chair, a bureau, a vanity table filled with cosmetics and lotions, and two huge bathrooms, each with its own Jacuzzi. There's also a room with built-in bookshelves, a real leather couch and chairs and an oval table. Upstairs there are two more bedrooms and baths, which of course I really don't need. Luxury! I keep pinching myself.

"Baroness von Schreiber told me that the day starts at seven A.M. with a brisk walk, which everyone in the Spa is requested to take. After that I will be served a low-calorie breakfast in my own dining room. The maid will also bring my personal daily schedule, which will include things like a facial, a massage, a herbal wrap, a sloofing treatment—whatever that is—the steam cabinet, a pedicure and a manicure and a hair treatment. Imagine! After I have been checked out by the doctor, they will add my exercise classes.

"Now I'm going to take a little rest, and then it will be time to dress for dinner. I'm going to wear my rainbow caftan,which I bought at Martha's on Park Avenue. I showed it to the Baroness and she said it would be perfect, but not to wear the crystal beads I won at the shooting gallery in Coney Island."

Alvirah turned off the recorder and beamed in satisfaction. Who ever said writing was hard? With a recorder it was a cinch. Recorder! Quickly, she got up and reached for her pocketbook. From inside a zippered compartment she took out a small box containing a sunburst pin.

But not just *any* sunburst pin, she thought proudly. This one had a microphone, and the editor had told her to wear it to record conversations. "That way," he had explained, "no one can claim you misquoted them later on."

# 7

"Sorry to do this to you, Ted, but we simply don't have the luxury of time." Henry Bartlett leaned back in the upholstered armchair at the end of the library table.

Ted was aware that his left temple was throbbing, and shafts of pain were finding a target behind and above his left eye. Deliberately he moved his head to avoid the streams of late-afternoon sun that were coming through the window opposite him.

They were in the study of Ted's bungalow in the Meadowcluster area, one of the two most expensive accommodations at Cypress Point Spa. Craig was sitting diagonally across from him, his face grave, his hazel eyes cloudy with worry.

Henry had wanted a conference before dinner. "Time is running out," he had said, "and until we decide on our final strategy, we can't make any progress."

Twenty years in prison, Ted thought incredulously. That was the sentence he was facing. He'd be fifty-four years old when he got out. Incongruously, all the old gangster movies he'd used to watch late at night sprang into his mind. Steel bars, tough prison guards, Jimmy Cagney starring as a mad-dog killer. He used to revel in them.

"We have two ways we can go," Henry Bartlett said. "We can stick to your original story—"

"My *original* story," Ted snapped.

"Hear me out! You left Leila's apartment at about ten after nine. You went to your own apartment. You tried to phone Craig." He turned to Craig. "It's a damn shame you didn't pick up the phone."

"I was watching a program I wanted to see. The telephone recorder was on. I figured I'd call back anyone who left a message. And I can swear the phone rang at nine twenty, just as Ted says."

"Why *didn't* you leave a message, Ted?"

"Because I hate talking to machines, and especially that one." His lips tightened. Craig's habit of talking like a Japanese houseboy on his recorder irritated Ted wildly.

"What were you calling Craig about, anyhow?"

"It's blurry. I was drunk. My impression is that I wanted to tell him I was taking off for a while."

"That doesn't help us. Probably if you had reached him it wouldn't help us. Not unless he can

back you up that you were talking to him at precisely nine thirty-one P.M."

Craig slammed his hand on the table. "Then I'll
say it. I'm not in favor of lying under oath, but
neither am I in favor of Ted getting railroaded for
something he didn't do."

"It's too late for that. You've already made a statement. You change it now and the situation gets
worse." Bartlett skimmed the papers he had pulled
from his briefcase. Ted got up and walked to the
window. He had planned to go to the men's spa and
work out for a while. But Bartlett had been insistent
about this meeting. Already his freedom was being
infringed.

How many times had he come to Cypress Point
with Leila in their three-year relationship? Eight or
ten probably. Leila had loved it here. She'd been
amused by Min's bossiness, by the Baron's preten-
tiousness. She'd enjoyed long hikes along the cliffs.
"All right, Falcon, if you won't come with me, play
your darn golf and I'll meet you at my pad later."
That mischievous wink, the deliberate leer, her
long, slender fingers running along his shoulders.
"God, Falcon, you do turn me on." Lying with her
in his arms on the couch watching late-night movies. Her murmured "Min knows better than to give
us any of those damn narrow antiques of hers. She
knows I like to cuddle with my fellow." It was here
that he had found the Leila he loved; the Leila she
herself wanted to be.

What was Bartlett saying? "Either we attempt to

flatly contradict Elizabeth Lange and the so-called eyewitness or we try to turn that testimony to our benefit."

"How does one do that?" God, I hate this man, Ted thought. Look at him sitting there, cool and comfortable. You'd think he was discussing a chess game, not the rest of my life. Irrational fury almost choked him. He had to get out of this spot. Even being in a room with someone he disliked gave him claustrophobia. How could he share a cell with another man for two or three decades? He couldn't. At any price, he couldn't do it.

"You have no memory of hailing the cab, of the ride to Connecticut."

"Absolutely none."

"Your last conscious memory of that evening. Tell me again: what was it?"

"I had been with Leila for several hours. She was hysterical. Kept accusing me of cheating on her."

"Did you?"

"No."

"Then why did she accuse you?"

"Leila was—terribly insecure. She'd had bad experiences with men. She had convinced herself she could never trust one. I thought I'd gotten her over that as far as our relationship was concerned, but every once in a while she'd throw a jealous fit." That scene in the apartment. Leila lunging at him, scratching his face; her wild accusations. His hands on her wrists, restraining her. What had he felt? Anger. Fury. And disgust.

"You tried to give her back the engagement ring?"

"Yes, and she refused it."

"Then what happened?"

"Elizabeth phoned. Leila began sobbing into the phone and shouting at me to get out. I told her to put the phone down. I wanted to get to the bottom of what had brought all this on.

I saw it was hopeless and left. I went to my own apartment. I think I changed my shirt. I tried to call Craig. I remember leaving the apartment. I don't remember anything else until the next day when I woke up in Connecticut."

"Teddy, do you realize what the prosecutor will do to that story? Do you know how many cases are on record of people who kill in a fit of rage and then have a psychotic episode where they block it out? As your lawyer I have to tell you something: *That story stinks!* It's no defense. Sure, if it weren't for Elizabeth Lange there wouldn't be a problem. . . . Hell, there wouldn't even be a case. I could make mincemeat of that so-called eyewitness. She's a nut, a real off-the-wall nut. But with Elizabeth swearing you were in the apartment fighting with Leila at nine thirty, the nut becomes believable when she says you shoved Leila off the terrace at nine thirty-one."

"Then what do we do about it?" Craig asked.

"We gamble," Bartlett said. "Ted agrees with Elizabeth's story. He now remembers going back upstairs. Leila was still hysterical. She slammed the phone down and ran to the terrace. Everybody who was in Elaine's the night before can testify to her emotional state. Her sister admits she had been drinking. She was despondent about her career. She had decided to break off her relationship with you. She felt washed up. She wouldn't be the first one to take a dive in that situation."

Ted winced. *A dive.* Christ, were all lawyers so insensitive? And then the image came of Leila's broken body; the garish police pictures. He felt perspiration break out over his entire body.

But Craig looked hopeful. "It might work. What that eyewitness saw was Ted struggling to *save* Leila, and when Leila fell, he blacked out. That's when he had the psychotic episode. *That* explains why he was almost incoherent in the cab."

Ted stared through the window at the ocean. It was unusually calm now, but he knew the tide would soon be roaring in. The calm before the storm, he thought. Right now we're having a clinical discussion. In nine days I'll be in the courtroom. *The People of the State of New York* v. *Andrew Edward Winters III.* "There's one big hole in your theory," he said flatly. "If I admit I went back to that apartment and was on the terrace with Leila, I'm putting my head in a noose. If the jury decides I was in the process of killing her, I'll be found guilty of Murder Two."

"It's a chance you may have to take."

Ted came back to the table and began to stuff the open files into Bartlett's briefcase. His smile was not pleasant. "I'm not sure I can take that chance. There has to be a better solution, and at any cost I intend to find it. *I will not go to prison!*"

# 8

Min sighed gustily. "That feels good. I swear, you've got better hands than any masseuse in this place."

Helmut leaned down and kissed her cheek. "*Liebchen,* I love touching you, even if it's only to ease your shoulders."

They were in their apartment, which covered the entire third floor of the main house. Min was seated at her dressing table wearing a loose kimono. She had unpinned her heavy raven-colored hair, and it fell below her shoulders. She looked at her reflection in the mirror. Today she was no ad for this place. Shadows under her eyes—how long since she'd had her eyes done? Five years? Something hard to accept was happening. She was fifty-nine years old. Until this last year she could have passed for ten years younger. No more.

Helmut was smiling at her in the mirror. Deliberately, he rested his chin on her head. His eyes were a shade of blue that always reminded her of the waters in the Adriatic Sea around Dubrovnik, where she had been born. The long, distinguished face with its picture-perfect tan was unlined, the dark brown sideburns untouched by gray. Helmut was fifteen years her junior. For the first years of their marriage it hadn't mattered. But now?

She had met him at the spa in Baden-Baden, after Samuel died. Five years of catering to that fussy old man had paid off. He'd left her twelve million dollars and this property.

She hadn't been stupid about Helmut's sudden attentiveness to her. No man becomes enamored of a woman fifteen years his senior unless there's something he wants. At first she had accepted his attentions cynically, but by the end of two weeks she had realized that she was becoming deeply interested in him and in his suggestion that she convert the Cypress Point Hotel into a spa. . . . The cost had been staggering, but Helmut had urged her to consider it an investment, not an expenditure. The day the Spa opened, he had asked her to marry him.

She sighed heavily.

"Minna, what is it?"

How long had they been staring at each other in the mirror? "You know."

He bent down and kissed her cheek.

Incredibly, they'd been happy together. She had never dared tell him how much she loved him, instinctively afraid to hand him that weapon, always watching for signs of restlessness. But he ignored the young women who flirted with him. It was only

Leila who had seemed to dazzle him, only Leila who had made her churn in an agony of fear. . . .

Perhaps she had been wrong. If one could believe him, Helmut had actually disliked Leila, even hated her. Leila had been openly contemptuous of him—but then, Leila had been contemptuous of every man she knew well. . . .

The shadows had become long in the room. The breeze from the sea was sharply cooler. Helmut reached his hands under her elbows. "Rest a little. You'll have to put up with the lot of them in less than an hour."

Min clutched his hand. "Helmut, how do you think she'll react?"

"Very badly."

"Don't tell me that," she wailed. "Helmut, you know why I have to try. It's our only chance."

# 9

At seven o'clock, chimes from the main house announced the arrival of the "cocktail" hour, and immediately the paths to the main house became filled with people—singles, couples, groups of three or four. All were well dressed, in semiformal wear, the women in elegant caftans or flowing tunics, the men in blazers, slacks and sport shirts. Blazing gemstones were mixed with amusing costume pieces. Famous faces greeted each other warmly, or nodded distantly. Soft lights glowed on the veranda, where waiters in ivory-and-blue uniforms served delicate canapés and alcohol-free "cocktails."

Elizabeth decided to wear the dusty-pink silk jumpsuit with a magenta sash that had been Leila's last birthday present to her. Leila always wrote a note on her personal stationery. The note that had accompanied this outfit was tucked in the back of Elizabeth's wallet, a talisman of love. She'd written: *"It's a long, long way from May to December. Love and Happy Birthday to my darling Capricorn sister from the Taurus kid."*

Somehow, wearing that outfit, rereading that note made it easier for Elizabeth to leave the bungalow and start up the path to the main house. She kept a half-smile on her face as she finally saw some of the regulars. Mrs. Lowell from Boston, who had been coming here since Min opened the place; Countess d'Aronne, the brittle, aging beauty, who was at last showing most of her seventy years. The Countess had been an eighteen-year-old bride when her much older husband was murdered. She'd married four times since then, but after every divorce petitioned the French courts to restore her former title.

"You look gorgeous. I helped Leila pick out that jumpsuit on Rodeo Drive." Min's voice boomed in her ear; Min's arm was solidly linked in hers. Elizabeth felt herself being propelled forward. A scent of the ocean mingled with the perfume of roses. The well-bred voices and laughter of the people on the veranda hummed around her. The background music was Serber playing Mendelssohn's *Concerto for Violin in E minor.* Leila would drop everything to attend a Serber concert.

A waiter offered her a choice of beverages—nonalcoholic wine or a soft drink. She chose the nonalcoholic wine. Leila had been cynical about Min's firm no-alcohol rule. *"Listen, Sparrow, half the people who go to that joint are boozers. They all bring some stuff with them, but even so they have to cut down a lot. So they lose some weight, and Min claims credit for the Spa. Don't you think the Baron keeps a supply in that study of his? You bet he does!"*

I should have gone to East Hampton, Elizabeth thought. Anywhere—anywhere but here. It was as if she were filled with a sense of Leila's presence, as if Leila were trying to reach her. . . .

"Elizabeth." Min's voice was sharp. Sharp, but also nervous, she realized. "The Countess is talking to you."

"I'm terribly sorry." Affectionately, she reached out to grasp the aristocratic hand that was extended to her.

The Countess smiled warmly. "I saw your last film. You're developing into a very fine actress, *chérie.*"

How like Countess d'Aronne to sense she would not want to discuss Leila. "It was a good role. I was lucky." And then Elizabeth felt her eyes widen. "Min, coming down the path. Isn't that Syd and Cheryl?"

"Yes. They just called this morning. I forgot to tell you. You don't mind that they're here?"

"Of course not. It's only . . ." Her voice trailed off. She was still embarrassed over the way Leila. had humiliated Syd that night in Elaine's. Syd had made Leila a star. No matter what mistakes he'd talked her into those last few years, they didn't stack up against the times he'd nailed down the parts she wanted. . . .

And Cheryl? Under the veneer of friendship, she and Leila had shared an intense professional and personal rivalry. Leila had taken Ted from Cheryl. Cheryl had almost wrecked her career by stepping into Leila's play. . . .

Unconsciously, Elizabeth straightened her back. On the other hand, Syd had made a fortune off Leila's earnings. Cheryl had tried every trick in the book to get Ted back. If only she'd succeeded, Elizabeth thought, Leila might still be alive. . . .

They had spotted her. They both looked as surprised as she felt. The Countess murmured, "Not that dreadful tart, Cheryl Manning . . ."

They were coming up the steps toward her. Elizabeth studied Cheryl objectively. Her hair was a tangled web around her face. It was much darker than it had been the last time she had seen her, and very becoming. The last time? That had been at Leila's memorial service.

Reluctantly Elizabeth conceded to herself that Cheryl had never looked better. Her smile was dazzling; the famous amber-colored eyes assumed a tender expression. Her greeting would have fooled anyone who didn't know her. "Elizabeth, my darling, I never dreamed I'd see you here, but how wonderful! Has it gone fairly well?"

Then it was Syd's turn. Syd, with his cynical eyes and mournful face. She knew he'd put a million dollars of his own money into Leila's play—money he had probably borrowed. Leila had called him "the Dealer." *"Sure, he works hard for me, Sparrow, but that's because I make a lot of money for him. The day I quit being an asset to him, he'll walk over my dead body."*

Elizabeth felt a chill as Syd gave her a perfunctory show-business kiss. "You look good; I may have to steal you from your agent. I didn't expect to see you till next week."

*Next week.* Of course. The defense was probably going to use Cheryl and Syd to testify to Leila's emotional state that night in Elaine's.

"Are you filling in for one of the instructors?" Cheryl asked.

"Elizabeth is here because I invited her," Min snapped.

Elizabeth wondered why Min seemed so terribly nervous. Min's eyes were darting around, and her hand was still gripping Elizabeth's elbow as though she were afraid of losing her.

"Cocktails" were offered to the newcomers.

Friends of the Countess drifted over to join them. The host of a famous talk show greeted Syd genially. "Next time you want us to book one of your clients, make sure he's sober."

"That one's never sober."

Then she heard a familiar voice coming from behind her, an astonished voice: "Elizabeth, what are you doing here?"

She turned and felt Craig's arms around her—the solid, dependable arms of the man who had rushed to her when he heard the news flash, who had stayed with her in Leila's apartment, listening as she babbled out her grief, who had helped her to answer the questions of the police, who had finally located Ted. . . .

She'd seen Craig three or four times in the last year. He'd look her up when she was filming. "I can't be in the same city without at least saying hello," he'd say. By tacit agreement they avoided discussing the impending trial, but they never got through a dinner without some reference to it. It was through Craig that she'd learned that Ted was staying in Maui, that he was jumpy and irritable, that he was practically ignoring business and out of touch with his friends. It was from Craig, inevitably, that she'd heard the question "Are you *sure*?"

The last time she'd seen him, she'd burst out, "How can anyone be sure of anything or anybody?" and asked him not to contact her again until after the trial. "I know where your loyalty has to be."

But what was he doing here now? She'd have

thought he'd be with Ted preparing for the trial. And then as she stepped back from his embrace, she saw Ted coming up the steps of the veranda.

She felt her mouth go dry. Her arms and legs trembled; her heart beat so wildly she could hear its pounding in her ears. Somehow in these months she had managed to bar his image from her conscious mind, and in her nightmares, he was always shadowy—she'd seen only the murderous hands, pushing Leila over the railing, the merciless eyes watching her fall. . . .

Now he was walking up these stairs with his usual commanding presence. Andrew Edward Winters III, his dark hair contrasting with the white dinner jacket, his strong, even features deeply tanned, looking all the better for his self-imposed exile in Maui.

Outrage and hatred made Elizabeth want to lunge at him; to push him down those steps as he had pushed Leila, to scratch that composed, handsome face as Leila had scratched it, trying to save herself. The brackish taste of bile filled her mouth and she gulped, trying to fight back nausea.

"There he is!" Cheryl cried. In an instant she was sliding through the clusters of people on the veranda, her heels clattering, the scarf of her red silk evening pajamas trailed behind her. Conversation stopped, heads turned as she threw herself into Ted's arms.

Like a robot, Elizabeth stared down at them. It was as though she were looking through a kaleidoscope. Loose fragments of colors and impressions rotated before her. The white of Ted's jacket; the red of Cheryl's outfit; Ted's dark brown hair; his long, well-shaped hands holding Cheryl's shoulders as he tried to free himself.

At the grand jury hearing, Elizabeth remembered, she had brushed past him, filled with self-loathing that she had been so deceived, so taken in by his performance as Leila's grief-stricken fiancé. Now he glanced up, and she knew he had seen her. He looked shocked and dismayed—or was that just another act? Pulling his arm away from Cheryl's clinging fingers, he came up the steps. Unable to move, she was dimly aware of the hushed silence of the people around them, the murmurs and laughter of those farther away who did not realize what was happening, of the last strains of the concerto, of the bouquet of fragrances from the flowers and ocean.

He looked older. The lines around his eyes and mouth that had appeared at the time of Leila's death had deepened and were now permanently etched on his face. Leila had loved him so, and he had killed her. A fresh passion of hatred surged through Elizabeth. All the intolerable pain, the awful sense of loss, the guilt that permeated her soul like a cancer because at the end she had failed Leila. This man was the cause of all of it.

"Elizabeth . . ."

*How dare he speak to her?* Shocked out of her immobility, she spun around, stumbled across the veranda and into the foyer. She heard the click of heels behind her. Min had followed her in. Elizabeth turned to her fiercely. "Damn you, Min. What in hell do you think you're pulling?"

"In here." Min's head jerked toward the music room. She did not speak until she had closed the door behind them. "Elizabeth, I know what I'm doing."

"I don't." With an acute sense of betrayal, Elizabeth stared at Min. No *wonder* she had seemed nervous. And she was even more nervous now—she, who always seemed impervious to stress, who always gave off the commanding air of one who could change and resolve any problem, was actually trembling.

"Elizabeth, when I saw you in Venice, you told me yourself that something in you still couldn't believe Ted would hurt Leila. I don't care how it looks. I've known him longer than you—years longer. . . . You're making a mistake. Don't forget, I was in Elaine's that night too. Listen, Leila had gone crazy. There's no other way of saying it. And *you* knew it! You say you set your clock the next day. You were distraught about her. Are you so infallible that maybe you didn't set it wrong? When Leila was on the phone with you just before she died, were you watching the clock? Look at Ted these next few days as if he's a human being, not a monster. Think about how good he was to Leila."

Min's face was impassioned. Her low, intense voice was more piercing than a scream. She grasped Elizabeth's arm. "You're one of the most honest people I know. From the time you were a little girl you always told the truth. Can't you face the fact that your mistake means that Ted will rot in prison for the rest of his life?"

The melodious sound of chimes echoed through the room. Dinner was about to be served. Elizabeth put her hand on Min's wrist, forcing Min to release her. Incongruously, she remembered how a few minutes ago Ted had pulled away from Cheryl.

"Min, next week a jury will begin to decide who is telling the truth. You think you can run everything, but you're out of your element this time. . . . Get someone to call me a taxi."

"Elizabeth, you can't leave!"

"Can't I? Do you have a number where I can reach Sammy?"

"No."

"Exactly when is she expected back?"

"Tomorrow night after dinner." Min clasped her hands beseechingly. "Elizabeth, I beg you."

From behind her, Elizabeth heard the door open. She whirled around. Helmut was in the doorway. He put his hands on her arms in a gesture that both embraced and restrained her. "Elizabeth." His voice was soft and urgent. "I tried to warn Minna. She had the crazy idea that if you saw Ted you would think of all the happy times, would remember how much he loved Leila. I implored her not to do this. Ted is as shocked and upset as you are."

"He should be. Will you please let go of me!"

Helmut's voice became soothing, pleading. "Elizabeth, next week is Labor Day. The Peninsula is alive with tourists. There are hundreds of college kids having one last fling before school opens. You could drive around half the night and not find a room. Stay here. Be comfortable. See Sammy tomorrow night, then go if you must."

It was true, Elizabeth thought. Carmel and Monterey were meccas for tourists in late August.

"Elizabeth, please." Min was weeping. "I was so foolish. I thought, I believed that if you just saw Ted . . . not in court, but here . . . I'm sorry."

Elizabeth felt her anger drain away, to be replaced by bone-weary emptiness. Min was Min. Incongruously, she remembered the time Min had sent a reluctant Leila to a casting for a cosmetics commercial. Min had stormed, "Listen, Leila, I don't need you to tell me they didn't ask to see you. Get over there. Force your way in. You're just what they're looking for. You make your breaks in this world."

Leila got the job and became the model the cosmetic company used in all its commercials for the next three years.

Elizabeth shrugged. "Which dining room will Ted be in?"

"The Cypress Room," Helmut answered hopefully.

"Syd? Cheryl?"

"The same."

"Where did you plan to put me?"

"With us as well. But the Countess sends her love and asks you to join her table in the Ocean Room."

"All right. I'll stay over till I see Sammy." Elizabeth looked sternly at Min, who seemed almost to cringe. "Min, I'm the one who's warning *you* now," she said. "Ted is the man who killed my sister. Don't dare try to arrange any more 'accidental' meetings between him and me."

# 10

Five years before, in an attempt to resolve the vociferous differences between smokers and non-smokers, Min had divided the spacious dining room into two areas, separating them by a glass wall. The Cypress Room was for nonsmokers only; the Ocean Room accommodated both. The seating was open, except for the guests who were invited to share Min and Helmut's table. When Elizabeth stood at the door of the Ocean Room, she was waved to a table by Countess d'Aronne. The problem, she soon realized, was that from her seat she had an unbroken view of Min's table in the other room. It was with a sense of *déjà vu* that she saw them all sitting together: Min, Helmut, Syd, Cheryl, Ted, Craig.

The two other people at Min's table were Mrs. Meehan, the lottery winner, and a distinguished-looking older man. Several times she caught him glancing over at her.

Somehow she got through the dinner, managing to nibble at the chop and salad, to make some attempts at conversation with the Countess and her friends. But as though drawn to a magnet, she found herself again and again watching Ted.

The Countess noticed it, naturally. "Despite everything he looks quite wonderful, doesn't he? Oh, I'm sorry, my dear. I made a pact with myself not to mention him at all. It's just that you do realize I've known Ted since he was a little boy. His grandparents used to bring him here, when this place was a hotel."

As always, even among celebrities, Ted was the center of attention. Everything he did was effortless, Elizabeth thought—the attentive bend of his head toward Mrs. Meehan, the easy smile for the people who came to his table to greet him, the way he allowed Cheryl to slip her hand into his, then managed to disengage it casually. It was a relief to see him and Craig and the older man leave the table early.

She did not linger for the coffee that was served in the music room. Instead, she slipped out onto the veranda and down the path to her bungalow. The mist had blown off, and stars were brilliant in the dark night sky. The crashing and pounding of the surf blended with the faint sounds of the cello. There was always a musical program after dinner.

An intense sense of isolation came over Elizabeth, an indefinable sadness that was beyond Leila's death, beyond the incongruity of the company of these people who had been so much a part of her life. Syd, Cheryl, Min. She'd known them since she was the eight-year-old Miss Tag Along. The Baron. Craig. Ted.

They went back a long way, these people whom she had considered close friends and who had now closed ranks on her, who sympathized with Leila's murderer, who would come to New York to testify for him. . . .

When she reached her bungalow, Elizabeth hesitated and then decided to sit outside for a while. The veranda furniture was comfortable—a padded sofa swing and matching deck chairs. She settled on a corner of the sofa and, with one foot against the floor, set it moving. Here in the almost-dark, she could see the lights of the big house and quietly think about the people who had incongruously been gathered here tonight.

Gathered at whose request?

And why?

# 11

"For a nine-hundred-calorie dinner, it wasn't bad."
Henry Bartlett came from his bungalow carrying a
handsome leather case. He placed it on the table in
Ted's sitting room and opened it, revealing a porta-
ble mini-bar. He reached for the Courvoisier and
brandy snifters. "Gentlemen?"

Craig nodded assent. Ted shook his head. "I think
you should know that one of the firm rules at this
spa is no liquor."

"When I—or should I say *you*?—pay over seven
hundred dollars a day for me to be at this place, I
decide what I drink."

He poured a generous amount into the two
glasses, handed one to Craig and walked over to the
sliding glass doors. A full, creamy moon and a galaxy
of brilliant silver stars lighted the inky darkness of
the ocean; the crescendo of the waves attested to
the awesome power of the surf. "I'll never know
why Balboa called this the *Pacific* Ocean," Bartlett
commented. "Not when you hear that sound coming from it." He turned to Ted. "Having Elizabeth
Lange here could be the break of the century for
you. She's an interesting girl."

Ted waited. Craig turned the stem of the glass in
his hand. Bartlett looked reflective. "Interesting in
a lot of ways, and most particularly for something

neither one of you could have seen. Every expression in the gamut marched across her face when she saw you, Teddy. Sadness. Uncertainty. Hatred. She's been doing a lot of thinking, and my guess is that something in her is saying two plus two doesn't equal five."

"You don't know what you're talking about," Craig said flatly.

Henry pushed open the sliding glass door. Now the crescendo of the ocean became a roar. "Hear that?" he asked. "Makes it kind of hard to concentrate, doesn't it? You're paying me a lot of money to get Ted out of this mess. One of the best ways to do it is to know what I'm up against and what I have going for me."

A sharply cool gust of air interrupted him. Quickly he pulled the door shut and walked back to the table. "We were very fortunate the way the seating worked out. I spent a good part of the dinner studying Elizabeth Lange. Facial expressions and body language tell a lot. She never took her eyes off you, Teddy. If ever a woman was caught in a love-hate situation, she's it. Now my job is to figure out how we can make it work for you."

# 12

Syd walked an unnaturally silent Cheryl back to her bungalow. He knew that dinner had been an ordeal for her. She'd never gotten over losing Ted Winters to Leila. Now it must absolutely gall her that even with Leila out of the way, Ted wouldn't respond to her. In a crazy way, that lottery winner had been a good diversion for Cheryl. Alvirah Meehan knew all about the series, told her she was perfect for the role of Amanda. "You know how sometimes you can just see a star in a role," Alvirah had said. "I read *Till Tomorrow* when it was in paperback, and I said, 'Willy, that would make a great television series, and only one person in the world should play Amanda, and that's Cheryl Manning.'" Of course, it was unfortunate she had also told Cheryl that Leila was her favorite actress in the whole world.

They were walking along the highest point of the property back to Cheryl's bungalow. The paths were lighted with ground-level Japanese lanterns which threw shadows on the cypress trees. The night was sparkling with stars, but the weather was supposed to change, and already the air was carrying the touch of dampness that preceded a typical Monterey Peninsula fog. Unlike the people who considered Pebble Beach the nearest spot to heaven, Syd had always felt somewhat uncomfortable around cypress trees, with their crazy twisted shapes. No wonder some poet had compared them to ghosts. He shivered.

Matter-of-factly, he took Cheryl's arm as they turned from the main path to her bungalow. Still he waited for her to begin to talk, but she remained silent. He consoled himself with the thought that he'd had enough of her moods anyway for one day; but when he started to say good night, she interrupted him: "Come inside."

Groaning to himself, he followed her in. She wasn't ready to quit on him yet. "Where's the vodka?" he asked.

"Locked in my jewelry case. It's the only place these damn maids don't check for booze." She tossed him the key and settled herself on the striped satin couch. He poured vodka on ice for the two of them, handed her a glass and sat down opposite her, sipping his drink, watching her make a production out of tasting hers. Finally she looked squarely at him. "What did you think about tonight?"

"I'm not sure I get your meaning."

She looked scornful. "Of course you do. When Ted drops his guard, he looks haunted. It's obvious Craig is worried sick. Min and the Baron make me think of a pair of high-wire acrobats on a slippery rope. That lawyer never took his eyes off Elizabeth, and *she* was spying on our table all night. I've always suspected she had a case on Ted. As for that crazy lottery winner—if Min puts me next to her tomorrow night, I'll *strangle* her!"

"The hell you will! Listen, Cheryl, you may get the part. Great. There's still always the chance the series will die in the ratings. A slight chance, I grant you, but a chance. If that happens, you're going to need a movie role. There are plenty of them around, but movies need backing. That lady's gonna have a lot of bucks for investment capital. Keep smiling at her."

Cheryl's eyes narrowed. "Ted could be talked into financing a movie for me. I know he could. He told me it wasn't fair that I was stuck with the play last year."

"Get this straight: Craig is a lot more cautious than Ted. If Ted goes to prison, he'll run the show. And another thing. You're crazy if you think Elizabeth has the hots for Ted. If she did, why the hell would she be putting a noose around his neck? All she has to do is say she was wrong about the time and how wonderful Ted was to Leila. Period. Case dismissed."

Cheryl finished her drink and imperiously held out her empty glass. Silently, Syd got up, refilled it and added a generous splash of vodka to his own. "Men are too dumb to see," Cheryl told him as he placed the drink in front of her. "You remember the kind of kid Elizabeth was. Polite, but if you asked her a direct question, you got a direct answer. And she never made excuses. She just doesn't know *how* to lie. She'd never lie for herself, and unfortunately she won't lie for Ted. But before this is over she's going to look under stones to try to find some sort of positive proof of what happened that night. That can make her very dangerous.

"Something else, Syd. You heard that nutty Alvirah Meehan say she read in a fan magazine that Leila LaSalle's apartment was like a motel? That Leila gave out keys to all her friends in case they wanted to stay over?"

Cheryl got up from the couch, walked over to Syd, sat beside him and put her hands on his knees. "*You* had a key to the apartment, didn't you, Syd?"

"So did you."

"I know it. Leila got a kick out of patronizing me, knowing I couldn't afford one room in that building, never mind a duplex. But when she died, the bartender in the Jockey Club can testify I was lingering over a drink. My dinner date was late. *You* were my dinner date, Syd, dear. How much did you put up for that goddamn play?"

Syd felt his knuckles harden and hoped that Cheryl could not feel the instant rigidity of his body. "What are you driving at?"

"The afternoon before Leila died, you told me you were going to see Leila, to beg her to reconsider. You had at least a million tied up in that play. Your million or borrowed money, Syd? You shoved me into that disaster as a replacement, just the way you'd send a lamb to slaughter. Why? Because you were willing to risk *my* career on the faint chance that maybe the play could still work. And my memory has improved a lot. You're *always* on time. That night, you were fifteen minutes late. You came into the Jockey Club at nine forty-five. You were dead white. Your hands kept trembling. You spilled a drink on the table. Leila had died at nine thirty-one. Her apartment was less than a ten-minute walk from the Jockey Club."

Cheryl put her hands on the sides of his face. "Syd, I want that part. See that I get it. If I do, I promise you, drunk or sober, I'll never remember that you were late that night, that you looked terrible, that you had a key to Leila's apartment and that Leila had virtually driven you into bankruptcy. Now get the hell out of here. I need my beauty sleep."

# 13

Min and Helmut kept their smiles fixed and warm until they were safely in their own apartment. Then, wordlessly, they turned to each other. Helmut put his arms around Min. His lips brushed her cheeks. With practiced skill, his hands massaged her neck. *"Liebchen."*

"Helmut, was it as bad as I think?"

His voice was soft. "Minna, I tried to warn you it would be a mistake to bring Elizabeth here, yes? You understand her. Now she's furious at you, but beyond that, something else has happened. Your back was to her at dinner, but I could see the way she was observing us from her table. It was as if she were seeing us for the first time."

"I thought if she just *saw* Ted . . . You know how much she cared about him . . . I've always suspected that she was in love with him herself."

"I know what you thought. But it hasn't worked. So, no more about it tonight, Minna. Get into bed. I'm going to make a cup of hot milk for you, and give you a sleeping pill. Tomorrow you'll be your usual overbearing self."

Min smiled wanly and allowed him to lead her toward the bedroom. His arm was still around her; she was half-leaning against him. Her head fitted into the crook of his shoulder. After ten years she still loved the scent of him, the hint of expensive cologne, the feel of his superbly tailored jacket. In his arms, she could forget about his predecessor, with his cold hands and his petulance.

When Helmut returned with the hot milk, she was propped up in bed, the silken pillows framing her loosened hair. She knew the rose-tinted shade on the night table threw a flattering glow on her high cheekbones and dark eyes. The appreciation she saw in her husband's eyes when he handed her the delicate Limoges cup was gratifying. *"Liebchen,"* he whispered, "I wish you knew how I feel about you. After all this time, you still don't trust that feeling, do you?"

Seize the moment. She had to do it. "Helmut,

something is terribly wrong, something you haven't told me. What is it?"

He shrugged. "You know what's wrong. Spas are springing up all over the country. The rich are restless people, fickle. . . . The cost of the Roman bath has exceeded my expectation—I admit it. . . . Nevertheless, I am sure that when we finally open it—"

"Helmut, promise me one thing. No matter what, we won't touch the Swiss account. I'd rather let this place go. At my age, I can't be broke again." Min tried to keep her voice from rising.

"We won't touch it, Minna. I promise." He handed her the sleeping pill. "So. As your husband . . . as a doctor . . . I *order* you to swallow this, immediately."

"I'll take it, gladly."

He sat on the edge of the bed as she sipped the milk. "Aren't you coming to bed?" Her voice was drowsy.

"Not yet. I'll read for a bit. That's my sleeping pill."

After he turned out the light and left the room, Min felt herself drifting off to sleep. Her last conscious thought became an inaudible whisper. "Helmut," she pleaded, "what are you hiding from me?"

# 14

At quarter of ten Elizabeth saw the guests begin to stream from the main house. She knew that in a few minutes the whole place would be silent, curtains drawn, lights extinguished. The day began early at the Spa. After the strenuous exercise classes and the relaxing beauty treatments, most people were more than ready to retire by ten o'clock.

She sighed when she saw one figure leave the main path and turn in her direction. Instinctively she knew it was Mrs. Meehan.

"I thought you might be a little lonesome," Alvirah said as, uninvited, she settled herself on one of the deck chairs. "Wasn't dinner good? You'd never guess you were counting calories, would you? Buhlieve me, I wouldn't weigh one hundred and sixty-five pounds if I'd eaten like this all my life."

She rearranged the shawl on her shoulders. "This thing keeps slipping." She looked around. "It's a beautiful night, isn't it? All those stars. I guess they don't have as much pollution here as in Queens. And the ocean. I love that sound. What was I saying? Oh, yes—dinner. You could have knocked me over when the waiter—or was he a butler?—put that tray in front of me, with the spoon and fork. You know, at home we just kind of dig *in*. I mean who needs a spoon *and* fork to get at string beans, or an itsy-bitsy lamb chop? But then I remembered the way Greer Garson helped herself from the fancy silver platter in *Valley of Decision,* and I was okay. You can always count on the movies."

Unwillingly, Elizabeth smiled. There was something so genuinely honest about Alvirah Meehan. Honesty was a rare commodity at the Spa. "I'm sure you did fine."

Alvirah fiddled with her sunburst pin. "To tell the truth, I couldn't take my eyes off Ted Winters. I was all set to hate him, but he was so *nice* to me. Boy, was I surprised at how snippy that Cheryl Manning is. She certainly hated Leila, didn't she?"

Elizabeth moistened her lips. "What makes you think that?"

"I just happened to say at dinner that I thought Leila would become a legend like Marilyn Monroe, and *she* said that if it's still fashionable to consider a washed-up drunk a legend, Leila just might make it." Alvirah felt a pang of regret at having to tell this to Leila's sister. But as she'd always read, a good reporter gets the story.

"How did the others respond to that?" Elizabeth asked quietly.

"They all laughed, except Ted Winters. He said that was a sickening thing to say."

"You can't mean Min and Craig thought it was funny?"

"It's hard to be sure," Alvirah said hastily. "Sometimes people laugh when they're embarrassed. But

even that lawyer who's with Ted Winters said something like it's pretty clear Leila wouldn't win any
popularity contests around here."

Elizabeth stood up. "It was nice of you to drop by,
Mrs. Meehan. I'm afraid I have to change now. I
always like to take a swim before I go to bed."

"I know. They talked about that at the table.
Craig—is that his name, Mr. Winters' assistant—?"

"Yes."

"He asked the Baroness how long you were going
to stay. She told him probably until day after tomorrow because you were waiting to see someone
named Sammy."

"That's right."

"And Syd Melnick said that he has a hunch you're
going to avoid all of them. Then the Baroness said
that the one place you can always find Elizabeth is
swimming in the Olympic pool around ten o'clock
at night. I guess she was right."

"She knows I like to swim. Do you know your way
to your cottage, Mrs. Meehan? If not, I'll walk with
you. It can be confusing in the dark."

"No, I'm fine. I enjoyed talking to you." Alvirah
pulled herself up from the chair and, ignoring the
path, began to cut across the lawn to her bungalow.
She was disappointed that Elizabeth hadn't said
anything that would be helpful for her articles. But
on the other hand, she had gotten a lot of material at
dinner. She certainly could do a meaty article on
jealousy!

Wouldn't the reading public be interested to hear that Leila LaSalle's very best friends all acted as if they were glad she was dead!

# 15

*Carefully, he drew the shades and extinguished the lights. He was frantic to hurry. It might already be too late, but there was no way he could have ventured out before now. When he opened the outside door, he shivered for a moment. The air had become chilly, and he was wearing only swim trunks and a dark T-shirt.*

*The grounds were quiet, lighted only by the now-dimmed lanterns along the footpaths and in the trees. It was easy to stay hidden in the shadows as he hurried toward the Olympic pool. Would she still be there?*

*The change in wind had caused a mist to blow in from the sea. In minutes, the stars had been covered by clouds, the moon had disappeared. Even if anyone happened to stand at a window and look out, he would not be seen.*

*Elizabeth planned to stay at the Spa until she saw Sammy tomorrow night. That gave him only a day and a half—until Tuesday morning—to arrange her death.*

*He stopped at the shrubbery that edged the patio around the Olympic pool. In the darkness he could barely see Elizabeth's moving form as she swam with swift, sure strokes from one end of the pool to the other. Carefully, he calculated his chance of success. The idea had come to him when Min said Elizabeth was always in this pool around ten o'clock. Even strong swimmers have accidents. A sudden cramp, no one within hearing distance if she cried out, no marks, no signs of struggle . . . His plan was to slip into the pool when she was almost at the opposite end, wait and pounce on her as she passed him, hold her down until she stopped struggling. Now, he edged his way from behind the shrubbery. It was dark enough to risk a closer look.*

*He had forgotten how fast she swam. Though she was so slender, the muscles in her arms were like steel. Suppose she was able to fight long enough to attract attention? And she was probably wearing one of those damn whistles Min insisted lone swimmers put on.*

*His eyes narrowed in anger and frustration as he crouched nearer and nearer the edge of the pool, ready to spring, not sure if this was the precisely right moment. She was a faster swimmer than he was. In the water she might have the advantage over him. . . .*

*He could not afford to make a second mistake.*

IN AQUA SANITAS. The Romans had chiseled the motto into the walls of their bathhouses. If I believed in reincarnation, I would think I had lived in those times, Elizabeth thought as she glided across the dark recess of the pool. When she had begun to swim, it had been possible to see not only the perimeter of the pool, but the surrounding area with its lounge chairs and umbrella tables and flowering hedges. Now they were only dark silhouettes.

The persistent headache she'd had all evening began to ebb, the sense of enclosure faded; once again she began to experience the release she had always found in water. "Do you think it started in the womb?" she'd once joked to Leila. "I mean this absolute sensation of being free when I'm immersed."

Leila's answer had shocked her: "Maybe Mama was happy when she was carrying you, Sparrow. I've always thought that your father was Senator Lange. He and Mama had a big thing going after my daddy-dear split the scene. When *I* was in the womb, I gather they called me 'the mistake.'"

It was Leila who had suggested that Elizabeth use the stage name *Lange*. "It probably should be your real name, Sparrow," she had said. "Why not?"

As soon as Leila began making money, she had sent a check to Mama every month. One day the check was returned uncashed by Mama's last boyfriend. Mama had died of acute alcoholism.

Elizabeth touched the far wall, brought her knees to her chest and flipped her body over, changing from a backstroke to a breaststroke in one fluid movement. Was it possible that Leila's fear of personal relationships had begun at the moment of conception? Can a speck of protoplasm sense that the climate is hostile, and can that realization color a whole life? Wasn't it because of Leila that she'd never experienced that terrible sense of parental rejection? She remembered her mother's description of bringing her home from the hospital: "Leila took her out of my arms. She moved the crib into her room. She was only eleven, but she became that child's mother. I wanted to call her Laverne, but Leila put her foot down. She said, *'Her name is Elizabeth!'* " One more reason to be grateful to Leila, Elizabeth thought.

The soft ripple that her body made as she moved through the water masked the faint sound of footsteps at the other end of the pool. She had reached the north end and was starting back. For some reason she began to swim furiously, as though sensing danger.

*The shadowy figure edged its way along the wall. He coldly calculated the speed of her swift, graceful progress. Timing was essential. Grab her from behind as she passed, lie over her body, hold her face in the water until she stopped struggling. How long would it take? A minute? Two? But suppose she wasn't that easy to subdue? This had to appear to be an accidental drowning.*

*Then an idea came to him, and in the darkness his lips stretched in the semblance of a smile. Why hadn't he thought of the scuba equipment earlier?*

*Wearing the oxygen tank would make it possible for him to hold her at the bottom of the pool until he was certain she was dead. The wet suit, the gloves, the mask, the goggles were a perfect disguise, if anyone happened to see him cutting across the grounds.*

*He watched as she began to swim toward the steps. The impulse to get rid of her now was almost overwhelming. Tomorrow night, he promised himself. Carefully he moved closer as she placed her foot on the bottom step of the ladder and straightened up. His narrowed eyes strained to watch as she slipped on her robe and began to walk along the path to her bungalow.*

*Tomorrow night he would be waiting here for her. The next morning someone would spot her body at the bottom of the pool, as the workman had spotted Leila's body in the courtyard.*

*And he would have nothing left to fear.*

# Monday,
## August 31

QUOTE FOR THE DAY:
*A witty woman is a treasure; a witty beauty is a power.*

—George Meredith

Good morning, dear guests.

We hope you have slept blissfully. The weatherman promises us yet another beautiful Cypress Point Spa day.

A little reminder. Some of us are forgetting to fill out our luncheon menu. We don't want you to have to wait for service after all that vigorous exercise and delicious pampering of the morning. So do please take a tiny moment to circle your choices before you leave your room now.

In just a moment, we'll be greeting you on our morning walk. Hurry and join us.

And remember, another day at Cypress Point Spa means another set of dazzling hours dedicated to making you a more beautiful person, the kind of person people long to be with, to touch, to love.

Baron and Baroness Helmut von Schreiber

# 1

Elizabeth woke long before dawn on Monday morning. Even the swim had not performed its usual magic. For what seemed most of the night, she had been troubled with broken dreams, fragments that came and went intermittently. They were all in the dreams: Mama, Leila, Ted, Craig, Syd, Cheryl, Sammy, Min, Helmut—even Leila's two husbands, those transitory charlatans who had used her success to get themselves into the spotlight: the first an actor, the second a would-be producer and socialite. . . .

At six o'clock she got out of bed, pulled up the shade, then huddled back under the light covers. It was chilly, but she loved to watch the sun come up. It seemed to her that the early morning had a dreamy quality of its own, the human quiet was so absolute. The only sounds came from the seabirds along the shore.

At six thirty there was a tap on the door. Vicky, the maid who brought in the wake-up glass of juice, had been with the Spa for years. She was a sturdy sixty-year-old woman who supplemented her husband's pension by what she sardonically called "carrying breakfast roses to fading blossoms." They greeted each other with the warmth of old friends.

"It feels strange to be on the guest end of the place," Elizabeth commented.

"You earned your right to be here. I saw you in *Hilltop*. You're a damn good actress."

"I still feel surer of myself teaching water aerobics."

"And Princess Di can always get a job teaching kindergarten. Come off it."

She deliberately waited until she was sure that the daily procession called The Cypress Hike was in progress. By the time she went out, the marchers, led by Min and the Baron, were already nearing the path that led to the coast. The hike took in the Spa property, the Crocker wooded preserve and Cypress Point, wound past the Pebble Beach golf course, circled the Lodge and backtracked to the Spa. In all, it was a brisk fifty-minute exercise, followed by breakfast.

Elizabeth waited until the hikers were out of sight before she began jogging in the opposite direction from them. It was still early, and traffic was light. She would have preferred to run along the coast, where she could have an unbroken view of the ocean, but that would have meant risking being noticed by the others.

If only Sammy were back, she thought as she began to quicken her pace. I could talk to her and be

on a plane this afternoon. She wanted to get away
from here. If Alvirah Meehan was to be believed,
Cheryl had called Leila a "washed-up drunk" last
night. And except for Ted, her murderer, everyone
else had laughed.

Min, Helmut, Syd, Cheryl, Craig, Ted. The people who had been closest to Leila; the weeping
mourners at her memorial service. Oh, Leila! Elizabeth thought. Incongruously, lines from a song she
had learned as a child came back to her.

*Though all the world betray thee,*
*One sword at least thy rights shall guard,*
*One faithful heart shall praise thee.*

I'll sing your praises, Leila! Tears stung her eyes,
and she dabbed at them impatiently. She began to
jog faster, as if to outrun her thoughts. The early-
morning mist was being burned away by the sun;
the thick shrubbery that bordered the homes along
the road was bathed in morning dew; the sea gulls
arced overhead and swooped back to the shore.
How accurate a witness was Alvirah Meehan?
There was something oddly intense about the
woman, something that went beyond her excitement at being here.

She was passing the Pebble Beach golf links.
Early golfers were already on the course. She had
taken up golf in college. Leila had never played.
She used to tell Ted that someday she'd make time
to learn. She never would have, Elizabeth thought,

and a smile touched her lips; Leila was too impatient to traipse after a ball for four or five hours. . . .

Her breath was coming in gulps, and she slowed her pace. I'm out of shape, she thought. Today she would go to the women's spa and take a full schedule of exercises and treatments. It would be a useful way to pass the time. She turned down the road that led back to the Spa—and collided with Ted.

He grasped her arms to keep her from falling. Gasping at the force of the impact, she struggled to push him away from her. "Let go of me." Her voice rose. *"I said, let go of me."* She was aware that there was no one else on the road. He was perspiring, his T-shirt clinging to his body. The expensive watch Leila had given him glistened in the sun.

He released her. Stunned and frightened, she watched as he stared down at her, his expression inscrutable. "Elizabeth, I've got to talk to you."

He wasn't even going to pretend he hadn't planned this.

"Say what you have to say in court." She tried to pass him, but he blocked her way. Inadvertently she stepped back. Was this what Leila had felt at the end: this sense of being trapped?

"I said listen to me." It seemed that he had sensed her fear and was infuriated by it.

"Elizabeth, you haven't given me a chance. I know how it looks. Maybe—and this is something I just don't know—*maybe* you're right, and I went back upstairs. I *was* drunk and angry, but I was also terribly worried about Leila. Elizabeth, think about this: if you are right, if I did go back up, if that woman is right who says she saw me struggling with Leila, won't you at least grant that I might have been trying to *save* her? You know how depressed Leila was that day. She was almost out of her mind."

"*If* you went back upstairs. Are you telling me now that you're willing to concede you went back upstairs?" Elizabeth felt as though her lungs were closing. The air seemed suddenly humid and heavy with the scent of still-damp cypress leaves and moist earth. Ted was just over six feet tall, but the three-inch difference in their heights seemed to disappear as they stared at each other. She was aware again of the intensity of the lines that seared the skin around his eyes and mouth.

"Elizabeth, I know how you must feel about me, but there is something you *have* to understand. I don't remember what happened that night. I was so damn drunk; so damn upset. Over these months I've begun to have some vague impression of being at the door of Leila's apartment, of pushing it open. So maybe you're right, maybe you *did* hear me call something to her. *But I have absolutely no memory beyond that!* That is the truth as I know it. The next question: do you think, drunk or sober, that I'm capable of murder?"

His dark blue eyes were clouded with pain. He bit his lip and held his hands out imploringly. "Well, Elizabeth?"

In a quick move she darted around him and ran

for the gates of the Spa. The district attorney had predicted this. If Ted didn't think he could lie his way out of being on the terrace with Leila, he would say he was trying to save her.

She didn't look back until she was at the gates. Ted had not attempted to follow her. He was standing where she had left him, staring after her, his hands on his hips.

Her arms were still burning from the force with which his hands had grabbed her. She remembered something else the district attorney had told her.

Without her as a witness, Ted would go free.

# 2

At eight A.M., Dora "Sammy" Samuels backed her car out of her cousin Elsie's driveway and with a sigh of relief began the drive from the Napa Valley to the Monterey Peninsula. With any luck, she'd be there about two o'clock. Originally she'd planned to leave in the late afternoon, and Elsie had been openly annoyed that she'd changed her mind, but she was eager to get back to the Spa and go through the rest of the mailbags.

She was a wiry seventy-one-year-old woman with steel-gray hair pulled back in a neat bun. Old-fashioned rimless glasses sat on the bridge of her small, straight nose. It had been a year and a half since an aneurism had nearly killed her, and the massive surgery had left her with a permanent air of fragility, but until now she had always impatiently shaken off any talk of retirement.

It had been a disquieting weekend. Her cousin had always disapproved of Dora's job with Leila. "Answering fan mail from vapid women" was the way she put it. "I should think with your brains, you'd find a better way to spend your time. Why don't you do volunteer teaching?"

Long ago, Dora had given up trying to explain to Elsie that after thirty-five years of teaching, she never wanted to see a textbook again, that the eight years she'd worked for Leila had been the most exciting of her own uneventful life.

This weekend had been particularly trying, because when Elsie saw her going through the sack of fan mail, she'd been astonished. "You mean to tell me that seventeen months after that woman died, you're *still* writing to her fans? Are you crazy?"

No, she wasn't, Dora told herself as she drove well within the speed limit through the wine country. It was a hot, lazy day, but even so, busloads of sightseers were already passing her, heading for vineyard tours and wine-tasting parties.

She had not tried to explain to Elsie that sending personal notes to the people who had loved Leila was a way of assuaging her own sense of loss. She had also *not* told her cousin the reason why she had brought up the heavy sack of mail. She was searching to see if Leila had received other poison-pen letters than the one she had already found.

That one had been mailed three days before Leila died. The address on the envelope and the enclosed note were put together with words and phrases snipped from magazines and newspapers. It read:

Leila,

How many Times Do I Have to write? Can't YOU get it straight ThAT Ted is sick OF You? His new girl is beautiful and much younger THaN you. I told you ThAT the emerald necklace HE gave Her matcHes the bracelet he gave you. It cost Twice as much And looks ten Times better. I hear your play is Lousy. You really should Learn your lines. I'll write again soon.

Your friend.

Thinking of that note, of the others that must have preceded it, brought a fresh burst of outrage. Leila, Leila, she whispered. Who would *do* that to you?

She of all people had understood Leila's terrible vulnerability, understood that her outward confidence, her flamboyant public image was the facade of a deeply insecure woman.

She remembered how Elizabeth had gone off to school just at the time she'd started working for Leila. She'd seen Leila come back from the airport, lonely, devastated, in tears. "God, Sammy," she said. "I can't believe I may not see Sparrow for months. But a Swiss boarding school! Won't that be a great experience for her? A big difference from Lumber Creek High, my alma mater." Then she said hesitantly, "Sammy, I'm not doing anything tonight. Will you stay, and let's get something to eat?"

The years went by so quickly, Dora thought as another bus honked impatiently and passed her. Today, for some reason, the memory of Leila seemed particularly vivid to her: Leila with her wild extravagances, spending money as fast as she made it; Leila's two marriages. . . . Dora had begged her not to marry the second one. *"Haven't you learned your lesson yet?"* she pleaded. *"You can't afford another leech."*

*Leila with her arms hugging her knees. "Sammy, he's not that bad. He makes me laugh, and that's a plus."*

*"If you want to laugh, hire a clown."*

*Leila's fierce hug. "Oh, Sammy, promise you'll always say it straight. You're probably right, but I guess I'll go through with it."*

*Getting rid of the funnyman had cost her two million dollars.*

*Leila with Ted. "Sammy, it can't last. Nobody's that wonderful. What does he see in me?"*

*"Are you crazy? Have you stopped looking in the mirror?"*

*Leila, always so apprehensive when she started a new film. "Sammy, I stink in this part. I shouldn't have taken it. It's not me."*

*"Come off it. I saw the dailies too. You're wonderful."*

She'd won the Oscar for that performance.

But in those last few years she had been miscast in three films. Her worry about her career became an obsession. Her love for Ted was equaled only by her fear of losing him. And then Syd had brought her the play. "Sammy, I swear I don't have to act in this one. I just have to be me. I love it."

Then it was over, Dora thought. In the end, each of us left her alone. I was sick, she told herself; Elizabeth was touring with her own play; Ted was constantly away on business. And someone who knew Leila well attacked her with those poison-pen letters, shattered that fragile ego, precipitated the drinking. . . .

Dora realized that her hands were trembling. She scanned the road for signs of a restaurant. Perhaps she would feel better if she stopped for a cup of tea. When she got to the Spa, she would begin going through the rest of the unopened mail.

She knew that Elizabeth would somehow find a way to trace the poison-pen mail back to its sender.

# 3

When Elizabeth reached her bungalow, she found a note from Min pinned with her schedule to the terry-cloth robe folded on the bed. It read:

My dear Elizabeth,

I do hope that while you are here you will enjoy a day of treatment and exercise at the Spa. As you know, it is necessary that all new guests consult briefly with Helmut before beginning any activities. I have scheduled you for his first appointment.

Please know that your ultimate happiness and well-being are very important to me.

The letter had been written in Min's florid, sweeping penmanship. Quickly, Elizabeth scanned her schedule. Interview with Dr. Helmut von Schreiber at 8:45; aerobic dance class at 9; massage at 9:30; trampoline at 10; advanced water aerobics at 10:30—that had been the class she taught when she worked here; facial at 11; cypress curves 11:30; herbal wrap at noon. The afternoon schedule included a loofah, a manicure, a yoga class, a pedicure, two more water exercises . . .

She would have preferred to avoid seeing Helmut, but she didn't want to make an issue of it.

Her interview with him was brief. He checked her pulse and blood pressure, then examined her skin under a strong light. "Your face is like a fine carving," he told her. "You are one of those fortunate women who will become more beautiful as you age. It's all in the bone structure."

Then, as if he were thinking aloud, he murmured, "Wildly lovely as Leila was, her beauty was the kind that peaks and begins to slip away. The last time she was here I suggested that she begin collagen treatments, and we had planned to do her eyes as well. Did you know that?"

"No." Elizabeth realized with a pang of regret that her reaction to the Baron's remark was to be hurt that Leila had not confided her plans to her. Or was he lying?

"I am sorry," Helmut said softly. "I should not have brought up her name. And if you wonder why she did not confide in you, I think you must realize that Leila had become very conscious of the three-year age difference between her and Ted. I was able to assure her honestly that it made no difference between people who love each other—after all, I should know—but even so, she had begun to worry. And to see you growing lovelier, as she began to find those small signs of age in herself, was a problem for her."

Elizabeth got up. Like all the other offices at the Spa, this one had the look of a well-appointed living room. The blue-and-green prints on the couches and chairs were cool and restful, the draperies tied back to allow the sunshine to stream in. The view included the putting green and the ocean.

She knew Helmut was studying her intently. His extravagant compliments were the sugar coating on a bitter pill. He was trying to make her believe that Leila had begun to consider her a competitor. But why? Remembering the hostility with which he had studied Leila's picture when he thought he was unobserved, she wondered if Helmut was viciously trying to get even for Leila's barbs by suggesting she had been beginning to lose her beauty.

Leila's face flashed in her mind: the lovely mouth; the dazzling smile; the emerald-green eyes; the glorious red hair, like a blazing fire around her shoulders. To steady herself, she pretended to be reading one of the framed ads about the Spa. One phrase caught her eye: *a butterfly floating on a cloud.* Why did it seem familiar?

The belt of her terry-cloth robe had loosened. As she tightened it, she turned to Helmut. "If one tenth of the women who spend a fortune in this place had even a fragment of Leila's looks, you'd be out of business, Baron."

He did not reply.

The women's spa was busier than it had been the previous afternoon, but certainly not at the level she remembered. Elizabeth went from exercise class to treatment, glad to really work out again, then equally glad to relax under the skillful hands of the masseuse or facialist. She encountered Cheryl several times in the ten-minute breaks between appointments. *A washed-up drunk*. She was barely civil to Cheryl, who didn't seem to notice. Cheryl acted preoccupied.

Why not? Ted was on the premises, and Cheryl was obviously still dazzled by him.

Alvirah Meehan was in the same aerobic dance class—a surprisingly agile Alvirah, with a good sense of rhythm. Why in the name of heaven did she wear that sunburst pin on her robe? Elizabeth noticed that Alvirah fiddled with the pin whenever she got into a conversation. She also noticed, with some amusement, Cheryl's unsuccessful efforts not to be cornered by Mrs. Meehan.

She went back to her own bungalow for lunch; she did not want to risk running into Ted again by lunching at one of the poolside tables. As she ate the fresh-fruit salad and sipped the iced tea, she phoned the airline and changed her reservation. She could get a ten-o'clock flight to New York from San Francisco the next morning.

She had been frantic to get out of New York. Now, with equal fervor, she wanted to be out of here.

She put on her robe and prepared to go back to the spa for the afternoon session. All morning she had tried to push Ted's face from her mind. Now it filled her vision again. Pain-racked. Angry. Imploring. Vengeful. What expression had she seen in it? And would she spend the rest of her life trying to escape it, after the trial—and the verdict?

# 4

Alvirah collapsed on her bed with a grateful sigh. She was dying for a nap, but knew it was important to record her impressions while they were fresh in her mind. She propped herself on her pillows, reached for the recorder and began to speak.

"It is four o'clock and I am resting in my bungalow. I have finished my first full day of activities at the Spa and I must report I am absolutely exhausted. Go, go, go. We started with a hike; then I came back here and the maid brought in my schedule for the day on my breakfast tray. Breakfast was a poached egg on a couple of crumbs of whole-wheat toast and coffee. My schedule, which is on a tag that you tie to your robe, showed me as having two water aerobics classes, a yoga class, a facial, a massage, two dance classes, a warm hose treatment, fifteen minutes in the steam box and a whirlpool dip. . . .

"The water aerobics classes are very interesting. I push a beach ball around in the water, which sounds very easy, but now my shoulders hurt and I've got muscles in my thighs I didn't know existed. The yoga class wasn't bad except that I can't get my knees in the Lotus position. The dance exercise was fun. If I do say so myself I was always a good dancer, and even though this is just hopping from one foot to the other and doing a lot of kicking, I put some of the younger women to shame. Maybe I should have been a Rockette.

"The warm hose treatment is another word for crowd control. I mean they turn these powerful hoses on you while you're standing in the buff, and you hang on to a metal bar hoping you won't get washed away. But supposedly it breaks down fatty cells, and if so, I'm ready for two treatments a day.

"The clinic is a very interesting building. From the outside it looks just like the main house, but inside it's totally different. All the treatment rooms have private entrances, with high hedges leading to them. The idea is that people don't bump into each other coming and going for appointments. I mean, I really don't care that the whole world knows I'm going to have some collagen injections to fill out the lines around my mouth, but I can well understand why someone like Cheryl Manning would be very upset if that was general knowledge.

"I had my interview with Baron von Schreiber about my collagen injections this morning. The Baron is a charming man. So handsome, and the way he bowed over my hand made me very fluttery. If I were his wife, I think I'd be pretty nervous about holding him, especially if I had fifteen years on him. I think it *is* fifteen years, but I'll check that when I write my article.

"The Baron examined my face under a strong light and said that I had remarkably tight skin and the only treatment he would suggest besides the regular facials and a peeling mask would be the collagen injections. I explained to him that when I made my reservations, his receptionist, Dora Samuels, suggested that I have a test to see if I'd be allergic to collagen, and I did. I'm not allergic, but I told the Baron how scared I am of needles, and how many would he have to use?

"He was so nice. He said that a lot of people feel that way about needles, and when I go for my treatment the nurse will give me a double-strength Valium, and by the time he's ready to start the injections, I'll think I'm just getting a couple of mosquito bites.

"Oh, one more thing. The Baron's office has lovely paintings in it, but I was really fascinated by the ad for the Spa that has appeared in magazines like *Architectural Digest* and *Town and Country* and *Vogue*. He told me there's a copy of it on the wall in all the bungalows. It's so cleverly worded.

"The Baron seemed pleased that I noticed. He said he'd had a hand in creating it."

# 5

Ted spent the morning working out in the gym in the men's spa. With Craig at his side, he rowed stationary boats, pedaled stationary bicycles and methodically made his way through the aerobics machines.

They decided to finish with a swim and found Syd pacing laps in the indoor pool. Impulsively, Ted challenged him and Craig to a race. He had been swimming daily in Hawaii, but finished barely ahead of Craig. To his surprise, even Syd was only a few feet behind him. "You're keeping in shape," he told him. He had always thought of Syd as sedentary, but the man was surprisingly strong.

"I've had time to keep in shape. Sitting in an office waiting for the phone to ring gets boring." With unspoken consent, they walked to deck chairs far enough away from the pool to avoid being overheard.

"I was surprised to find you here, Syd. When we talked last week, you didn't tell me you were coming." Craig's eyes were cold.

Syd shrugged. "You didn't tell me you people were coming either. This place isn't my idea. Cheryl made the decision." He glanced at Ted. "She must have found out you'd be around."

"Min would know better than to blab—"

Syd interrupted Craig. With one finger, he beckoned to the waiter who was going from table to table offering soft drinks. "Perrier."

"Make it three," Craig said.

"Do you want to swallow it for me too?" Ted snapped. "I'll have a Coke," he told the waiter.

"You never drink colas," Craig commented mildly. His light hazel eyes were tolerant. He

amended the order. "Bring two Perriers and an
orange juice."

Syd chose to ignore the byplay. "Min wouldn't
blab, but don't you think there are people on the
staff who get paid to tip the columnists? Bettina
Scuda called Cheryl yesterday morning. She probably put the bug in her ear that you were on the way.
What's the difference? So she makes a play for you
again. Is that new? Use it. She's dying to be a witness
for you at the trial. If anyone can convince a jury
how nutty Leila acted in Elaine's, Cheryl can. And
I'll back her up."

He put a friendly hand on Ted's shoulder. "This
whole thing stinks. We're going to help you beat it.
You can count on us."

"Translated, that means you owe him one," Craig
commented as they walked back to Ted's bungalow.
"Don't fall for it. So what if he lost a million bucks in
that goddamn play? You lost *four* million, and he
talked you into investing."

"I invested because I read the play and felt that
someone had managed to capture the essence of
Leila; created a character who was funny and vulnerable and willful and impossible and sympathetic
all at the same time. It ought to have been a tri-
umph for her."

"It was a four-million-dollar mistake," Craig said.
"Sorry, Ted, but you do pay me to give you good
advice."

* * *

Henry Bartlett spent the morning in Ted's bungalow reviewing the transcript of the grand jury hearing and on the phone to his Park Avenue office. "In case we go for a temporary-insanity defense, we'll need plenty of documentation of similar successful pleas," he told them. He was wearing an opennecked cotton shirt and baggy khaki walking shorts. The Sahib! Ted thought. He wondered if Bartlett wore knickers on the golf course.

The library table was covered with annotated piles of paper. "Remember how Leila and Elizabeth and you and I used to play Scrabble at this table?" he asked Craig.

"And you and Leila always won. Elizabeth was stuck with me. As Leila put it, 'Bulldogs can't spell.' "

"What's that supposed to mean?" Henry asked.

"Oh, Leila had nicknames for all her close friends," Craig explained. "Mine was Bulldog."

"I'm not sure I'd have been flattered."

"Yes, you would have. When Leila gave you a nickname, it meant you were part of her inner circle."

Was that true? Ted wondered. When you looked up the definitions of the nicknames Leila bestowed, there was always a double edge to them. Falcon: a hawk trained to hunt and kill. Bulldog: a shorthaired, square-jawed, heavily built dog with a tenacious grip.

"Let's order lunch," Henry said. "We've got a long afternoon of work ahead of us."

Over a club sandwich, Ted described his encounter with Elizabeth. "So you can forget yesterday's suggestion," he told Henry. "It's just as I thought. If I admit the possibility that I went back to Leila's apartment, when Elizabeth gets through testifying I'll be on my way to Attica."

It *was* a long afternoon. Ted listened as Henry Bartlett explained the theory of temporary insanity. "Leila had publicly rejected you; she had quit a play in which you invested four million dollars. The next day you pleaded with her for a reconciliation. She continued to insult you, to demand that you match her drink for drink."

"I could afford the tax write-off," Ted interrupted.

"You know that. I know it. But the guy on the jury who's behind in his car payments won't believe it."

"I refuse to concede that I might have killed Leila. I won't even consider it."

Bartlett's face was becoming flushed. "Ted, you'd better understand I'm trying to help you. All right, you were smart to get a reading on Elizabeth Lange's reaction today. So we can't admit you might have gone back upstairs. If we don't claim a total blackout on your part, we have to destroy both Elizabeth Lange's testimony and the eyewitness'. One or the other: maybe. I've told you this before. Both: no."

"There's one possibility I'd like to explore," Craig

suggested. "We've got psychiatric information on that so-called eyewitness. I'd suggested to Ted's first lawyer that we put a detective on her trail and get a more rounded picture of her. I still think that's a good idea."

"It is." Bartlett's eyes disappeared beneath a heavy-lidded frown. "I wish it had been done a long time ago."

They are talking about me, Ted thought. They are discussing what can and cannot be done to win my eventual freedom as though I weren't here. A slow, hard anger that now seemed to be part of his persona made him want to lash out at them. Lash out at them? The lawyer who supposedly would win his case? The friend who had been his eyes and ears and voice these last months? But I don't want them to take my life out of my hands, Ted thought, and tasted the acid that suddenly washed his mouth. I can't blame them, but I can't trust them either. No matter what, it's as I've known right along: I have to take care of this myself.

Bartlett was still talking to Craig. "Have you an agency in mind?"

"Two or three. We've used them when there's been an internal problem we had to solve without publicity." He named the investigative agencies.

Bartlett nodded. "They're all fine. See which one can get right on the case. I want to know if Sally Ross is a drinker; if she has friends she confides in; if she's ever discussed the case with them; if any of them were with her the night Leila LaSalle died.

Don't forget, everyone's taking her word that she was in her apartment and happened to be looking at Leila's terrace at the precise moment Leila plunged off it."

He glanced at Ted. "With or without *Teddy's* help."

When Craig and Henry finally left him at quarter of five, Ted felt drained. Restlessly he switched on the television set and in a reflex gesture switched it off. He certainly wouldn't clear his mind by watching soap operas. A walk would feel good, a long, long walk where he could breathe in the salty spray of the ocean and maybe wander past his grandparents' house where he'd spent so much time as a kid.

Instead, he elected to shower. He went into the bathroom and for a moment stared at his reflection in the paneled mirror that covered half the wall around the oversize marble sink. Flecks of gray around his temples. Signs of strain around his eyes. A tautness around his mouth. *Stress manifests itself both mentally and physically.* He'd heard a pop psychologist deliver that line on a morning news program. No kidding, he thought.

Craig had suggested that they might share a two-bedroom unit. Ted hadn't answered, and obviously Craig got the message; he hadn't pursued the idea.

Wouldn't it be nice if everybody understood without being told that you needed a certain amount of space? He stripped and tossed his discarded clothes into the bathroom hamper. With a half-smile he remembered how Kathy, his wife, had gotten him out of the habit of dropping clothes as he stepped out of them. "I don't care how rich your family is," she would chide. "I think it's disgusting to expect another human being to pick your laundry off the floor."

"But it's distinguished laundry."

His face in her hair. The scent she always used, a twenty-dollar cologne. "Save your money. I can't wear expensive perfume. It overwhelms me."

The icy shower helped to relieve the dull, throbbing headache. Feeling somewhat better, Ted wrapped the terry-cloth robe around him, rang for the maid and requested iced tea. It would have been enjoyable to sit on the deck, but too much of a risk. He didn't want to get into a conversation with someone walking by. Cheryl. It would be just like her to "accidentally" pass. Good God, would she never get over their casual affair? She was beautiful, she had been amusing and she did have a certain hardheaded ability to cut through the bull—but even if he didn't have the trial hanging over his head, there was no way he would get involved with her again.

He settled on the couch, where he could look out on the ocean and watch the sea gulls arcing over the foaming surf, beyond the threat of the undertow, beyond the power of the waves to crash them against the rocks.

He felt himself begin to perspire as the prospect of the trial loomed in his mind. Impatiently, he got up and pushed open the door to the side deck. Late August usually carried this welcome tang of chill. He put his hands on the railing.

When had he begun to realize that he and Leila wouldn't make it, in the long run? The mistrust for men so ingrained in her head had become intolerable. Was that the reason he'd overruled Craig's advice and put the millions in her play? Subconsciously had he hoped that she would get so caught up in a smash hit that she would decide she didn't want to accept the social demands of his life, or his desire for a family? Leila was an actress—first, last, always. She *talked* about wanting a child, but it wasn't true. She had satisfied her maternal instincts by raising Elizabeth.

The sun was beginning to lower over the Pacific. The air was filled with the humming of the crickets and the katydids. Evening. Dinner. He could already see the expressions on the faces around the table. Min and Helmut, phony smiles, worried eyes. Craig trying to read his mind. Syd, a certain defiant nervousness about him. How much did Syd owe the wrong people for the money he'd put into the play? How much was Syd hoping to borrow? How much was his testimony worth? Cheryl, all seductive enticement. Alvirah Meehan, fiddling with that damn sunburst pin, her eyes snapping with curiosity. Henry watching Elizabeth through the glass partition. Elizabeth, her face cold and scornful, studying them all.

Ted glanced down. The bungalow was set on sloping ground, and the side veranda jutted out over a ten-foot drop. He stared at the red-flowered bushes below. Images formed in his mind, and he rushed back inside.

He was still trembling when the maid came with the iced tea. Heedless of the delicate satin puff, he threw himself down on the massive king-size bed. He wished that dinner were over; that the night, with all it entailed, were over.

His mouth curved in a grim attempt at a smile. Why was he wishing the evening away? What kind of dinners do they serve in prison? he wondered.

He would have plenty of evenings to find out.

# 6

Dora arrived back at the Spa at two o'clock, dropped her bag in her room and went directly to her desk in the reception office.

Min had allowed her to keep the sacks of unanswered fan mail in a closet in the file room. Dora usually took out a handful at a time and kept them in the bottom drawer of her desk. She knew the sight of Leila's mail was an irritant to Min. Now she didn't care if Min was annoyed. She had the rest of the day off, and she intended to search for any further letters.

For the tenth time since she had found it, Dora re-examined the poison-pen letter. With each reading, her conviction grew that there might have been at least an element of truth in it. Happy as Leila had been with Ted, her distress over the last three or four films had often made her temperamental and moody. Dora had noticed Ted's increasing impatience with the outbursts. Had he become involved with another woman?

That was exactly the way Leila would have been thinking if she opened this kind of letter or a series of these letters. It would explain the anxiety, the drinking, the despondency of those last months. Leila often said, "There are just two people I know I can trust in this world: Sparrow and Falcon. Now you, Sammy, are getting there." Dora had felt honored. "And the *Q.E. Two*"—Leila's name for Min—"is a do-or-die friend, provided there's a buck in it for her and it doesn't conflict with anything the Toy Soldier wants."

Dora reached the office and was glad to see that Min and Helmut weren't there. Outside, the day was sunny, the breeze from the Pacific gentle. Far down on the rocky embankments over the ocean, she could see the traces of ice plants, the henna-and-green-and-rust-shaded leaves that lived on water and air. Elizabeth and Ted had been water and air to Leila.

Quickly she went into the file room. With Min's passion for beautiful surroundings, even this small storage area was extravagantly designed. The cus-

tom-made files were a sunny yellow, the ceramic-
tile floor was in shades of gold and umber, a Jaco-
bean sideboard had been converted into a supply
cupboard.

There were still two full sacks of letters to Leila.
They ranged from lined paper torn from a child's
notebook to expensive, perfumed stationery. Dora
scooped a batch of them into her arms and brought
them to her desk.

It was a slow process. She could not assume that
another anonymous letter would necessarily come
addressed with snipped and pasted words and numbers like the one she had found. She began with the
letters already opened, the ones Leila had seen. But
after forty minutes she'd gotten nowhere. Most of
the mail was the usual. *You're my favorite actress
. . . I named my daughter after you . . . I saw you
on Johnny Carson. You looked beautiful, and you
were so funny . . .* But there were also several surprisingly harsh critical notes. *That's the last time I
spend five dollars to see you. What a lousy movie
. . . Do you read your scripts, Leila, or just take
what roles you can get?*

Her rapt concentration caused her to be unaware
of Min and Helmut's four-o'clock arrival. One minute she was alone; the next they were approaching
her desk. She looked up, tried to summon a natural
smile and with a casual movement of her hand slid
the anonymous letter into the pile.

It was clear that Min was upset. She did not seem

to notice that Dora was early. "Sammy, get me the file on the bathhouse."

Min waited while she went for it. When she returned, Helmut reached out his hand to take the manila folder, but Min literally grabbed it first. Min was ghastly pale. Helmut patted her arm. "Minna, please, you are hyperventilating."

Min ignored him. "Come inside," she ordered Dora.

"I'll just tidy up first." Dora indicated her desk.

"Forget it. It's not going to make any difference."

There was nothing she could do. If she made any attempt to put the anonymous letter into her drawer, Min would demand to see it. Dora patted her hair and followed Min and Helmut into their private office. Something was dreadfully wrong, and it had to do with that blasted Roman bath.

Min went to her own desk, opened the file and began to race through the papers in it. Most of the correspondence was in the form of bills from the contractor. "Five hundred thousand down, three hundred thousand, twenty-five thousand . . ." She kept reading, her voice going higher and higher. *"And now another four hundred thousand dollars before he can continue working on the interior rooms."* She slapped the papers down and slammed her fist on them.

Dora hurried to get a glass of ice water from the office refrigerator. Helmut rushed around the desk, put his hands on Min's temples and made soft, shushing sounds. "Minna, Minna, you must relax.

Think about something pleasant. You'll bring on high blood pressure."

Dora handed the glass to Min and looked contemptuously at Helmut. That spendthrift, she thought, would put Min in her grave with his crazy projects! Min had been absolutely right when she'd suggested that they add a self-contained budget-price spa on the back half of the property. *That* would have worked. Secretaries as well as socialites were going to spas these days. Instead, this pompous fool had persuaded Min to build the bathhouse. "It will make a statement about us to the world" was his favorite phrase when he talked Min into plunging into debt. Dora knew the finances of this place as well as they did. It couldn't go on. She cut through Helmut's soothing "Minna, Minna—"

"Stop work on the bathhouse immediately," she suggested crisply. "The outside is finished, so the place looks all right. Say the special marble you ordered for the interior has been held up. No one will know the difference. The contractor's pretty much paid to date, isn't he?"

"Very nearly," Helmut agreed. He smiled brightly at Dora as though she had just solved an intricate puzzle. "Dora is right, Minna. We'll put off finishing the bathhouse."

Min ignored him. "I want to go over those figures again." For the next half-hour they had their heads together comparing the contracts, the estimates and the actual figures. At one point Min and then Helmut left the room. Don't let them go to my desk,

Dora prayed. She knew the minute Min calmed down, she would be annoyed to see clutter in the reception area.

Finally Min tossed the original sketches across her desk. "I want to talk to that damn lawyer. It looks to me as if the contractor is entitled to price over-runs on every phase of the job."

"This contractor has soul," Helmut said. "He understands the concept of what we are doing. Minna, we stop building for the moment. Dora is right. We turn the problem into a virtue. We are awaiting shipment of Carrara marble. We still settle for nothing less, yes? So. We shall be admired as purists. *Liebchen*, don't you know that to *create* a desire for something is every bit as important as *fulfilling* it?"

Dora was suddenly aware of another presence in the room. She looked up quickly. Cheryl was standing there, her shapely body curved against the doorframe, her eyes amused. "Have I come at a bad time?" she asked brightly. Without waiting for an answer, she strolled over and leaned past Dora. "Oh, I see you're going over the sketches of the Roman bath." She bent over to examine them.

"Four pools, steam rooms, saunas, more massage rooms, *sleeping* rooms? I love the idea of nap time after a strenuous romp through the mineral baths! Incidentally, won't it cost a fortune to provide real mineral water for the baths? Do you intend to fake it or pipe it in from Baden-Baden?" She straightened up gracefully. "It looks as though you two

could use a little investment capital. Ted respects
my opinion, you know. In fact, he used to listen to
me quite a bit before Leila got her fangs into him.
See you people at dinner."

At the door she turned back and looked over her
shoulder. "Oh, by the way, Min, dear, I left my bill
on Dora's desk. I'm sure it was just an oversight that
one was left in my bungalow. I *know* you planned to
have me as your guest, dear."

*Cheryl had left the bill on her desk.* Dora knew
that meant she had gone through the mail. Cheryl
was what she was. She had probably seen the letter
to Leila.

Min looked at Helmut. Frustrated tears welled in
her eyes. "She knows we're in a bad financial bind,
and it would be just like her to tip the columnists off!
Now we have another freebie—and don't think she
won't use this place as a second home!" Despair-
ingly, Min jammed the scattered bills and sketches
back into the file.

Dora took it from her and replaced it in the file
room. Her heart fluttering rapidly, she went back to
the reception room. The letters to Leila were scattered on her desk; the poison-pen one was missing.

Dismayed, Dora tried to assess what harm that
letter might do. Could it be used to blackmail Ted?
*Or was whoever sent it anxious to have it back, just
in case someone tried to trace it?*

If only she hadn't been reading it when Min and
Helmut came in! Dora sat down at her desk; only

then did she notice that propped against her calendar was Cheryl's bill for her week at the Spa.

Scrawled across it Cheryl had written *Paid in full*.

# 7

At six thirty the phone in Elizabeth's bungalow rang. It was Min. "Elizabeth, I want you to have dinner with Helmut and me tonight. Ted, his lawyer, Craig, Cheryl, Syd—they're all going out." For a moment she sounded like the familiar Min, imperious, brooking no refusal. Then, before Elizabeth could answer, her tone softened. "Please, Elizabeth. You're going home in the morning. We have missed you."

"Is this another one of your games, Min?"

"I was absolutely wrong to have forced that meeting last night. I can only ask you to forgive me."

Min sounded weary, and Elizabeth felt reluctant sympathy. If Min chose to believe in Ted's innocence, so be it. Her scheme to throw them together had been outrageous, but that was Min's way.

"You're *certain* none of them will be in the dining room . . . ?"

"I am certain. Do join us, Elizabeth. You're leaving tomorrow. I've hardly seen you."

It was totally out of character for Min to plead. This would be her only chance to visit with Min, and besides, Elizabeth was not sure she welcomed the prospect of a solitary dinner.

She had had a full afternoon at the Spa, including a loofah treatment, two stretch-exercise classes, a pedicure and manicure, and finally a yoga class. In the yoga class, she'd tried to free her mind, but no matter how much she concentrated, she could not obey the soothing suggestions of the instructor. Over and over, against her will, she kept hearing Ted's question: *If I did go back upstairs . . . Was I trying to save her?*

"Elizabeth . . . ?"

Elizabeth gripped the phone and glanced around, drinking in the restful monochromatic color scheme of this expensive bungalow. "Leila green," Min called it. Min had been sickeningly high-handed last night, but she had certainly loved Leila. Elizabeth heard herself accepting the invitation.

The large bathroom included a step-in tub, whirlpool, stall shower and personal steam-room facility. She chose Leila's favorite way to wind down. Lying in the tub, she took advantage of both steam and whirlpool. Eyes closed, her head cushioned by a terry-cloth neck rest, she felt tension slip away under the soothing mist and churning water.

Again she marveled at the cost of this place. Min must be racing through the millions she'd inherited.

She had noticed that that worry was shared by all the old-timers on the staff. Rita, the manicurist, had told her virtually the same story that she'd heard from the masseuse. "I tell you, Elizabeth," she had complained, "Cypress Point just doesn't have the same excitement since Leila died. The celebrity followers are going to La Costa now. Sure you see some pretty big names, but the word is half of them aren't paying."

After twenty minutes the steam automatically turned off. Reluctantly Elizabeth stood under a cold shower, then draped herself in a thick terry robe and twisted a towel around her hair. There was something else she had overlooked in her anger at finding Ted here. Min had genuinely loved Leila. Her anguish after Leila's death had not been faked. But Helmut? The hostile way he had looked at Leila's picture, his sly suggestion that Leila was losing her looks . . . What had *provoked* that venom? Surely not just the cracks about his being a "toy soldier" that Leila made at his expense? When he overheard them, he was always amused. She remembered the time he'd arrived for dinner at Leila's apartment wearing the tall, old-fashioned cap of a toy soldier.

"I was passing a costume shop, saw it in the window and couldn't resist," he explained as they all applauded. Leila had laughed uproariously and kissed him. "You're a good sport, Your Lordship," she said. . . .

Then what had triggered his anger? Elizabeth

toweled her hair dry, brushed it back and caught it
in a Psyche knot. As she applied makeup and
touched her lips and cheeks with gloss, she could
hear Leila's voice: "My God, Sparrow, you get bet-
ter-looking all the time. I swear you were lucky
Mama was having an affair with Senator Lange
when you were conceived. You remember some of
her other men. How would you like to have been
Matt's kid?"

Last year she'd been in summer stock. When the
show got to Kentucky, she'd gone to the leading
newspaper in Louisville and searched for references to Everett Lange. His obituary notice was
four years old at that time. It gave details of his
family background, his education, his marriage to a
socialite, his achievements in Congress. In his pho-
tograph, she had seen a masculine version of her
own features. . . . Would her life have been different if she had known her father? She suppressed the
thought.

It was a fact of life that everyone at Cypress Point
Spa dressed for dinner. She decided to wear a white
silk jersey tunic with a knotted cord belt and silver
sandals. She wondered if Ted and the others had
gone to the Cannery in Monterey. That used to be
his favorite spot.

One night, three years ago, when Leila had to
leave unexpectedly to shoot extra scenes, Ted had
taken her to the Cannery. They had sat for hours
talking, and he had told her about spending summers with his grandparents in Monterey, about his

mother's suicide when he was twelve, about how much he had despised his father. And he told her about the automobile accident that took the lives of his wife and child. "I couldn't function," he said. "For nearly two years I was a zombie. If it hadn't been for Craig, I'd have had to turn over executive control of my business to someone else. He functioned for me. He became my voice. He practically *was* me."

The next day he told her, "You're too good a listener."

She had known that he was uncomfortable about having revealed so much of himself to her.

She deliberately waited until the "cocktail" hour was nearly over before she left her bungalow. As she followed the path that led to the main house, she stopped to observe the scene on the veranda. The lighted main house, the well-dressed people standing in twos and threes, sipping their make-believe cocktails, talking, laughing, separating, forming into new social units.

She was acutely aware of the breathtaking clarity of the stars against the backdrop of the sky, the artfully placed lanterns that illuminated the path and accentuated the blossoms on the hedges, the placid slap of the Pacific as it washed against the shoreline; and behind the main house, the looming shadow of the bathhouse, its black marble exterior glistening in the reflected light.

Where *did* she belong? Elizabeth wondered. When she was in Europe working, it had been easier to forget the sense of isolation, the alienation from every other human being that had become a fact of her existence. As soon as the movie was in the can, she rushed home, so sure that her apartment would be a haven, the familiarity of New York a welcoming comfort, but in ten minutes, she had been frantic to flee, had grasped at Min's invitation like a drowning woman. Now she was marking the hours until she could go back to New York, and the apartment. She felt as if she had no home.

Would the trial be a purge for her emotions? Would knowing that she had helped to bring about the punishment of Leila's murderer in some way release her, let her reach out to other people, start a new life for herself? "Excuse me." A young couple were behind her. She recognized him as a top-seeded tennis player. How long had she been blocking their path?

"I'm sorry. I guess I'm woolgathering." She stepped aside, and he and the young woman, whose hand was entwined in his, smiled indifferently and passed her. She followed them slowly to the end of the path, up the steps of the veranda. A waiter offered her a drink. She accepted it and quickly moved to the far railing. She had no small talk in her.

Min and Helmut were circulating among their guests with the practiced skill of veteran party givers. Min was triumphantly visible in a flowing yellow satin caftan and cascading diamond earrings. With a measure of surprise, Elizabeth realized that

Min was really quite slim. It was her full breasts and overbearing manner that created the imposing illusion.

As always, Helmut was impeccable, in a navy silk jacket and light gray flannel slacks. He exuded charm as he bowed over hands, smiled, raised one perfectly arched eyebrow—the perfect gentleman.

But why did he hate Leila?

Tonight the dining rooms were decorated in peach: peach tablecloths and napkins, centerpieces of peach roses, Lenox china in a delicate peach-and-gold design. Min's table was set for four. As Elizabeth approached it, she saw the *maître d'* touch Min's arm and direct her to the phone on his desk.

When Min came back to the table, she was visibly annoyed. Nevertheless, her greeting seemed genuine. "Elizabeth, at last a little time to be with you. I had hoped to give both you and Sammy a happy surprise. Sammy returned early. She must have missed my note and didn't realize you were here. I invited her to join us at table, but she's just phoned to say she doesn't feel very well. I told her you were with us and she'll see you in your bungalow after dinner."

"Is she ill?" Elizabeth asked anxiously.

"She had a long drive. Still, she ought to eat. I wish she had made the effort." Min clearly wanted to dismiss any more discussion.

Elizabeth watched as, with a practiced eye, Min surveyed the surroundings. Woe to a waiter who did not have the proper demeanor, who rattled, or spilled, or brushed against the chair of a guest. The thought struck her that it was not like Min to invite Sammy to join her table. Was it possible that Min had guessed there was a special reason she had waited to see Sammy, and wanted to know what it was?

And was it possible that Sammy had shrewdly avoided that trap?

"I'm sorry I'm late." Alvirah Meehan yanked out the chair before the waiter could help her. "The cosmetician did a special makeup after I got dressed," she said, beaming. "How do you like it?"

Alvirah was wearing a scoop-necked beige caftan with intricate brown beading. It looked very expensive. "I bought this in the boutique," she explained. "You have lovely things there. And I bought every single product the makeup woman suggested. She was so helpful."

As Helmut came to the table, Elizabeth studied Min's face with amusement. One was *invited* to join Min and Helmut—something which Mrs. Meehan did not understand. Min could explain that and place her at another table. On the other hand, Mrs. Meehan was in the most expensive bungalow in the Spa; she was clearly buying everything in sight, and offending her could be very foolish. A strained smile tugged at the corners of Min's lips. "You look charming," she told Alvirah. "Tomorrow I shall personally help you select other outfits."

"That's very nice of you." Alvirah fiddled with

her sunburst pin and turned to Helmut. "Baron, I have to tell you I was re-reading your ad—you know, the one you have framed in the bungalows."

"Yes?"

Elizabeth wondered if it was just her imagination that made Helmut suddenly seem wary.

"Well, let me tell you that everything you say about the place is true. Remember how the ad says, 'At the end of a week here, you will feel as free and untroubled as a butterfly floating on a cloud'?"

"The ad reads something like that, yes."

"But you wrote it—didn't you tell me that?"

"I had some input, I said. We have an agency."

"Nonsense, Helmut. Mrs. Meehan obviously agrees with the text of the ad. Yes, Mrs. Meehan, my husband is very creative. He personally writes the daily greeting, and ten years ago when we converted the hotel into the Spa, he simply would not accept the advertising copy we were given, and rewrote it himself. That ad won many awards, which is why we have a framed copy in every bungalow."

"It certainly made important people want to come here," Alvirah told them. "How I wish I'd been a fly on the wall to listen to all of them. . . ." She beamed at Helmut. "Or a butterfly floating on a cloud."

They were eating the low-calorie mousse when it dawned on Elizabeth how skillfully Mrs. Meehan had drawn out Helmut and Min. They had told her stories Elizabeth had never heard before: about an eccentric millionaire who had arrived on opening day on his bicycle, with his Rolls-Royce majestically trailing him, or about how a chartered plane had been sent from Arabia to pick up a fortune in jewels that one of a sheikh's four wives had left behind on a table near the pool. . . .

As they were about to leave the table, Alvirah posed her final question: "Who was the most exciting guest you've ever had?"

Without hesitation, without even looking at each other, they answered "Leila LaSalle."

For some reason, Elizabeth shivered.

Elizabeth did not linger for coffee or the musical program. As soon as she reached her bungalow, she phoned Sammy. There was no answer in her apartment. Puzzled, she dialed Sammy's office.

Sammy's voice had an excited urgency to it when she answered. "Elizabeth, I nearly fainted when Min told me you were here. No, I'm perfectly all right. I'll be right over."

Ten minutes later, Elizabeth flung open the door of her bungalow and threw her arms around the frail, fiercely loyal woman who had shared with her the last years of Leila's life.

Sitting opposite each other on the matching sofas, they took each other's measure. Elizabeth was shocked to see how much Dora had changed. "I know," Dora said with a wry smile. "I don't look that hot."

"You don't look *well*, Sammy," Elizabeth said. "How's it really going?"

Dora shrugged. "I still feel so guilty. You were away, and couldn't see the day-to-day change in Leila. When she came to visit me in the hospital, *I* could see it. Something was destroying her, but she wouldn't talk about it. I ought to have contacted you. I feel I let her down so terribly. And now it's as if I have to find out what happened. I can't let it rest until I do."

Elizabeth felt tears begin to spill from her eyes. "Now don't you dare get *me* started," she said. "For the entire first year I had to carry dark glasses with me. I just never knew when I'd start crying. I used to call the glasses my grief equipment."

She clasped her hands together. "Sammy, tell me. Is there *any* chance I'm wrong about Ted? I was *not* mistaken about the time, and if he pushed Leila off that terrace he has to pay for it. But is it possible he *was* trying to hold her? Why was she so upset? Why was she drinking? You heard her talk about how disgusted she was with people who drank too much. That night, a few minutes before she died, I was nasty to her. I tried to do what she used to do to Mama—shock her, make her see what she was doing to herself. Maybe if I'd been more sympathetic. Sammy, if I'd only asked her *why* !"

In a spontaneous gesture they moved together. Dora's thin arms encircled Elizabeth, felt the trembling in the slender young body and remembered the teenager who had so worshiped her big sister.

"Oh, Sparrow," she said, unthinkingly using Leila's name for Elizabeth, "what would Leila think about the two of us going on like this?"

"She'd say, 'Quit moaning and do something about it.'" Elizabeth dabbed at her eyes and managed a smile.

"Exactly." With quick, nervous movements, Dora smoothed the thin strands of hair that always wanted to slip out from her bun. "Let's backtrack. Had Leila started to act upset before you left on the tour?"

Elizabeth frowned as she tried to focus, to weed out extraneous memories. "It was just before I left that Leila's divorce had come through. She'd been with her accountant. It was the first time in years I'd seen her worried about money. She said something like 'Sparrow, I've made an awful lot of loot, and honest to God, now I'm on thin ice.'

"I told her that two deadbeat husbands had put her in that bind, but I didn't consider being about to marry a multimillionaire like Ted being on thin ice. And she said something like 'Ted really *does* love me, doesn't he?' I told her to, for God's sake, get off that line. I said, 'You keep doubting him and you'll drive him away. He's *nuts* about you. Now go earn the four million bucks he just invested in you!'"

"What did she say?" Dora asked.

"She started to laugh—you know that big, gorgeous laugh of hers—and she said, 'As usual, you're right, Sparrow.' She was terribly excited about the play."

"And then when you were gone, and I was sick, and Ted was traveling, someone began a campaign to destroy her." Dora reached into the pocket of her cardigan. "Today the letter I wrote you about was stolen from my desk. But just before you phoned I found *another* one in Leila's mail. She never got to read it either—it was still sealed—but it speaks for itself."

Horrified, Elizabeth read and reread the uneven, carelessly pasted words:

Leila,

Why won't you admit Ted is trying
to Dump you? His new girl is
getting tired of waiting.
That four million Dollars was his
Kiss-off to you. And more than you're
worth. Don't blow it, honey.
The word's Out it's A Lousy
play–And you're Ten years too old for
the part Too.

Your friend.

Dora watched as Elizabeth's face turned stony pale.

"Leila hadn't seen this?" Elizabeth asked quietly.

"No, but she must have been receiving a series of them."

"Who could have taken the other one today?"

Briefly Dora filled her in on the explosion over the expenses for the bathhouse and about Cheryl's unexpected arrival. "I know Cheryl was at my desk. She left her bill there. But so could anyone else have taken it."

"This smacks of Cheryl's touch." Elizabeth held the letter by the corner, loath to handle it. "I wonder if this can be traced."

"Fingerprints?"

"That, and typeface has a code. Even knowing what magazines and newspapers these words were snipped from could be helpful. Wait a minute." Elizabeth went into the bedroom and returned with a plastic bag. Carefully she slipped the anonymous note into it. "I'll find out where to send this to be analyzed." She sat down again and folded her arms on her knees. "Sammy, do you remember exactly what the other letter said?"

"I think so."

"Then write it down. Just a minute. There's paper in the desk."

Dora wrote, crossed out, rewrote, finally handed the paper to Elizabeth. "That's pretty close."

Leila,
How many times do I have to write? Can't you get it straight that Ted is sick of you? His new girl is beautiful and *much* younger than you. I told

you that the emerald necklace he gave her matches the bracelet he gave you. It cost twice as much and looks ten times better. I hear your play is lousy. You really should learn your lines. I'll write again soon.

Your friend.

This letter Elizabeth read and reread. "That bracelet, Sammy. When did Ted give it to Leila?"

"Sometime after Christmas. The anniversary of their first date, wasn't it? She had me put it in the safety-deposit box because she was starting rehearsals and knew she wouldn't be wearing it."

"That's what I mean. How many people could have known about that bracelet? Ted gave it to her at a dinner party. Who was there?"

"The usual people. Min. Helmut. Craig. Cheryl. Syd. Ted. You and I."

"And the same group of people knew how much Ted put into the play. Remember, he didn't want it publicized. Sammy, have you finished going through the mail?"

"Besides the one I started this afternoon, there's one more large sack. It may have six or seven hundred letters in it."

"Tomorrow morning I'm going to help you go through them. Sammy, think about who might have written these letters. Min and the Baron had nothing to do with the play; they had everything to gain by having Ted and Leila together here, with all the people they attracted. Syd had a million dollars in the play. Craig acted as though the four million Ted invested was out of his own pocket. He certainly wouldn't do anything to wreck the play's chances. But Cheryl never forgave Leila for taking Ted from her. She never forgave Leila for becoming a superstar. She knew Leila's vulnerabilities. And she would be the very one who'd want the letters back now."

"What good are they to her?"

Elizabeth stood up slowly. She walked to the window and pushed back the curtain. The night was still brilliantly clear. "Because if some way they can be traced to her, they can ruin her career? How would the public feel if it learned that Leila had been driven to suicide by a woman she considered a friend?"

"Elizabeth, did you hear what you just said?"

Elizabeth turned. "Don't you think I'm right?"

"You have just conceded the fact that Leila might have committed suicide."

Elizabeth gasped. She stumbled across the room, fell to her knees, and put her head on Sammy's lap. "Sammy, help me," she pleaded. "I don't know what to believe anymore. I don't know what to do."

# 8

It was at Henry Bartlett's suggestion that they went out for dinner and invited Cheryl and Syd to join them. When Ted protested that he did not want to get involved with Cheryl, Henry cut him off sharply. "Teddy, like it or not, you *are* involved with Cheryl. She and Syd Melnick can be very important witnesses for you."

"I fail to see how."

"If we don't admit that you may have gone back upstairs, we've got to prove that Elizabeth Lange was confused about the exact time of that phone conversation and we've got to make the jury believe that Leila may have committed suicide."

"What about the eyewitness?"

"She saw a tree on the terrace moving. Her lively imagination decided it was you struggling with Leila. She's a nut case."

They went to the Cannery. A chattering, happy end-of-summer crowd filled the popular restaurant; but Craig had phoned ahead, and there was a window table with a sweeping view of Monterey Harbor awaiting them. Cheryl slipped in beside Ted. Her hand rested on his knee. "This is like old times," she whispered. She was wearing a lamé halter and matching skin-tight pants. A buzz of excitement had followed her as she walked across the room.

In the months since he'd seen her, Cheryl had phoned him repeatedly but he'd never returned the calls. Now as her warm, restless fingers caressed his knee, Ted wondered if he was being a fool for not taking what was being offered to him. Cheryl would say anything he wanted that might help his defense. But at what price?

Syd, Bartlett and Craig were visibly relieved to be here instead of at the Spa. "Wait till you start eating," Syd told Henry. "You'll know what seafood is all about."

The waiter came. Bartlett ordered a Johnnie Walker Black Label. His champagne-toned linen jacket was an impeccable fit; his sport shirt in the exact champagne shade and cinnamon-colored trousers were obviously custom-made. His thick but meticulously barbered white hair contrasted handsomely with his unlined, tanned face. Ted imagined him by turn informing, wooing, scolding a jury. A grandstander. Obviously, it worked for him. But what percentage of the time? He started to order a vodka martini and changed it to a beer. This was no time to dull any of his faculties.

It was early for dinner, only seven o'clock. But he had insisted on that. Craig and Syd were having an animated conversation. Syd seemed almost cheerful. Testimony for sale, Ted thought. Make Leila sound like a maniacal drunk. *It could all backfire, kids, and if it does, I'm the one who pays.*

Craig was asking Syd about his agency; was sympathizing with him over the money he'd lost in Leila's play. "We took a bath too," he said. He looked over at Cheryl and smiled warmly. "And we think you were a hell of a good sport to try to save the ship, Cheryl."

*For God's sake, don't shovel it on!* Ted bit his lip to keep from shouting at Craig. But everyone else was smiling broadly. He was the alien in the group, the Unidentified Flying Object. He could sense the eyes of the other diners on this table, on him. He might as well have been able to overhear the *sotto voce* conversations. "His trial starts next week." . . . "Do you think he did it?" . . . "With his money, he'll probably get off. They always do."

Not necessarily.

Impatiently, Ted looked out at the bay. The harbor was filled with boats—large, small, sailing vessels, yachts. Whenever she could, his mother had brought him to visit here. It was the only place where she'd been happy.

"Ted's mother's family came from Monterey," Craig was telling Henry Bartlett.

Again Ted experienced the wild irritation that Craig had begun to trigger in him. When had it started? In Hawaii? Before that? *Don't read my thoughts. Don't speak for me. I'm sick of it.* Leila used to ask him if he didn't get sick of having the Bulldog at his heels all the time. . . .

The drinks came. Bartlett took over the conversation. "As you know, you are all listed as potential defense witnesses for Teddy. Obviously you can testify to the scene at Elaine's. So can about two hundred other people. But on the stand, I'd like you to help me paint for the jurors a more complete picture of Leila. You all know her public image. But you also know that she was a deeply insecure woman who had no faith in herself, who was haunted by a fear of failure."

"A Marilyn Monroe defense," Syd suggested. "With all the wild stories about Monroe's death, everyone has pretty well conceded that she committed suicide."

"Exactly." Bartlett favored Syd with a friendly smile. "Now the question is motive. Syd, tell me about the play."

Syd shrugged. "It was perfect for her. It could have been written about her. She loved the script. The rehearsals started like a cakewalk. I used to tell her we could open in a week. And then something happened. She came into the theater smashed at nine in the morning. After that it was all downhill."

"Stage fright?"

"Lots of people get stage fright. Helen Hayes threw up before every performance. When Jimmy Stewart finished a movie, he was sure no one would ever ask him to be in another one. Leila threw up *and* worried. That's show biz."

"That's just what I don't want to hear on the stand," Henry said sharply. "I intend to paint the picture of a woman with a drinking problem who was experiencing severe depression."

A teenager was standing over Cheryl. "Could I please have your autograph?" He plunked a menu in front of her.

"Of course." Cheryl beamed and scrawled her signature.

"Is it true you're going to be Amanda in that new series?"

"Keep your fingers crossed. I think so." Cheryl's eyes drank in the adolescent's homage.

"You'll be great. Thank you."

"Now, if we just had a tape of this to send to Bob Koenig," Syd said drily.

"When will you know?" Craig asked.

"Maybe in the next few days."

Craig held up his glass. "To Amanda."

Cheryl ignored him and turned to Ted. "Aren't you going to drink to that?"

He raised his glass. "Of course." He meant it. The naked hope in her eyes was in an odd way touching. Leila had always overshadowed Cheryl. Why had they kept up the farce of friendship? Was it because Cheryl's endless quest to become bigger than Leila had been a challenge for Leila, a constant prod that she welcomed, that kept her on her mettle?

Cheryl must have seen something in his face, because her lips brushed his cheek. He did not pull away.

It was over coffee that Cheryl leaned her elbows on the table and cupped her chin in her hands. The champagne she had drunk had clouded her eyes so that they now seemed to smolder with secret promises. Her voice was slightly blurred as she half-whispered to Bartlett, "Suppose Leila believed that Ted wanted to dump her for another woman? What would that do to help the suicide theory?"

"I was not involved with another woman," Ted said flatly.

"Darling, this isn't True Confessions. You don't have to say a word," Cheryl chided. "Henry, answer my question."

"If we had *proof* that Ted was interested in someone else, and that Leila knew it, we give Leila a reason to be despondent. We damage the prosecutor's claim that Ted killed Leila because she rejected him. Are you telling me there was something going on between you and Ted before Leila died?" Bartlett asked hopefully.

"I'll answer that," Ted snapped. "No!"

"You didn't listen," Cheryl protested. "I said I may have proof that Leila *thought* Ted was ready to dump her for someone else."

"Cheryl, I suggest you shut up. You don't know what you're talking about," Syd told her. "Now let's get out of here. You've had too much to drink."

"You're right," Cheryl said amiably. "You're not often right, Syd, dear, but this time you are."

"Just a minute," Bartlett interrupted. "Cheryl, unless this is some sort of game, you'd better put your cards on the table. Anything that clarifies Leila's state of mind is vital to Ted's defense. What do you call 'proof'?"

"Maybe something that wouldn't even interest you," Cheryl said. "Let me sleep on it."

Craig signaled for a check. "I have a feeling this conversation is a waste of time."

It was nine thirty when the limousine dropped them at the Spa. "I want Ted to walk me to my place." Now Cheryl's voice had an edge on it.

"I'll walk you," Syd snapped.

"Ted will walk me," Cheryl insisted.

She leaned against him as they went down the path toward her bungalow. Other guests were just beginning to leave the main house. "Wasn't it fun to be out together?" Cheryl murmured.

"Cheryl, is this 'proof' talk one of your games?" Ted pushed the cloud of black hair away from her face.

"I like it when you touch my hair." They were at her bungalow. "Come in, darling."

"No. I'll say good night."

She pulled his head down until their lips were barely apart. In the starlight her eyes blazed up at him. Had she faked the business of acting tight? he wondered. "Darling," she whispered feverishly, "don't you understand that I'm the one who can help you walk out of that courtroom a free man?"

Craig and Bartlett said good night to Syd and made their way to their bungalows. Henry Bartlett was visibly satisfied. "Teddy looks as if he's finally getting the message. Having that little lady in his corner at the trial will be important. What do you think she meant by that mumbo jumbo about Ted being involved with another woman?"

"Wishful thinking. She probably wants to volunteer for the part."

"I see. If he's smart, he'll accept."

They reached Craig's bungalow. "I'd like to come in for a minute," Bartlett told him. "It's a good chance to talk alone." Inside the bungalow, he glanced around. "This is a different look."

"It's Min's masculine, rustic effect," Craig explained. "She didn't miss a trick—pine tables, wide-planked floors. The bed even has a cord spring. She automatically puts me in one of these units. I think she subconsciously views me as the simple type."

"Are you?"

"I don't think so. And even though I lean to king-size beds with box springs, this *is* a hell of a step up from Avenue B and Eighth Street, where my old man had a deli."

Bartlett studied Craig carefully. "Bulldog" was an apt description for him, he decided. Sandy hair, neutral complexion, cheeks that would fold into jowls if he let himself put weight on. A solid citizen. A good person to have in your corner. "Ted is lucky to have you," he said. "I don't think he appreciates it."

"That's where you're wrong. Ted has to rely on me now to front for him in the business, and he resents it. To clarify that, he only *thinks* he resents me. The problem is, my very presence in his place is a symbol of the jam he's in."

Craig went to the closet and pulled out a suitcase. "Like you, I carry my private supply." He poured Courvoisier into two glasses, handed one of them to Bartlett and settled on the couch, leaning forward, turning his glass in his hand. "I'll give you the best example I can. My cousin was in an accident and flat on her back in the hospital for nearly a year. Her mother knocked herself out taking care of the kids. You want to know something? My cousin was jealous of her mother. She said her mother was enjoying her children and *she* should be the one with them. It's like that with Ted and me. The minute my cousin got out of the hospital, she was singing her mother's praises for the good job she did. When Ted is acquitted, things will be back to normal between us. And let me tell you, I'd a lot rather put up with his outbursts than be in his boots."

Bartlett realized that he had been too quick to dismiss Craig Babcock as a glorified lackey. The problem, he told himself sourly, of being too cocky. He chose his response carefully. "I see your point, and I think you're quite perceptive."

"Unexpectedly perceptive?" Craig asked with a half-smile.

Bartlett chose to ignore the bait. "I also am starting to feel somewhat better about this case. We might be able to put together a defense that will at least create reasonable doubt in a jury's mind. Did you take care of the investigative agency?"

"Yes. We've got two detectives finding out everything they can about the Ross woman. We've got another detective trailing her. Maybe that's overkill, but you never know."

"Nothing that helps is overkill." Bartlett moved to the door. "As you can certainly see, Ted Winters resents the hell out of me for probably the same reason he's jumping at *you*. We both want him to walk out of that courtroom a free man. One line of defense that I hadn't considered before tonight is to convince the jury that shortly before Leila LaSalle died, he and Cheryl had gotten back together, and the money he put in the play was a kiss-off for Leila."

Bartlett opened the door and glanced back over his shoulder. "Sleep on it, and come back to me in the morning with a game plan."

He paused. "But we've got to prevail on *Teddy* to go along with us."

When Syd reached his bungalow the message light on the phone was flashing. He sensed immediately that it was Bob Koenig. The president of World Motion Pictures was famed for his habit of placing after-hours calls. It could only mean that a decision had been made about Cheryl and the role of Amanda. He broke into a cold sweat.

With one hand he reached for a cigarette, with the other for the phone. As he barked "Syd Melnick," he cradled the receiver against his shoulder and lit the cigarette.

"Glad you reached me tonight, Syd. I had a six-o'clock call in to you in the morning."

"I'd have been awake. Who can sleep in this business?"

"I sleep like a top, myself. Syd, I've got a couple of questions."

He had been sure that Cheryl had lost the part. Something about the flashing light had signaled doom. *But Bob had questions. No decision had been made.*

He could visualize Bob at the other end of the line, leaning back in the leather swivel chair in his library at home. Bob hadn't gotten to be head of the studio by making sentimental decisions. Cheryl's test was great, Syd told himself hopefully. But then what? "Shoot," he said, trying to sound relaxed.

"We're still battling it out between Cheryl and Margo Dresher. You know how tough it is to launch a series. Margo's a bigger name. Cheryl was good, damn good—probably better than Margo, even though I'll deny having said that. But Cheryl hasn't done anything big in years, and that fiasco on Broadway kept coming up at the meeting."

The play. Once again the play. Leila's face drifted across Syd's mind. The way she'd screamed at him in Elaine's. He had wanted to bludgeon her then, to drown out that cynical, mocking voice forever. . . .

"That play was a vehicle for Leila. I take full blame for rushing Cheryl into it."

"Syd, we've been through all that. I'm going to be absolutely candid with you. Last year, as all the columnists reported, Margo had a little drug problem. The public is getting damn sick of stars who spend half their lives in drug-rehab centers. I want it straight. Is there anything about Cheryl that could embarrass us, if we choose her?"

Syd gripped the phone. Cheryl had the inside track. A burst of hope made his pulse fluctuate wildly. Sweat poured from his palms. "Bob, I swear to you—"

"Everybody swears to me. Try telling me the truth instead. If I put myself on the line and decide on Cheryl, will it backfire on me? If it ever does, Syd, you're finished."

"I swear. I swear on my mother's grave. . . ."

Syd hung up the phone, hunched over and put his face in his hands. Clammy perspiration broke over his entire body. Once again the golden ring was within his grasp.

Only this time it was Cheryl, not Leila, who could screw it up for him. . . .

# 9

When she left Elizabeth, Dora carried the plastic-wrapped anonymous letter in the pocket of her cardigan. They had decided that she would make a copy of the letter on the office machine, and in the morning Elizabeth would take the original to the sheriff's office in Salinas.

Scott Alshorne, the county sheriff, was a regular dinner guest at the Spa. He'd been friendly with Min's first husband and was always discreetly helpful when a problem, like missing jewelry, arose. Leila had adored him.

"Poison-pen letters aren't the same as missing jewelry," Dora warned Elizabeth.

"I know, but Scott can tell us where to send the letter for analysis, or if I should just give it to the district attorney's office in New York. Anyway, I want a copy myself."

"Then let me make it tonight. Tomorrow, when Min is around, we can't risk having her reading it."

As Dora was leaving, Elizabeth wrapped her in her arms. "You don't believe Ted is guilty, do you, Sammy?"

"Of calculated murder? No, I simply can't believe that. And if he was interested in another woman, there was no motive for him to kill Leila."

Dora had to go back to the office anyhow. She'd left mail scattered on the desk and the unsearched plastic bags on the floor of the reception room. Min would have a fit if she saw them.

Her dinner tray was still on a table near her desk, almost untouched. Funny how little appetite she had these days. Seventy-one really wasn't that old. It was just that between the operation and losing

Leila, there was a spark gone, the old zest that Leila had always teased her about.

The copy machine was camouflaged by a walnut cabinet. She opened the top of the cabinet and turned on the machine, took the letter from her pocket and slipped it free of the plastic bag, carefully touching it only by the edges. Her movements were quick. There was always the worry that Min might take it into her head to come down to the office. Helmut was undoubtedly locked in his study. He was an insomniac and read late into the night.

She happened to glance out the half-open window. Just the sound of the Pacific—its truculent roar —and the smell of the salty breeze were invigorating. She did not mind the rush of cool air that caused her to shiver. But what had caught her attention?

All the guests were settled by now. Lights were visible from behind the curtained windows of the bungalows. Just against the horizon she could see the outlines of the umbrella tables around the Olympic pool. To the left, the silhouette of the Roman bathhouse loomed against the sky. The night was starting to turn misty. It was getting harder to see. Then Dora leaned forward. Someone was walking not on the path, but in the shadows of the cypress trees, as though afraid of being seen. She adjusted her glasses and was astonished to realize that whoever was there was wearing a scuba-diving outfit. What ever was he doing on the grounds? He seemed to be heading toward the Olympic pool.

Elizabeth had told her she was going swimming. An unreasoning fear gripped Dora. Shoving the letter into the pocket of her cardigan, she hurried out of the office and as swiftly as she could move her arthritic body rushed down the stairs, across the darkened foyer and out the seldom-used side door. Now the interloper was passing the Roman bathhouse. She hurried to cut him off. It was probably one of the college kids who were staying at Pebble Beach Lodge, she told herself. Every once in a while they'd sneak onto the grounds and go for a swim in the Olympic pool. But she didn't like the idea of this one coming upon Elizabeth if she was alone there.

She turned and realized that he had seen her. The lights of the security guard's golf cart were coming up the hill from near the gates. The figure in the scuba outfit ran toward the Roman bathhouse. Dora could see that the door was ajar. That fool Helmut probably hadn't bothered to close it this afternoon.

Her knees were trembling as she hurried behind him. The guard would drive by in a moment, and she didn't want the intruder to get away. Tentatively she stepped inside the doorway of the bathhouse.

The entrance foyer was a giant open expanse of marbled walls with twin staircases at the far end. There was enough light from the Japanese lanterns in the trees outside for Dora to see that this area was empty. They actually had done quite a bit more work since she'd looked in a few weeks ago.

Through the open doorway to the left, she saw the beam of a flashlight. The archway led to the lockers, and beyond was the first of the saltwater pools.

For an instant, her indignation was replaced by fear. She decided to go out and wait for the guard.

"Dora, in here!"

The familiar voice made her weak with relief. Carefully making her way across the darkened foyer, she went through the locker room and into the area of the indoor pool.

He was waiting for her, flashlight in hand. The blackness of the wet suit, the thick underwater goggles, the bend of the head, the sudden convulsive movement of the flashlight made her step back uncertainly. "For goodness' sake, don't shine that thing at me. I can't see," she said.

One hand, thick and menacing in the heavy black glove, stretched out toward her, reaching for her throat. The other flashed the light directly in her eyes, blinding her.

Horrified, Dora began to back up. She raised her hands to protect herself and was unaware that she had brushed the letter from her pocket. She barely felt the empty space under her feet before her body toppled backward.

Her last thought as her head smashed against the piles of jagged concrete at the bottom of the pool was that at last she knew who had killed Leila.

# 10

Elizabeth swam from one end of the pool to the other at a demanding, furious pace. The fog was just beginning to roll in—uneven bits of mist that at one moment blew like a dark vapor over the surrounding area, the next were gone. She preferred it when it was dark. She could work every inch of her body knowing that the punishing physical effort somehow would diffuse the built-up emotional anxiety.

She reached the north end of the pool, touched the wall, inhaled, turned, pivoted and with a furious breaststroke began racing toward the opposite end. Now her heart was pounding with the strain of the pace she had set herself. It was crazy. She wasn't in condition for this kind of swimming. But still she raced, trying with the expenditure of physical energy to outrun her thoughts.

At last she felt herself begin to calm down, and flipping onto her back, she began to tread water, her arms rotating in even, sweeping motions.

The letters. The one they had; the one someone had taken; the others they might find in the unopened mail. The ones Leila had probably seen and destroyed. *Why didn't Leila tell me about them? Why did she shut me out? She always used me as a sounding board. She always said I could snap her out of taking criticism too seriously.*

Leila hadn't told her because she had believed that Ted was involved with someone else, that there was nothing she could do about it. But Sammy was right: *If Ted was involved with someone else, he had no motive to kill Leila.*

But I wasn't mistaken about the time of the call.

Suppose Leila had fallen—had slipped from his grasp—and he'd blacked out? Suppose those letters had driven her to suicide? I've got to find out who sent them, Elizabeth thought.

It was time to go in. She was dead tired, and at last somewhat calmer. In the morning, she'd go through the rest of the mail with Sammy. She'd take the letter they'd found to Scott Alshorne. He might want her to take it directly to the district attorney in New York. Was she handing Ted an alibi? And whom had he been involved with?

As she climbed the ladder from the pool, she shivered. The night air was chilly now, and she'd stayed longer than she'd realized. She slipped on her robe and reached into the pocket for her wristwatch. The luminous dial showed that it was half-past ten.

She thought she heard a rustling sound from behind the cypress trees that bordered the patio. "Who's there?" She knew her voice sounded nervous. There was no answer, and she walked to the edge of the patio and strained her eyes to see past the hedges and between the scattered trees. The silhouettes of the cypress trees seemed grotesque and ominous in the dark, but there was no movement other than the faint rustling of the leaves. The cool sea breeze was becoming more forceful. That was it, of course.

With a gesture of dismissal, she wrapped the robe around her and pulled the hood over her hair.

But somehow the feeling of uneasiness persisted, and her footsteps quickened along the path to her bungalow.

*He hadn't touched Sammy. But there would be questions. What was she doing in the bathhouse? He cursed the fact that the door had been open, that he had run in there. If he had simply gone around it, she'd never have caught him.*

*Something so simple could betray him.*

*But the fact that she had the letter with her, that it had fallen from her pocket—that had been simple good luck. Should he destroy it? He wasn't sure. It was a double-edged sword.*

*Now the letter was buried against his skin inside the wet suit. The door of the bathhouse was snap-locked. The guard had made his desultory rounds and wouldn't be back tonight. Slowly, with infinite caution, he made his way toward the pool. Would she be there? Probably. Should he take the chance tonight? Two accidents. Was that more risky than letting her live? Elizabeth would demand answers when Sammy's body was found. Had Elizabeth seen that letter?*

*He heard the lapping of the water in the pool. Cautiously he stepped from behind the tree and watched the swiftly moving body. He would have to wait until she slowed down. By then she would be tired. It might be the time to go ahead. Two unrelated accidents in one night. Would the ensuing confusion keep people off the track? He took a step forward toward the pool.*

*And saw him. Standing behind the shrubbery. Watching Elizabeth. What was he doing there? Did he suspect she was in danger? Or had he too decided she was an unacceptable risk?*

*The wet suit glistened with mist as its wearer slipped behind the sheltering branches of cypress and vanished into the night.*

# Tuesday,
## September 1

Good morning. *Bonjour,* to our dear guests.

It is to be a bit brisker this morning, so brace yourselves for the exciting tingle of the fresh sunlit air.

For the nature lovers, we offer a 30-minute after-luncheon walk along our beautiful Pacific coast, to explore the native flowers of our beloved Monterey Peninsula. So if you are of a mind, do join our expert guide at the main gate at 12:30.

A fleeting thought. Our menu tonight is especially exquisite. Wear your prettiest or handsomest outfit, and feast on our gourmet offerings knowing that the delicate taste treats are balanced by the delicate amount of calories you are consuming.

A fascinating thought: Beauty is in the eye of the beholder, but when you look in the mirror, *you* are the beholder.

—Baron and Baroness Helmut von Schreiber

# 1

The first hint of dawn found Min lying wide awake in the canopied king-size bed she shared with Helmut. Moving carefully to keep from disturbing him, she turned her head and pulled herself up on one elbow. Even in sleep he was a handsome man. He was lying on his side, facing her, his one hand outstretched as though reaching for her, his breath now quiet and soft.

He had not slept like that all night. She didn't know what time he'd come to bed, but at two she'd awakened to the awareness of agitated movement, his head shaking, his voice angry and muffled. There had been no more sleep for her when she heard what he was saying: "Damn you, Leila, damn you."

Instinctively, she had laid her hand on his shoulder, murmured a soft shushing sound, and he had settled back. Would he remember the dream, remember that he had cried out? She had given no indication of having heard him. It would be useless to expect him to tell her the truth. Incredible as it seemed, had something been going on between him and Leila after all? Or had it been a one-sided attraction on Helmut's part toward Leila?

That didn't make it any easier.

The light, more golden than rosy now, began to brighten the room. Carefully Min eased out of bed. Even in her heartsick distress, she felt a moment of appreciation for the beauty of this room. Helmut had chosen the furnishings and color scheme. Who else would have visualized the exquisite balance of the peach satin draperies and bedding against the deep blue-violet tone of the carpet?

How much longer would she be living here? This could be their last season. The million dollars in the Swiss account, she reminded herself. Just the interest on that will be enough. . . .

Enough for whom? Herself? Maybe. Helmut? Never! She'd always known that a large part of her attraction for him was this place, the ability to strut around with this background, to mingle with celebrities. Did she really think he'd be content to follow a relatively simple lifestyle with an aging wife?

Noiselessly, Min glided across the room, slipped on a robe and went down the stairs. Helmut would sleep for another half-hour. She always had to awaken him at six thirty. In this half-hour it would be safe to go through some of the records, particularly the American Express bills. In those weeks before Leila died, Helmut had been away from the Spa frequently. He'd been asked to speak at several medical seminars and conventions; he'd lent his name to some charity balls and flown in to attend them. That was good for business. But what else had he been doing when he was on the East Coast? That was the time Ted had been traveling a great deal. She understood Helmut. Leila's obvious scorn for him would be a challenge. Had he been seeing her?

The night before Leila died, they'd attended the last preview of her show; they'd been at Elaine's. They'd stayed at the Plaza and in the morning flown to Boston to attend a charity luncheon. He'd put her on a plane to San Francisco at six thirty in the evening. Had he gone to the dinner he was supposed to attend in Boston, or had he taken the seven-o'clock shuttle to New York?

The possibility haunted her.

At midnight California time, three A.M. Eastern time, Helmut had phoned to make sure she was home safely. She had assumed he was calling from the hotel in Boston.

That was something she could check.

At the bottom of the staircase, Min turned left and, key in hand, went to the office. The door was unlocked. Her senses were assaulted by the condition of the room. The lights were still on; a dinner tray was on a table at one side of Dora's desk; the desk itself was piled with letters. Plastic bags, their contents spilling on the floor, bordered the desk. The window was partly open, and a cold breeze was rustling the letters. Even the copy machine was on.

Min stalked over to the desk and flipped through the mail. Angrily she realized that everything was fan mail to Leila. Her lips tightened ominously. She was sick to death of that mournful look Dora got whenever she answered those letters. At least till now she'd had the brains not to mess up the office with that silly drivel. From now on, if she wants to do that mail, she'll do it in her apartment. Period. Or maybe it was time to get rid of anyone who insisted on canonizing Leila. What a field day Cheryl would have had if she'd come in here and started going through the personal files. Dora had probably gotten tired and decided to wait to clear up the office this morning. But to leave the copy machine and the lights on was unforgivable. In the morning she'd tell Dora to start making plans for her retirement.

But now she had to get about the reason she had come here. In the storage room, Min went to the file marked "TRAVEL EXPENSES, BARON VON SCHREIBER."

It took less than two minutes to find what she wanted. The phone call from the East Coast to the Spa the night Leila died was listed on his telephone credit-card bill.

It had been made from New York.

# 2

Sheer fatigue made Elizabeth fall into sleep; but it was a restless sleep, filled with dreams. Leila was standing in front of stacks of fan mail; Leila was reading the letters to her; Leila was crying. "I can't trust anyone . . . I can't trust anyone."

In the morning, there was no question in her mind of going on the walk. She showered, pulled her hair into a topknot, slipped on her jogging suit and after waiting just long enough for the hikers to be on their way, headed for the main house. She knew Sammy was always at her desk by a few minutes after seven.

It was a shock to find the usually impeccable receptionist's office cluttered with stacks of mail on and around Dora's desk. A large sheet of paper with the ominous words *See me* and signed by Min clearly revealed that Min had seen the mess.

How unlike Sammy! Never once in all the years she'd known her had Sammy left her desk cluttered. It was unthinkable she'd have chanced leaving it this way in the reception area. It was a surefire way of bringing on one of Min's famous rages.

But suppose she was ill? Quickly Elizabeth hurried down the stairs to the foyer of the main house and rushed to the stairway leading to the staff wing. Dora had an apartment on the second floor. She knocked briskly at the door, but there was no answer. The sound of a vacuum came from around the corner. The maid, Nelly, was a longtime employee who had been here when Elizabeth was working as an instructor. It was easy to get her to open Sammy's door. With a growing sense of panic, Elizabeth walked through the pleasant rooms: the sitting room in shades of lime green and white, with Sam-

my's carefully tended plants on the windowsills and
tabletops; the single bed primly neat, with Sammy's
Bible on the night table.

Nelly pointed to the bed. "She didn't sleep here
last night, Miss Lange. And look!" Nelly walked to
the window. "Her car's in the parking lot. Do you
suppose she felt sick and sent for a cab or something
to go to the hospital? That would be just like Miss
Samuels. You know how independent she is."

But there was no record of a Dora Samuels' having signed herself into the community hospital.
With growing apprehension, Elizabeth waited for
Min to come back from the morning walk. In an
effort to keep her mind from the fearful worry that
something had happened to Sammy, she began to
scan the fan mail. Where was the unsigned letter
Dora had planned to copy?

Was she still carrying it?

# 3

At five of seven, Syd walked up the path to join the
others for the morning hike. Cheryl could read him
like a book. He'd have to be careful. Bob wasn't
making his final decision until this afternoon. If it
weren't for that damn play, it would be in the bag
now.

*"You hear that, everybody? I quit!"*

And you wiped me out, you bitch, he thought. He managed to twist his face into the contortion of a smile. The Greenwich, Connecticut, set were there, all turned out for the morning hike, every hair in place, flawless skin, manicured hands. Pretty clear none of *them* had ever hung by their fingernails waiting for a call, ever clawed their way up in a cutthroat business, ever had someone throw them into the financial gutter with the toss of a head.

It would be a perfect Pebble Beach day. The sun was already warming the cool morning air; the faint smell of salt from the Pacific mingled with the fragrance of the flowering trees that surrounded the main house. Syd remembered the tenement in Brooklyn where he'd been raised. The Dodgers had been in Brooklyn then. Maybe they should have stayed there. Maybe *he* should have stayed there too.

Min and the Baron came out onto the veranda. Syd was immediately aware of how drawn Min looked. Her expression was frozen on her face, the way people get when they've witnessed an accident and cannot believe what they've seen. *How much had she guessed?* He did not glance at Helmut but instead turned his head to watch Cheryl and Ted coming up the path. Syd could read Ted's mind. He'd always felt guilty about dumping Cheryl for Leila, but it was obvious he didn't want to pick up with her again. Obvious to everyone except Cheryl.

What in hell had she meant with that dumb remark about "proof" that Ted was innocent? What was she up to now?

"Good morning, Mr. Melnick." He turned to see Alvirah Meehan beaming up at him. "Why don't we just walk together?" she asked. "I know how disappointed you must be that Margo Dresher is probably going to be Amanda in the series. I'm telling you, they're making a terrible mistake."

Syd did not realize how hard he had grasped her arm until he saw her flinch. "Sorry, Mrs. Meehan, but you don't know what you're talking about."

Too late, Alvirah realized that only the insiders had that tip—the reporter from the *Globe* who was her contact for her article had told her to study Cheryl Manning's reaction when she got the news. She'd made a bad slip. "Oh, am I wrong?" she asked. "Maybe it's just that my husband was saying that he read it's neck and neck between Cheryl and Margo Dresher."

Syd made his voice confidential. "Mrs. Meehan, do me a favor, won't you? Don't talk about that to anyone. It isn't true, and you can imagine how it would upset Miss Manning."

Cheryl had her hand on Ted's arm. Whatever she had been saying, she had him laughing. She was a hell of a good actress—but not good enough to keep her cool if she lost the Amanda role. And she'd turn on him like an alley cat. Then, as Syd watched, Ted raised his hand in a careless salute and started jogging toward the front gate.

"Good morning, everyone," Min boomed in a hollow attempt at her usual vigor. "Let us be on our way. Remember, a brisk pace and deep breathing, please."

Alvirah stepped back as Cheryl caught up with them. They fell into line on the walkway that led to the woods. Scanning the clusters of people ahead, Syd picked out Craig walking with the lawyer, Henry Bartlett. The Countess and her entourage were directly behind them. The tennis pro and his girlfriend were holding hands. The talk-show host was with his date for the week, a twenty-year-old model. The various other guests in twos and threes were unfamiliar.

When Leila made this place her hangout, she put it on the map, Syd thought. You never knew when you'd find her here. Min needs a new superstar. He had noticed the way all eyes drank in Ted as he jogged away. Ted was a superstar.

Cheryl was clearly in a buoyant mood. Her dark hair exploded around her face. Her coal-black brows arced above the huge amber eyes. Her petulant mouth was carved into a seductive smile. She began to hum "That Old Feeling." Her breasts were high and pointed under her jogging suit. No one else could make a jogging suit look like a second coat of skin.

"We've got to talk," Syd told her quietly.

"Go ahead."

"Not here."

Cheryl shrugged. "Then later. Don't look so sour,

Syd. Breathe deeply. Get rid of poisonous thoughts."

"Don't bother being cute with me. When we get back, I'll come to your place."

"What is this about?" Cheryl clearly did not want to have the euphoric mood spoiled.

Syd glanced over his shoulder. Alvirah was directly behind them. Syd could almost feel her breath on his neck.

He gave Cheryl's arm a warning pinch.

When they reached the road, Min continued to lead in the direction of the lone cypress tree, and Helmut began dropping back to chat with the hikers. "Good morning . . . Wonderful day . . . Try to pick up the pace . . . You're doing marvelously." His artificial cheerfulness grated on Syd. Leila had been right. The Baron was a toy soldier. Wind him up and he marches forward.

Helmut stopped abreast of Cheryl. "I hope you two enjoyed your dinner last night." His smile was dazzling and mechanical. Syd could not remember what he had eaten. "It was okay."

"Good." Helmut dropped back to ask Alvirah Meehan how she was feeling.

"Absolutely fine." Her voice was hard and strident. "You might say I'm as bright as a butterfly floating on a cloud." Her noisy laugh sent a chill through Syd.

Had even Alvirah Meehan caught on?

* * *

Henry Bartlett was not feeling good about the world or his particular situation. When he was asked to take on the case of Ted Winters, he'd rearranged his calendar immediately. Few criminal lawyers would be too busy to represent a prominent multi-millionaire. But there was an ongoing problem between him and Ted Winters. The definitive word was "chemistry," and it was bad between them.

As he grudgingly plodded on the forced march behind Min and the Baron, Henry admitted to himself that this place was luxurious, that the setting was beautiful, that under different circumstances he could come to appreciate the charms of the Monterey Peninsula and Cypress Point Spa. But now he was on a countdown. The trial of *The People of the State of New York* v. *Andrew Edward Winters III* would begin in exactly one week. Publicity was eminently desirable when you won a headline case; but unless Ted Winters started cooperating, this case would not be won.

Min was picking up the pace. Henry quickened his footsteps. He hadn't missed the appreciative glances of the fiftyish ash-blonde who was with the Countess. Under different circumstances he'd check that out. But not now.

Craig was marching at a solid, steady pace behind him. Henry still couldn't put his finger on what made Craig Babcock tick. On the one hand he'd talked about Pop's deli on the Lower East Side. On the other, he was clearly the hatchet man for Ted

Winters. It was a pity that it was too late for him to
testify that he and Ted had been on the phone when
that so-called eyewitness claimed she saw Ted. That
thought reminded Henry of what he wanted to ask
Craig.

"What's with the investigator on Sally Ross?"

"I put *three* investigators on her—two for background, one to shadow her."

"It should have been done months ago."

"I agree. Ted's first lawyer didn't think it was
necessary."

They were leaving the path that exited the Spa
grounds and proceeding onto the road that led to
the Lone Cypress.

"How did you arrange to get reports?"

"The head guy will call me every morning, nine
thirty New York time, six thirty here. I just spoke to
him. Nothing too important to report yet. Pretty
much what we know already. She's been divorced a
couple of times; she fights with her neighbors; she's
always accusing people of staring at her. She treats
911 like it's her own personal hot line, always calling to report suspicious-looking characters."

"I could chew her up and spit her out on the
stand," Bartlett said. "Without Elizabeth Lange's
testimony, the prosecution would be flying on one
wing. Incidentally, I want to know how good her
eyesight is, if she needs glasses, what strength
glasses, when they were changed last, and so on
. . . everything about her vision."

"Good. I'll phone it in."

For a few minutes they walked in silence. The morning was silvery bright; the sun was absorbing the dew from the leaves and bushes; the road was quiet, with only an occasional car passing; the narrow bridge that led to the Lone Cypress was empty.

Bartlett glanced over his shoulder. "I'd hoped to see Ted holding hands with Cheryl."

"He always jogs in the morning. Maybe he was holding hands with her all night."

"I hope so. Your friend Syd doesn't look happy."

"The rumor is Syd's broke. He was riding high with Leila as a client. He'd sign her up for a picture and part of the deal was they'd use a couple of his other clients somewhere else. That's how he kept Cheryl working. Without Leila and with all the money he lost in that play, he's got problems. He'd love to put the arm on Ted right now. I won't let him."

"He and Cheryl are the most important defense witnesses we have," Henry snapped. "Maybe you'd better be more generous. In fact, I'm going to make that suggestion to Ted."

They had passed the Pebble Beach Lodge and were on the way back to the Spa. "We'll get to work after breakfast," Bartlett announced. "I've got to decide the strategy of this case and whether to put Ted on the stand. My guess is that he'll make a lousy witness for himself; but no matter how much the judge instructs the jury, it makes a big psychological difference when a defendant won't subject himself to questioning."

* * *

Syd walked back to Cheryl's bungalow with her. "Let's make this short," she said when the door closed behind them. "I want to shower, and I invited Ted for breakfast." She pulled the sweat shirt over her head, stepped out of the sweat pants and reached for her robe. "What *is* it?"

"Always practicing, aren't you?" Syd snapped. "Save it for the dopes, honey. I'd rather wrestle with a tiger." For a long minute he studied her. She had darkened her hair for the Amanda audition, and the effect was startling. The softer color had obliterated the brassy, cheap-at-the-core look she'd never quite conquered and had accentuated those marvelous eyes. Even in a terry-cloth robe she looked like someone with class. Inside, Syd knew, she was the same scheming little hooker he'd been dealing with for nearly two decades.

Now she smiled dazzlingly at him. "Oh, Syd, let's not fight. What do you want?"

"I'll be happy to make it brief. Why did you suggest that Leila might have committed suicide? Why would she have believed that Ted was involved with another woman?"

"Proof."

"What kind of proof?"

"A letter." Quickly she explained. "I went up to see Min yesterday. They had the nerve to leave a bill here, when they know perfectly well I'm a draw for this place. They were inside, and I just happened to notice all that fan mail on Sammy's desk,

and when I looked around I saw this crazy letter.
And I took it."

*"You took it!"*

"Of course. Let me show it to you." She hurried
into her bedroom, brought it back, and leaning over
his shoulder, read it with him.

Leila,

*How* many *Times* Do I Have *to*
write? Can-t YOU get it *straight*
ThAT Ted is sick OF You? *His*
new girl is beautiful and much younger
THaN you. *I* told you ThAT the
emerald necklace HE gave Her matcHes
the bracelet he gave you. It cost
*Twice* as much And looks ten Times
better. I hear your play is Lousy.
You really should Learn your lines.
I'll write again soon.

Your friend.

"Don't you see? Ted must have been having a
fling with someone else. But wouldn't that make
him glad to break up with Leila? And if he wants to
say it was with me, that's fine. I'll back him up."

"You stupid bitch."

Cheryl straightened up and walked over to the other couch. She sat down, leaned forward and spoke precisely, as though she were addressing a not-very-bright child. "You don't seem to realize that this letter is my chance to make Ted understand that I have his best interests at heart."

Syd walked over, grabbed the letter from Cheryl's hand and shredded it. "Last night Bob Koenig phoned me to make sure there was nothing unfavorable that might come out about you. You know why, as of this minute, you have the inside track for Amanda? Because Margo Dresher's had more than her share of lousy publicity. What kind of publicity do you think *you'd* get if Leila's fans find out you drove her to suicide with poison-pen letters?"

"I didn't write that letter."

"The hell you didn't! How many people knew about that bracelet? I saw your eyes when Ted gave it to Leila. You were ready to stab her right then. Those rehearsals were closed. How many people knew Leila was having trouble with her lines? You knew. Why? Because I told you myself. You wrote that letter and others like it. How much time did it take you to cut and paste? I'm surprised you had the patience. How many more are there, and are they likely to show up?"

Cheryl looked alarmed. "Syd, I swear to you I did not write that letter or any others. Syd, tell me about Bob Koenig."

Now it was Syd who, enunciating slowly, repeated the conversation. When he finished, Cheryl reached out her hand. "Got a match? You know I gave up smoking."

Syd watched as the shredded letter with its bizarre, uneven scraps of print curled and disappeared in the ashtray.

Cheryl came over to him and put her arms around his neck. "I knew you were going to get that part for me, Syd. You're right about getting rid of the letter. I think I should still testify at the trial. The publicity will be wonderful. But don't you think my attitude should be shock that my very dearest friend was so distraught and depressed? Then I could explain how even those of us at the top have terrible periods of anxiety."

Her eyes opened wide; two tears ran down her cheeks. "I think Bob Koenig would like that approach, don't you?"

# 4

"Elizabeth!" Min's startled voice made her jump. "Is something wrong? Where is Sammy?"

Min and Helmut were in matching jogging outfits; Min's black hair was pulled regally into a chignon, but her makeup only partially masked the unfamiliar wrinkles around her eyes, the puffiness of her lids. The Baron seemed, as always, to be striking a pose, his legs slightly parted, his hands clasped behind his back, his head bent forward, his eyes puzzled and guileless.

Briefly, Elizabeth told them what had happened. Sammy was missing; her bed had not been slept in.

Min looked alarmed. "I came down at about six o'clock. The lights were on; the window was open; the copy machine was on. I was annoyed. I thought Sammy was getting careless."

"*The copy machine was on!* Then she *did* come back to the office last night." Elizabeth darted across the room. "Did you look to see if the letter she wanted to copy is in the machine?"

It was not there. But next to the copier Elizabeth found the plastic bag the letter had been wrapped in.

Within fifteen minutes a search party had been quietly organized. Reluctantly, Elizabeth acceded to Min's pleadings not to call the police immediately. "Sammy was very ill last year," Min reminded her. "She had a slight stroke and was disoriented. It may have happened again. You know how she hates fuss. Let us try to find her first."

"I'll give it until lunchtime," Elizabeth said flatly, "and then I'm going to report her missing. For all we know, if she did have some kind of attack, she's wandering on the beach somewhere."

"Minna gave Sammy a job out of pity," Helmut snapped. "The essence of this place is privacy, seclusion. We have deputies swarming about and half the guests will pack up and go home."

Elizabeth felt red-hot anger, but it was Min who answered. "Too much has been concealed around here," she said quietly. "We will delay calling the sheriff's office for Sammy's sake, not for ours."

Together they scooped the piled-up letters back into the bags. "This is Leila's mail," Elizabeth told them. She twisted the tops of the bags into intricate knots. "I'll take these to my bungalow later." She studied the knots and was satisfied no one could undo them without tearing the bags.

"Then you're planning to stay?" Helmut's attempt to sound pleased did not come off.

"At least until Sammy is found," Elizabeth told him. "Now let's get some help."

The search party consisted of the oldest and most trusted employees: Nelly, the maid who had let her into Dora's apartment; Jason, the chauffeur; the head gardener. They stood huddled at a respectful distance from Min's desk waiting for instructions.

It was Elizabeth who addressed them. "To protect Miss Samuels' privacy, we don't want anyone to suspect that there is a problem." Crisply she divided their responsibilities. "Nelly, check the empty bungalows. Ask the other maids if they've seen Dora. Be casual. Jason, you contact the cab companies. Find out if anyone made a pickup here between nine o'clock last night and seven this morning." She nodded to the gardener. "I want every inch of the grounds searched." She turned to Min and the Baron. "Min, you go through the house and the women's spa. Helmut, see if she's anywhere in the clinic. I'm going around the neighborhood."

She looked at the clock. "Remember, noon is the deadline for finding her."

As she headed for the gates, Elizabeth realized it had not been for Min and Helmut that she had made the concession, but because she knew that for Sammy it was already too late.

# 5

Ted flatly refused to begin working on his defense until he'd spent an hour in the gym. When Bartlett and Craig arrived at his bungalow, he had just finished breakfast and was wearing a blue sport shirt and white shorts. Looking at him, Henry Bartlett could understand why women like Cheryl threw themselves at him, why a superstar like Leila LaSalle had been head over heels in love with him. Ted had that indefinable combination of looks and brains and charm which attracted men and women alike.

Over the years Bartlett had defended the rich and the powerful. The experience had left him cynical. No man is a hero to his valet. Or to his lawyer. It gave Bartlett a certain sense of power of his own to get guilty defendants acquitted, to shape a defense on loopholes in the law. His clients were grateful to him and paid his huge fees with alacrity.

Ted Winters was one of a kind. He treated Bartlett with contempt. He was the devil's advocate of his own defense strategy. He did not pick up the hints Bartlett threw to him, the hints which ethically Bartlett could not bluntly state. Now he said, "You start planning my defense, Henry. I'm going to the gym for an hour. And then I might just take a swim. And possibly jog again. By the time I get back, I'd like to see exactly what your line of defense is and see if I can live with it. I assume you understand that I have no intention of saying, Yes, perhaps, maybe I *did* stumble back upstairs?"

"Teddy, I . . ."

Ted stood up. He pushed the breakfast tray aside. His posture was menacing as he stared at the older man. "Let me explain something. Teddy is the name of a two-year-old boy. I'll describe him for you. He was what my grandmother used to call a towhead . . . very, very blond. He was a tough little guy who walked at nine months and spoke sentences at fifteen months. He was my son. His mother was a very sweet young woman who unfortunately could not get used to the idea she had married a very rich man. She refused to hire a housekeeper. She did her own marketing. She refused to have a chauffeur. She wouldn't hear of driving an expensive automobile. Kathy lived in fear that folks from Iowa City would think she was getting uppity. One rainy night she was driving back from grocery shopping and—we think—a goddamn can of tomato soup rolled out of the bag and under her foot. And so she couldn't stop at the stop sign, and a trailer truck plowed into that goddamn piece of tin she called a car. And she and that little boy, Teddy, *died*. That was eight years ago. Now have you got it straight that when you call me Teddy, I see a little blond kid who walked early and talked early and would be ten years old next month?"

Ted's eyes glistened. "Now *you* plan my defense. You're being paid for it. I'm going to the gym. Craig, take your pick."

"I'll work out with you."

They left the bungalow and started toward the men's spa. "Where did you *find* him?" Ted asked. "For Christ's *sake*!"

"Have a heart, Ted. He's the best criminal lawyer in the country."

"No, he *isn't*. And I'll tell you why. Because he came in with a preconceived notion and he's trying to mold me into the ideal defendant. And it's phony."

The tennis player and his girlfriend were coming out of their bungalow. They greeted Ted warmly. "Missed you at Forest Hills last time," the pro told Ted.

"Next year for sure."

"We're all rooting for you." This time it was the pro's girlfriend with her model's smile flashing.

Ted returned the smile. "Now, if I can just get you on the jury . . ." He raised his hand in a gesture of acknowledgment and walked on. The smile disappeared. "I wonder if they have celebrity tennis in Attica."

"You won't have to give a damn one way or the other. It will have nothing to do with you." Craig stopped. "Look, isn't that Elizabeth?"

They were almost directly in front of the main house. From across the vast lawn they watched as the slender figure ran down the steps of the veranda and turned toward the outer gates. There was no mistaking the honey-colored loop of hair twirled on the top of her head, the thrust of the chin, the innate grace of her movements. She was dabbing at her eyes, and as they watched, she pulled sunglasses from her pocket and put them on.

"I thought she was going home this morning." Ted's voice was impersonal. "Something's wrong."

"Do you want to see what it is?"

"Obviously my presence would only upset her more. Why don't *you* follow her? She doesn't think *you* killed Leila."

"Ted, for God's sake, knock it off! I'd put my hand in the fire for you and you know it, but being a punching bag isn't going to make me function any better. And I fail to see how it helps you."

Ted shrugged. "My apologies. You're quite right. Now see if you can help Elizabeth. I'll meet you back at my place in about an hour."

* * *

Craig caught up with her at the gate. Quickly she explained what had happened. His reaction was comforting. "You mean to say that Sammy may have been missing for hours and the police haven't been called?"

"They're going to be as soon as the grounds are searched, and I thought I'd just see if maybe . . ." Elizabeth could not finish. She swallowed and went on: "You remember when she had that first attack. She was so disoriented and then so embarrassed."

Craig's arm was around her. "Okay—steady. Let's walk a bit." They crossed the road toward the path that led to the Lone Cypress. The sun had dispersed the last of the morning mist, and the day was bright and warm. Sandpipers flurried over their heads, circled and returned to their perches on the rocky shore-line. Waves broke like foaming geysers against the rocks and retreated to the sea. The Lone Cypress, always a tourist attraction, was already the center of attention of the camera buffs.

Elizabeth began to question them. "We're looking for an older lady. . . . She may be ill. . . . She's quite small. . . ."

Craig took over. He gave an accurate description of Dora. "What was she wearing, Elizabeth?"

"A beige cardigan, a beige cotton blouse, a tan skirt."

"Sounds like my mother," commented a tourist in a red sport shirt with a camera slung over his shoulder.

"She's kind of everybody's mother," Elizabeth said.

They rang doorbells of the secluded homes hidden by shrubbery from the road. Maids, some sympathetic, some annoyed, promised to "keep an eye out."

They went to the Pebble Beach Lodge. "Sammy has breakfast here sometimes on her days off," Elizabeth said. With a clutch of hope, she searched the dining rooms, praying that her eyes would find the small straight figure, that Sammy would be surprised at all the fuss. But there were only the vacationers, dressed in casually expensive sport clothes, most of them awaiting their tee-off time.

Elizabeth turned to leave, but Craig held her arm. "I'll bet you didn't have any breakfast." He signaled to the headwaiter.

Over coffee they surveyed each other. "If there's no sign of her when we get back, we'll insist on calling the police," he told her.

"Something's happened to her."

"You can't be sure of that. Tell me exactly when you saw her, whether she said anything about going out."

Elizabeth hesitated. She was not sure if she wanted to tell Craig about the letter Sammy was going to copy or about the letter that had been stolen. She did know that the deep concern on his face was a tremendous comfort, that if it became necessary, he would put the awesome power of Winters Enterprises into the search for Sammy. Her response was careful. "When Sammy left me, she said she was going back to the office for a while."

"I can't believe that she's so overworked she has to burn midnight oil."

Elizabeth half-smiled. "Not quite midnight. Nine thirty." To avoid further questions, she gulped the rest of the coffee. "Craig, do you mind if we go back now? Maybe there's been some word."

But there was not. And if the maids, the gardener and the chauffeur could be believed, every inch of the grounds had been searched. Now even Helmut agreed not to wait until noon, that it was time to phone in a missing-person report.

"That's not good enough," Elizabeth told them. "I want you to ask for Scott Alshorne."

She waited for Scott at Sammy's desk. "Do you want me to hang around?" Craig asked.

"No."

He glanced at the trash bags. "What's all that?"

"Leila's fan mail. Sammy was answering it."

"Don't start going through it. It will only upset you." Craig glanced into Min and Helmut's office. They were sitting side by side on the Art Deco wicker couch, speaking in low tones. He leaned over the desk. "Elizabeth, you have to know I'm between a rock and a hard place. But when this is over, no matter how it ends, we've got to talk. I've missed you terribly." In a surprisingly agile move, he was around the desk; his hand was on her hair, his lips on her cheek. "I'm always here for you," he whispered. "If anything has happened to Sammy and you need a shoulder or an ear . . . You know where to find me."

Elizabeth clutched at his hand and for an instant held it against her cheek. She felt its solid strength, its warmth, the width of his blunt fingers. And incongruously thought of Ted's long-fingered graceful hands. She dropped his hand and pulled away. "Watch out or you'll get me crying." She tried to make her voice light, to dispel the intensity of the moment.

Craig seemed to understand. He straightened up and said matter-of-factly, "I'll be in Ted's bungalow if you need me."

Waiting was the hardest. It was like the night when she'd sat in Leila's apartment hoping, praying that Leila and Ted had made up, had gone off together and knowing with every nerve in her body that something was wrong. Sitting at Sammy's desk was agony. She wanted to run in a dozen different directions; to walk along the road and ask people if they'd seen her; to search the Crocker Woodland in case she'd wandered in there in a daze.

Instead, Elizabeth opened one of the bags of fan mail and brought out a handful of envelopes. At least she could accomplish something.

She could search for more anonymous letters.

# 6

Sheriff Scott Alshorne had been a lifelong friend of Samuel Edgers, Min's first husband, the man who had built the Cypress Point Hotel. He and Min had liked each other from the start, and it had pleased him to see that Min kept her part of her bargain. She gave the ailing and cantankerous octogenarian a new lease on life for the five years she was married to him.

Scott had watched with mingled curiosity and awe as Min and that titled jerk she married next had taken a comfortable, profitable hotel and turned it into a self-consuming monster. Min now invited him at least once a month to dinner at the Spa, and in the last year and a half he'd come to know Dora Samuels well. That was why when Min called with the news of her disappearance, he instinctively feared the worst.

If Sammy had had some kind of stroke and started wandering around, she'd have been noticed. Old sick people didn't get overlooked on the Monterey Peninsula. Scott was proud of his jurisdiction.

His office was in Salinas, the seat of Monterey County and twenty-two miles from Pebble Beach. Crisply he issued instructions for the posting of a missing-person notice and directed that deputies from the Pebble Beach area meet him at the Spa.

He was silent on the drive. The deputy who chauffeured him noticed there were unusually deep creases in his boss's forehead, that the craggy, tanned face under the wealth of unmanageable white hair was furrowed in thought. When the chief looked like this, it meant he anticipated a big problem.

It was ten thirty when they drove through the gates. The houses and grounds had an air of tranquillity. There were few people walking around. Scott knew that most of the guests were in the spas, working out, being pummeled and patted and scrubbed and plucked so that when they went home at the end of their stay, their families and friends would gush over how marvelous they looked. Or they were in the clinic having one of Helmut's sophisticated and ultra-expensive treatments.

He had heard that Ted Winters' private jet had landed at the airport on Sunday afternoon and that Ted was here. He'd debated with himself as to whether or not to call him. Ted was under indictment for second-degree murder. He was also the kid who used to delight in sailing with his grandfather and Scott.

Knowing that Ted was booked at the Spa caused Scott to register openmouthed astonishment when he saw Elizabeth sitting at Sammy's desk. She had not heard him come up the stairs, and he took a moment to study her unobserved. She was deathly pale, and her eyes were red-rimmed. Strands of hair had slipped from the knot on top of her head and curled around her face. She was pulling letters from envelopes, glancing at them and tossing them aside impatiently. Clearly she was searching for something. He noticed that her hands were trembling.

He knocked loudly on the open door and watched her jump up. Relief and apprehension mingled in her expression. Spontaneously she ran around the desk and with outstretched arms hurried toward him. Just before she reached him, she stopped abruptly. "I'm sorry . . . I mean, how are you, Scott? It's good to see you."

He knew what she was thinking. Because of his longtime friendship with Ted, he might regard her as the enemy. Poor kid. He gathered her in a quick bear hug. To disguise his own emotion, he said gruffly, "You're too skinny. I hope you're not on one of Min's celebrity diets."

"I'm on a get-fat-fast. Banana splits and brownies."

"Good."

Together they went into Min's office. Scott raised his eyebrows when he saw the haggard expression on Min's face, the wary, veiled eyes of the Baron. They were both worried, and somehow he felt it went beyond concern for Sammy. His direct questions garnered the information he needed. "I'd like to take a look at Sammy's apartment."

Min led the way. Elizabeth and Helmut trailed behind. Somehow Scott's presence gave Elizabeth a faint touch of hope. At least something would be done. She had seen the disapproval in his face at the realization they had waited so long to phone him.

Scott glanced around the sitting room and walked into the bedroom. He pointed to the suitcase on the floor near the closet. "Was she planning to go somewhere?"

"She just got back," Min explained, then looked puzzled. "It's not like Sammy not to unpack immediately."

Scott opened the bag. There was a cosmetic case on top filled with pill bottles. He read the directions: "One every four hours; twice a day; two at bedtime." He frowned. "Sammy was careful about her medication. She didn't want another siege. Min, show me the condition of the office as you found it."

It was the copy machine that seemed to intrigue him most. "The window was open. The machine was on." He stood in front of it. "She was about to copy something. She looked out the window, and then what? She felt dizzy? She wandered outside? But where was she trying to go?" He stared out the window. This view took in the expanse of the north lawn, the scattered bungalows along the way to the Olympic pool and the Roman bath—that god-awful monstrosity!

"You say every inch of the grounds, every building was searched?"

"Yes." Helmut answered first. "I personally saw to it."

Scott cut him off. "We'll start all over."

* * *

Elizabeth spent the next hours at Sammy's desk. Her fingers were dry from handling the dozens of letters she examined. They read alike—requests for Leila's autograph, requests for her picture. There was so far no sign of any more anonymous letters.

At two o'clock Elizabeth heard a shout. She raced to the window in time to see one of the policemen gesturing from the door of the bathhouse. Her feet flew on the stairs. At the next-to-last step, she tripped and fell, smashing her arms and legs against the polished tiles. Heedless of the sharp sting in her palms and knees, she ran across the lawn to the bathhouse, arriving as Scott disappeared inside. She followed him through the locker room into the pool area.

A policeman was standing at the side of the pool pointing down at Sammy's crumpled body.

Later, she vaguely remembered kneeling beside Sammy, reaching her hand to brush back the matted, bloody hair from her forehead, feeling Scott's iron grasp, hearing his sharp command: "Don't touch her!" Sammy's eyes were open, her features frozen in terror, her glasses still caught on her ears but dropped down on her nose, her palms outstretched as though pushing something back. Her beige cardigan was still buttoned, the wide patch pockets suddenly prominent. "See if she has the letter to Leila," Elizabeth heard herself say. "Look in the pockets." Then her own eyes widened. The beige wool cardigan became Leila's white satin pajamas, and she was kneeling over Leila's body again. . . .

Mercifully, she fainted.

When she regained consciousness, she was lying on the bed in her bungalow. Helmut was bending over her, holding something that smelled harsh and pungent under her nostrils. Min was chafing her hands. Uncontrollable sobs racked her body, and she heard herself wailing, "Not Sammy too, not Sammy too."

Min held her tightly. "Elizabeth, don't . . . Don't."

Helmut muttered, "This will help you." The prick of a needle in her arm.

When she awoke, the shadows were long in the room. Nelly, the maid who had helped in the search, was touching her shoulder. "I'm so sorry to disturb you, miss," she said, "but I did bring tea and something for you to eat. The sheriff can't wait any longer. He has to talk with you."

# 7

The news of Dora's death rippled through the Spa like an unwelcome rainstorm at a family picnic. There was mild curiosity: "What ever was she doing wandering in that place?" A sense of mortality: "How old was she, did you say?" An attempt to place her—"Oh, you mean that prim little woman in the office?"—then a quick return to the pleasant activities of the Spa. This was, after all, an extremely expensive retreat. One came here to escape problems, not find them.

In midafternoon Ted had gone for a massage, hoping to obtain some relief from tension in the pounding hands of the Swedish masseur. He'd just returned to his bungalow when Craig told him the news. "They found her body in the bathhouse. She must have gotten dizzy and fallen."

Ted thought of the afternoon in New York when Sammy had had that first stroke. They were all in Leila's apartment, and in the middle of a sentence Sammy's voice had trailed off. It was he who had realized there was something seriously wrong.

"How is Elizabeth taking it?" he asked Craig.

"Pretty badly. I gather she fainted."

"She was close to Sammy. She . . ." Ted bit his lip and changed the subject. "Where's Bartlett?"

"On the golf course."

"I wasn't aware I brought him out here to play golf."

"Ted, come off it! He's been on the job since early this morning. Henry claims he can think better if he gets some exercise."

"Remind him that I go on trial next week. He'd better curtail his exercise." Ted shrugged. "It was crazy to come here. I don't know why I thought it would help me calm down; it's not working."

"Give it a chance. It wouldn't be any better in New York or Connecticut. Oh, I just bumped into your old friend Sheriff Alshorne."

"Scott's here? Then they must think there's something peculiar about Sammy's death."

"I don't know about that. It's probably just routine for him to show up."

"Does he know I'm here?"

"Yes. As a matter of fact, he asked about you."

"Did he suggest that I call him?"

Craig's hesitation was barely perceptible. "Well, not exactly—but look, it wasn't a social conversation."

Another person avoiding me, Ted thought. Another person waiting to see the full evidence laid out in court. Restlessly he wandered around the living room of his bungalow. Suddenly it had become a cage to him. But all rooms had seemed like that since the indictment. It must be a psychological reaction. "I'm going for a walk," he said abruptly. Then, to forestall Craig's offer of company, he added, "I'll be back in time for dinner."

As he passed the Pebble Beach Lodge, he wondered at the sense of isolation that made him feel so totally apart from the people who wandered along the paths, heading for the restaurants, the tourist shops, the golf courses. His grandfather had started bringing him to these courses when he was eight. His father had detested California, and so when they came it was just his mother and himself, and he'd seen her shed her nervous mannerisms and become younger, lighthearted.

Why hadn't she left his father? he wondered. Her family didn't have the Winters millions, but she would certainly have had enough money. Wasn't it because she was afraid of losing custody of him that she'd stayed in that cursed marriage? His father had never let her forget that first suicide attempt. And so she had stayed and endured his periodic drunken rages, his verbal abuse, his mimicking of her mannerisms, his scorn of her private fears until one night she had decided she couldn't endure any more.

Unseeingly, Ted walked along the Seventeen Mile Drive, unaware of the Pacific, glimmering and gleaming below the houses that rose above Stillwater Cove and Carmel Bay, unaware of the luxuriant bougainvillea, heedless of the expensive cars that sped past him.

Carmel was still crowded with summer tourists, college students getting in one last fling before the fall semester. When he and Leila walked through town, she'd stopped traffic. The thought made him pull his sunglasses from his pocket. In those days, men used to look at him with envy. Now he was aware of hostility on the faces of strangers who recognized him.

Hostility. Isolation. Fear.

These last seventeen months had disrupted his entire life, had forced him to do things he would not have believed possible. Now he accepted the fact that there was one more monumental hurdle he had to overcome before the trial.

Drenching perspiration soaked his body at the image of what that would be.

# 8

Alvirah sat at the dressing table in her bungalow, happily surveying the shiny rows of creams and cosmetics that had been presented to her in the makeup class that afternoon. As the instructor had told her, she had flat cheekbones that could be beautifully enhanced with a soft blush rather than the crimson rouge she favored. She also had been persuaded to try wearing a brown mascara instead of the jet black which she believed drew attention to her eyes. "Less is better," the makeup expert had assured her, and truth to tell, there was a difference. In fact, Alvirah decided, the new makeup, combined with the way they'd toned down her hair to a rich brown, made her look just like the way she remembered Aunt Agnes, and Agnes always was the beauty in the family. It also felt good that her hands were starting to lose their calluses. No more heavy cleaning for her. Ever. Period.

"And if you think you look good now, wait till you

see how glamorous you are when Baron von Schreiber is finished with you," the makeup lady had said. "His collagen injections will make those little lines around your mouth, nose and forehead disappear. It's almost miraculous."

Alvirah sighed. She was bursting with happiness. Willy had always claimed that she was the finest-looking woman in Queens and that he liked being able to put his arms around her and feel that he had something to hold on to. But these last years, she'd put on weight. Wouldn't it be good to really look classy when they were hunting for a new house? Not that she had any intention of trying to get in with the Rockefellers—just middle-class people like themselves who'd made good. And if she and Willy made out a lot better than most others, were luckier than just about anybody else, it was nice to know that they could do some good for other people.

After she finished the articles for the *Globe*, she really would write that book. Her mother had always said, "Alvirah, you've got such a lively imagination, you're going to be a writer someday." Maybe *someday* was here.

Alvirah pursed her lips and carefully applied coral lip gloss with her newly acquired brush. Years ago, in the belief that her lips were too narrow, she'd gotten into the habit of making a kind of Kewpie doll curve to accentuate them, but now she'd been persuaded that that wasn't necessary. She put down the brush and surveyed the results.

Somehow she really did feel a little guilty about

being so happy and interested in everything when that nice little lady was stretched out somewhere in the morgue. But she was seventy-one, Alvirah comforted herself, and it must have been real quick. That's the way I want to go when it's my turn. Not that she expected it to be her turn for a long time to come. As her mother said, "Our women make old bones." Her mother was eighty-four and still went bowling every Wednesday night.

Her makeup adjusted to her satisfaction, Alvirah took her tape recorder from her suitcase and inserted the cassette from Sunday night's dinner. As she listened, a puzzled frown creased her forehead. Funny—when you're just listening to people, you get a different perspective than when you're sitting with them. Like Syd Melnick was supposed to be a big agent. But he sure let Cheryl Manning push him around. And *she* could turn on a dime, one minute hassling Syd Melnick about the water she'd spilled herself and then all sweetness and light, asking Ted Winters if she could go with him sometime to see the Winters Gym at Dartmouth College. *Dartmuth,* Alvirah thought, not *Dart-mouth.* Craig Babcock had corrected her on that. He had such a nice calm voice. She'd told him that. "You sound so educated."

He'd laughed. "You should have heard me in my teens."

Ted Winters' voice was so well-bred. Alvirah knew *he* hadn't had to work on it. The three of them had a nice talk on that subject.

Alvirah checked her microphone to see that it

was securely in place in the center flower of her sunburst pin and delivered an observation. "Voices," she declared, "tell a lot about people."

She was surprised to hear the phone ring. It was only nine o'clock New York time, and Willy was supposed to be at a union meeting. She wished that he'd quit his job, but he said to give him time. He wasn't used to being a millionaire.

It was Charley Evans, the special features editor of the *New York Globe.* "How's my star reporter?" he asked. "Any problems with the recorder?"

"It works like a charm," Alvirah assured him. "I'm having a wonderful time and meeting some very interesting people."

"Any celebrities?"

"Oh, yes." Alvirah couldn't help bragging. "I came from the airport in a limousine with Elizabeth Lange, and I'm at the same dinner table as Cheryl Manning and Ted Winters." She was rewarded by an audible gasp on the other end of the phone.

"Are you telling me that Elizabeth Lange and Ted Winters are together?"

"Oh, not exactly together," Alvirah said hastily. "In fact, she wouldn't go near him at all. She was going to leave right away, but she wanted to see her sister's secretary. The only trouble is Leila's secretary was found dead this afternoon in the Roman bathhouse."

"Mrs. Meehan, hold on a minute. I want you to repeat everything you just said, very slowly. Someone will be taking it down."

# 9

At Scott Alshorne's request, the coroner of Monterey County performed an immediate autopsy on the remains of Dora Samuels. Death had been caused by a severe head injury, pressure on the brain from skull fragments, contributing cause a moderately severe stroke.

In his office, Scott studied the autopsy report in reflective silence and tried to pinpoint the reasons he felt there was something sinister about Dora Samuels' death.

That bathhouse. It looked like a mausoleum; it had turned out to be Sammy's sepulcher. Who the hell did Min's husband think he was to have foisted that on her? Incongruously, Scott thought of the contest Leila had run: Should the Baron be called the *tin* soldier or the *toy* soldier? Twenty-five words or less. Leila bought dinner for the winner.

Why had Sammy been in the bathhouse? Had she just wandered in there? Was she planning to meet someone? That didn't make sense. The electricity wasn't turned on. It would have been pitch black.

Min and Helmut had both stated that the bathhouse should have been locked. But they'd also admitted they had left it in a hurry yesterday afternoon. "Minna was upset by the overrun costs," Helmut had explained. "I was worried about her emotional state. It is a heavy door. Possibly I did not pull it shut."

Sammy's death had been caused by the injuries to the back of her head. She had toppled backward into the pool. But had she fallen or been pushed? Scott got up and began backing across his office. A practical, if not a scientific test, he decided. No matter how dazed or confused you are, most people don't start walking backward unless they're backing *away* from someone, or something. . . .

He settled at his desk again. He was supposed to attend a civic dinner with the mayor of Carmel. He'd have to pass. He was going back to the Spa and he was going to talk to Elizabeth Lange. It was his hunch that she knew what urgent business had made Sammy go back to the office at nine thirty at night and what document had been so important to copy.

On the drive back to the Spa, two words flashed in his mind.

Fallen?

Pushed?

Then as the car passed the Pebble Beach Lodge, he realized what had been bothering him. That was the same question that was bringing Ted Winters to trial on a murder indictment!

# 10

Craig spent the rest of the afternoon in Ted's bungalow going through the bulky package of mail that had been expressed from the New York office. With a practiced eye he skimmed memos, reviewed printouts, studied projection charts. His frown deepened as he read. That group of Harvard and Wharton Business M.B.A.s Ted had hired a couple of years ago were a constant irritant to him. If they had their way, Ted would be building hotels on space platforms.

At least they had had the brains to recognize that they couldn't try to go around Craig anymore. The memos and letters were all addressed to him and Ted jointly.

Ted got back at five o'clock. Obviously the walk hadn't relaxed him any. He was in a foul mood. "Is there any reason you can't work in your place?" was his first question.

"None except that it seemed simpler to be here for you." Craig indicated the business files. "There are some things I'd like to go over."

"I'm not interested. Do what you think best."

"I think 'best' would be for you to have a Scotch and unwind a little. And I think 'best' for Winters Enterprises is to get rid of those two assholes from

Harvard. Their expense accounts amount to armed robbery."

"I don't want to go into that now."

Bartlett came in pink-faced from his afternoon in the sun. Craig noticed the way Ted's mouth tightened at Bartlett's genial greeting. There was no question Ted was starting to unravel. He drank the first Scotch quickly and didn't protest when Craig refilled it.

Bartlett wanted to discuss the list of defense witnesses Craig had prepared for him. He read it off to Ted—a glittering array of famous names.

"You don't have the President on it," Ted said sarcastically.

Bartlett fell into the trap. "Which president?"

"Of the United States, of course. I used to be one of his golf partners."

Bartlett shrugged and closed the file. "Obviously this isn't going to be a good working session. Are you planning to eat out tonight?"

"No, I'm planning to stay right here. And right now I'm planning to nap."

Craig and Bartlett left together. "You do realize this is getting hopeless," Bartlett told him.

At six thirty Craig received a call from the agency he'd hired to investigate the eyewitness, Sally Ross. "There was some excitement in Ross's apartment building," he was told. "The woman who lives directly above her walked in on an attempted burglary. They caught the guy—a petty thief with a long record. Ross didn't go out at all."

At seven o'clock, Craig met Bartlett at Ted's bungalow. Ted wasn't there. They started toward the main house together. "You're about as popular as I am with Teddy these days," Bartlett commented.

Craig shrugged. "Listen, if he wants to take it out on me, it's all right. In a way, I brought this on him."

"How do you figure that one?"

"I introduced him to Leila. She was my date first."

They reached the veranda in time to hear the newest witticism. *At Cypress Point, for four thousand dollars a week you get to use some of the pools. For five thousand you get to use the ones with water in them.*

There was no sign of Elizabeth during the "cocktail" hour. Craig watched for her to come up the path, but she did not appear. Bartlett drifted over to the tennis pro and his girlfriend. Ted was talking to the Countess and her group; Cheryl was hanging on his arm. A morose-looking Syd was standing off by himself. Craig went over to him. "That business about 'proof.' Was Cheryl drunk last night or just talking her usual drivel?" he asked.

He knew Syd wouldn't have minded taking a swing at him. Syd considered him to be, like all the parasites in Ted's world, the bottleneck to Ted's largesse. Craig considered himself more of a goalie —you had to pass him to score.

"I would say," Syd told him, "that Cheryl was giving her usual splendid dramatic performance."

Min and Helmut did not appear in the dining rooms until after the guests had settled. Craig noticed how gaunt they looked, how fixed their smiles were as they visited from table to table. Why not? They were in the business of staving off old age, illness and death. This afternoon Sammy had proved it was a pointless game.

As she sat down, Min murmured an apology for being late. Ted ignored Cheryl, whose hand clung persistently to his. "How *is* Elizabeth?"

Helmut answered him: "She's taking it very hard. I gave her a sedative."

Would Alvirah Meehan never stop fooling with that damn pin? Craig wondered. She had parked herself between him and Ted. He glanced around. Min. Helmut. Syd. Bartlett. Cheryl. Ted. The Meehan woman. Himself. There was one more place setting next to him. He asked Min who would be joining them.

"Sheriff Alshorne. He just came back. He's talking to Elizabeth now." Min bit her lip. "Please. We all know how sad we feel about losing Sammy, but I think it would be better if we do not discuss it during dinner."

"Why does the sheriff want to talk to Elizabeth Lange?" Alvirah Meehan asked. "He doesn't think there's anything funny about Miss Samuels dying in that bathhouse, does he?"

Seven stony pairs of eyes discouraged further questions.

The soup was chilled peach and strawberry, a specialty of the Spa. Alvirah sipped hers contentedly. The *Globe* would be interested to learn that Ted Winters was very clearly concerned about Elizabeth.

She could hardly wait to meet the sheriff.

# 11

Elizabeth stood at the window of her bungalow and glanced at the main house just in time to see the guests drifting inside for dinner. She had insisted that Nelly leave: "You've had a long day, and I'm perfectly all right now." She'd propped herself up in bed for the tea and toast, then showered quickly, hoping that the splashing cold water would clear her head. The sedative had left her groggy.

An off-white cable-knit sweater and tan stretch pants were her favorite comfortable clothes. Somehow, wearing them, her feet bare, her hair twisted up casually, she felt like herself.

The last of the guests had disappeared. But as she watched, she saw Scott cut across the lawn in her direction.

* * *

They sat across from each other, leaning slightly forward, anxious to communicate, wary of how to begin. Looking at Scott with his kind, questioning eyes made Elizabeth remember how Leila had once said, "He's the kind of guy I would have liked for a father." Last night Sammy had suggested that they take the anonymous letter to him.

"I'm sorry I couldn't wait until the morning to see you," Scott told her. "But there are too many things about Sammy's death that trouble me. From what I've learned so far, Sammy drove six hours from Napa Valley yesterday, arriving at about two o'clock. She wasn't due till late evening. She must have been pretty tired, but she didn't even stop to unpack. She went directly to the office. She claimed she wasn't feeling well and wouldn't come down to the dining room for dinner, but the maid tells me she had a tray in the office and was busily going through bags of mail. Then she came to visit you and left around nine thirty. Sammy should have been pretty beat by then, but she apparently went back to the office and turned on the copy machine. Why?"

Elizabeth got up and walked into the bedroom. From her suitcase she took the letter from Sammy that had been waiting for her in New York. She showed it to Scott. "When I realized Ted was here I would have left immediately, but I had to wait and see Sammy about this." She told him about the letter that had been taken from Sammy's office and showed him the transcript Sammy had made from memory. "This is pretty much the text of it."

Her eyes filled as she looked at Sammy's graceful penmanship. "She found another poison-pen letter in one of those sacks last evening. She was going to make a copy for me, and we were planning to give the original to you. I've written it down as I remembered. We had hoped the original could be traced. The typeface for magazines is coded, isn't it?"

"Yes." Scott read and re-read the transcripts of the letters. "Stinking business."

"Somebody was systematically trying to destroy Leila," Elizabeth said. "Somebody doesn't want those letters found. Somebody took one from Sammy's desk yesterday afternoon and perhaps the other one from Sammy's body last night."

"Are you saying that you think Sammy may have been murdered?"

Elizabeth flinched, then looked directly at him. "I simply can't answer that. I do know that someone was worried enough about those letters to want them back. I do know that a series of those letters would have explained Leila's behavior. Those letters precipitated that quarrel with Ted, and those letters have something to do with Sammy's death. I swear this to you, Scott. I'm going to find out who wrote them. Maybe there's no criminal prosecution possible, but there has to be a way of making that person pay. It's someone who was very close to Leila, and I have my suspicions."

Fifteen minutes later Scott left Elizabeth, the

transcripts of both anonymous letters in his pocket. Elizabeth believed Cheryl had written those letters. It made sense. It was Cheryl's kind of trick. Before he went into the dining room, he walked around to the right side of the main house. Up there was the window where Sammy had stood when she turned on the copy machine. If someone had been on the steps of the bathhouse and signaled to her to come down . . .

It was possible. But, of course, he told himself sadly, Sammy wouldn't have come down except for someone she knew. And trusted.

The others were halfway through the main course when he joined them. The empty seat was between Craig and a woman who was introduced as Alvirah Meehan. Scott took the initiative in greeting Ted. *Presumption of innocence.* Ted had always had outstanding looks. It was no wonder that a woman would go to any extreme to separate him from another woman. Scott did not miss the way Cheryl constantly managed to touch Ted's hand, to brush her shoulder against his.

He helped himself to lamb chops from the silver tray the waiter was offering him.

"They're delicious," Alvirah Meehan confided, her voice barely a whisper. "They'll never go broke in this place from the size of the portions, but I'm telling you when you're finished you feel as though you've had a big meal."

Alvirah Meehan. Of course. He'd read in the

*Monterey Review* about the forty-million-dollar lottery winner who was going to realize her fondest dream by coming to Cypress Point Spa. "Are you enjoying yourself, Mrs. Meehan?"

Alvirah beamed. "I sure am. Everyone has been just wonderful, and so friendly." Her smile encompassed the entire table. Min and Helmut attempted to return it. "The treatments make you feel like a princess. The nutritionist said that in two weeks I should be able to lose five pounds and a couple of inches. Tomorrow I'm having collagen to get rid of the lines around my mouth. I'm scared of injections, but Baron von Schreiber will give me something for my nerves. I'll leave here a new woman feeling . . . like . . . like a butterfly floating on a cloud." She pointed to Helmut. "The Baron wrote that. Isn't he a real author?"

Alvirah realized she was talking too much. It was just that she felt kind of guilty being an undercover reporter and wanted to say nice things about these people. But now she'd better be quiet and listen to see if the sheriff had anything to say about Dora Samuels' death. But, disappointingly, no one brought it up at all. It was only when they had just about finished the vanilla mousse that the sheriff asked, not quite casually, "You people will all be around here for the next few days? No one has plans to leave?"

"Our plans are undetermined," Syd told him. "Cheryl may have to go back to Beverly Hills on short notice."

"I think it would be better if she checks with me before she goes to Beverly Hills, or anywhere else," Scott said pleasantly. "And by the way, Baron— those bags of Leila's fan mail. I'll be taking them with me."

He put down the spoon he was holding and began to push back his chair. "It's funny," he said, "but it's my guess that one of the people at this table, with the exception of Mrs. Meehan, may have been writing some pretty rotten letters to Leila LaSalle. I'm real anxious to find out who that might be."

To Syd's dismay, Scott's now steely glance rested squarely on Cheryl.

# 12

It was nearly ten o'clock before they were alone in their apartment. Min had agonized all day about whether or not to confront Helmut with the proof that he had been in New York the night Leila died. To confront him was to force the admission that he had been involved with Leila. Not to confront him was to allow him to remain vulnerable. How stupid he had been not to destroy the record of the telephone call!

He went directly into his dressing room, and a few minutes later she heard the whirling of the

Jacuzzi in his bathroom. When he came back, she was waiting in one of the deep armchairs near the bedroom fireplace. Impersonally, she studied him. His hair was combed as precisely as though he were leaving for a formal ball; his silk dressing gown was knotted by a silk cord; his military posture made him seem taller than his true height. Five feet ten inches was barely above the average for men these days.

He prepared a Scotch and soda for himself and, without asking, poured a sherry for her. "It's been a difficult day, Minna. You handled it well," he said. Still she did not speak, and at last he seemed to sense that her silence was unusual. "This room is so restful," he said. "Aren't you glad you let me have my head with this color scheme? And it suits you. Strong, beautiful colors for a strong and beautiful woman."

"I would not consider peach a strong color."

"It *becomes* strong when it is wedded with deep blue. Like me, Minna. I become strong because I am with you."

"Then why this?" From the pocket of her robe she pulled out the telephone-credit-card bill and watched as his expression changed from bewilderment to fear. "Why did you lie to me? You were in New York that night. Were you with Leila? Had you gone to her?"

He sighed. "Minna, I'm glad you have found this. I wanted so much to tell you."

"Tell me now. You were in love with Leila. You were having an affair with her."

"No. I swear not."

"You're lying."

"Minna, I am telling the truth. I did go to her—as a friend—as a doctor. I got there at nine thirty. The door to her apartment was just barely open. I could hear Leila crying hysterically. Ted was shouting at her to put the phone down. She screamed back at him. The elevator was coming. I didn't want to be seen. You know the right angle the foyer takes. I went around that corner . . ."

Helmut sank to the floor at Min's feet. "Minna, it has been killing me not to tell you. Minna, Ted did push her. I heard her scream, *'Don't. Don't.'* And then her shriek as she fell."

Min paled. "Who got off the elevator? Did anyone see you?"

"I don't know. I ran down the fire stairs."

Then, as if his composure, his sense of order, had abandoned him, he leaned forward, his head in his hands, and began to cry.

# Wednesday,
## September 2

Good morning, treasured guests.

Are you feeling a bit lazy this morning? Never mind. After a few days we all begin to unwind into delicious and refreshing slumber and think that maybe, just maybe this morning we shall lie abed.

No. No. We beckon to you. Join us in that wonderful and invigorating morning walk through our beautiful grounds and along the coast. You will be glad. Perhaps by now you have already learned the pleasure of meeting new friends, of revisiting old ones on our sun-bright journey.

A gentle reminder. All guests who swim in any of the pools alone *must* wear the regulation Spa whistle. It has never been needed, but it is a safety factor that we deem essential.

Look in the mirror. Isn't all the exercise and pampering starting to show? Aren't your eyes brighter? Isn't your skin firmer? Won't it be fun showing off the new you to your family and friends?

And a final thought. Whatever troubles you brought with you to the Spa should by now be completely forgotten. *Think* happy.

Baron and Baroness Helmut von Schreiber

# 1

Elizabeth's phone rang at six o'clock. Sleepily she groped for it. Her eyelids were heavy and drooping. The aftereffects of the sedative made it impossible to think clearly.

It was William Murphy, the New York assistant district attorney. His opening words snapped her awake. "Miss Lange, I thought you wanted your sister's killer convicted." Without waiting for her to answer, he rushed on: "Can you please explain to me why you are in the same spa with Ted Winters?"

Elizabeth pulled herself up and swung her feet onto the floor. "I didn't know he was going to be here. I haven't been near him."

"That may be true, but the minute you saw him you should have been on the next plane home. Take a look at this morning's *Globe*. They've got a picture of you two in a clinch."

"I was never—"

"It was at the memorial service, but the way you're looking at each other is open to interpretation. Get out of there *now*! And what's this about your sister's secretary?"

"She's the reason I can't leave here." She told him about the letters, about Sammy's death. "I won't go near Ted," she promised, "but I am staying here until Friday. That gives me two days to find the letter Dora was carrying or to figure out who took it from her."

She would not change her mind, and finally Murphy hung up with a parting shot: "If your sister's killer walks, look to yourself for the reason." He paused. "And I told you before: *Be careful!*"

She jogged into Carmel. The New York papers would be on the stands there. Once again it was a glorious late-summer day. Sleek limousines and Mercedes convertibles followed each other on the road to the golf course. Other joggers waved at her amiably. Privacy hedges protected the estate homes from the curious eyes of the tourists, but in between, glimpses of the Pacific could be seen. A glorious day to be alive, Elizabeth thought, and she shuddered at the mental image of Sammy's body in the morgue.

Over coffee in a breakfast shop on Ocean Avenue, she read the *Globe*. Someone had snapped that picture at the end of the memorial service. She had started to weep. Ted was beside her. His arm had come around her and he'd turned her to him. She tried not to remember how it had felt to be in his arms.

With a surge of heartsick contempt for herself, she laid money on the table and left the restaurant.

On the way out she tossed the paper into a waste-basket. She wondered who at the Spa had tipped off the *Globe.* It could have been one of the staff. Min and Helmut were plagued with leaks. It could have been one of the guests who in exchange for personal publicity fed items to the columnists. It also could have been Cheryl.

When she got back to her bungalow, Scott was sitting on the porch waiting for her. "You're an early bird," she told him.

There were circles under his eyes. "I didn't do much sleeping last night. Something about Sammy falling backward into that pool just doesn't sit right with me."

Elizabeth winced as she thought of Sammy's bloodstained head.

"I'm sorry," Scott told her.

"It's all right. I feel exactly the same way. Did you find any more of those letters in the mailbags?"

"No. I've got to ask you to go through Sammy's personal effects with me. I don't know what I'm looking for, but you might spot something I'd miss."

"Give me ten minutes to shower and change."

"You're sure it won't upset you too much?"

Elizabeth leaned against the porch railing and ran her hand through her hair. "If that letter had been found, I could believe Sammy might have had some sort of attack and wandered into the bath-house. But with the letter gone . . . Scott, if some-one pushed her or frightened her so that she backed away, that person is a murderer."

The doors of the bungalows around them were opening. Men and women in identical ivory terrycloth robes headed for the spa buildings. "Treatments start in fifteen minutes," Elizabeth said. "Massages and facials and steam baths and God knows what-all. Isn't it incredible to think that one of the people being pampered here today left Sammy to die in that god-awful mausoleum?"

Craig's early-morning call was from the private investigator, and it was obvious he was troubled. "Nothing more on Sally Ross," he said, "but the word is that the burglar who was picked up in her building claims he has information about Leila LaSalle's death. He's trying to make a deal with the district attorney."

"What *kind* of information? This might be the break we're looking for."

"My contact doesn't get that feeling."

"What's *that* supposed to mean?"

"The district attorney is happy. You have to conclude his case is stronger, not weaker."

Craig phoned Bartlett and reported the conversation. "I'll put my office on it," Bartlett said. "My people may be able to find out something. We'll have to sit tight until we find out what's up. In the meantime I intend to see Sheriff Alshorne. I want a full explanation of those 'poison-pen' letters he talked about. You're *sure* Teddy wasn't involved with another woman, somebody he may be protecting? He doesn't seem to realize how much that

could help his case. Maybe you might mention that
to him."

Syd was about to leave for the hike when his
telephone rang. Something told him it would be
Bob Koenig. He was wrong. For three endless minutes he pleaded with a loan shark for a little more
time to pay the rest of his debts. "If Cheryl gets this
part, I can borrow against my commissions," he ar-
gued. "I swear she has the edge over Margo
Dresher. . . . Koenig told me himself . . . I
swear. . . ."

When he hung up the receiver, he sat on the edge
of the bed trembling. He had no choice. He had to
go to Ted and use what he knew to get the money
he needed.

Time had run out.

There was something indefinably different about
Sammy's apartment. Elizabeth felt it was as though
her aura as well as her physical being had departed.
Her plants had not been watered. Dead leaves
rimmed the planters. "Min was in touch with Sammy's cousin about the funeral arrangements," Scott
explained.

"Where is her body now?"

"It will be picked up from the morgue tomorrow
and shipped to Ohio for burial in the family plot."

Elizabeth thought of the concrete dust that had
smudged Sammy's skirt and cardigan. "Can I give
you clothes for Sammy?" she asked. "Is it too late?"

"It's not too late."

The last time she'd performed this service had been for Leila. Sammy had helped her select the dress in which Leila would be buried. "Remember, the casket won't be open," Sammy had reminded her.

"It isn't that," Elizabeth had said. "You know Leila. If she ever wore anything that didn't feel right, she was uncomfortable all evening even if everyone else thought she looked great. If there's such a thing as knowing . . ."

Sammy had understood. And together they had decided on the green chiffon-and-velvet gown Leila had worn the night she won the Oscar. They were the only two who had seen her in the casket. The undertaker had skillfully covered the bruises, had reconstructed the beautiful face, now curiously peaceful at last. For a time they had sat together reminiscing, Sammy holding Elizabeth's hand, finally reminding her that it was time to allow the fans to file past the bier, that the funeral director needed time to close the casket and drape it in the floral blanket that Elizabeth and Ted had ordered.

Now, with Scott watching her, Elizabeth examined the closet. "The blue tie silk," she murmured, "the one Leila gave her for her birthday two years ago. Sammy used to say that if she'd had clothes like this when she was young, her whole life might have been different."

She packed a small overnight case containing underthings, stockings, shoes and the inexpensive pearl necklace Sammy always wore with her "good dresses." "At least that's one thing I know I can do for her," she told Scott. "Now let's get about the business of finding what happened to her."

Sammy's dresser drawers revealed only personal items. Her desk held her checkbook, daily memo pad, personal stationery. On a shelf of the closet, pushed back behind a stack of sweaters, they found a year-old appointment book and a bound copy of *Merry-Go-Round* by Clayton Anderson.

"Leila's play," Elizabeth said. "I never did get to read it." She opened the folder and flipped through the pages. "Look, it's her working script. She always made so many notes and changed lines so that they sounded right for her."

Scott watched as Elizabeth ran her fingers over the ornate penmanship that dotted the margins of the pages. "Why don't you take that?" he asked.

"I'd like to."

He opened the appointment book. The entries were in the same curlicued handwriting. "This was Leila's too." There were no entries after March 31. On that page Leila had printed OPENING NIGHT! Scott flipped through the earlier pages. Most of them had the daily entry marked *Rehearsal* with a line drawn through.

There were appointments indicated for the hairdresser, for costume fittings, visit Sammy at Mount Sinai, send flowers, Sammy, publicity appearances. In the last six weeks, more and more of the extraneous appointments had been crossed out. There were also notations: *Sparrow, L.A.; Ted, Budapest; Sparrow, Montreal; Ted, Bonn.* . . . "She seems to have kept both your schedules right in front of her."

"She did. So she'd know where to reach us."

Scott stopped at one page. "You two were in the same city that night." He turned the pages more slowly. "Actually, Ted seems to have shown up fairly regularly in the same cities where your play was booked."

"Yes. We'd go out for supper after the performance and call Leila together."

Scott scrutinized Elizabeth's face. For just an instant something else had come over it. Was it possible that Elizabeth had fallen in love with Ted and refused to face that fact? And if so, was it possible that a sense of guilt was subconsciously demanding that Ted be punished for Leila's death, knowing that she would be punishing herself at the same time? It was a disquieting thought. He tried to dismiss it. "This appointment book probably doesn't have any bearing on the case, but I still think the district attorney in New York should have it," he said.

"Why?"

"No particular reason. But it could be considered an exhibit."

There was nothing more to be found in Sammy's apartment. "I've got a suggestion," Scott told her. "Go over to the spa and follow whatever schedule you had planned. As I told you, there are no more anonymous letters in that fan mail. My boys went through everything in those bags last night. Our chance of finding out who sent them is remote. I'll talk to Cheryl, but she's pretty cagey. I don't think she'll give herself away."

Together they walked down the long hall that led to the main house. "You haven't gone through Sammy's desk in the office, have you?" Scott asked.

"No." Elizabeth realized how tightly she was gripping the script. Something was compelling her to read it. She'd only seen that one terrible performance. She'd heard it was a good vehicle for Leila. Now she wanted to judge for herself. Reluctantly she accompanied Scott to the office. That had become another place she wanted to avoid.

Helmut and Min were in their private office. The door was open. Henry Bartlett and Craig were with them. Bartlett lost no time in demanding an explanation for the anonymous letters. "They may very well contribute to my client's defense," he told Scott. "We have a right to be fully briefed on them."

Elizabeth watched Henry Bartlett as he absorbed Scott's explanation of the anonymous letters. His look grew intense. His face was all sharp planes; his eyes were hard. This was the man who would be cross-examining her in court. He looked like a predator watching for prey.

"Let me get this straight," Bartlett said. "Miss Lange and Miss Samuels agreed that Leila LaSalle may have been profoundly upset by poison-pen letters suggesting that Ted Winters was involved with someone else? Those letters have now disappeared?

On Monday night Miss Samuels wrote her impressions of the first letter? Miss Lange has transcribed the second one? I want copies."

"I see no reason why you can't have them," Scott told him. He placed Leila's appointment book on Min's desk. "Oh, for the record, this is something else I'm sending on to New York," he said. "It was Leila's calendar for the last three months of her life."

Without asking for permission, Henry Bartlett reached for it. Elizabeth waited for Scott to protest, but he did not. Watching Bartlett thumb through Leila's personal daily diary, she felt an enormous sense of intrusion. What business had he? She threw an angry glance at Scott. He was looking at her impassively.

He's trying to prepare me for next week, she thought bleakly, and realized that maybe she should be grateful. Next week, all that Leila was would be laid out for twelve people to analyze; her own relationship with Leila, with Ted—nothing would be hidden, no privacy beyond violation. "I'll look through Sammy's desk," she said abruptly.

She was still holding the script of the play. She laid it on Sammy's desk and quickly went through the drawers. There was absolutely nothing personal in them. Spa letterheads; Spa publicity folders; Spa follow-up memos; the usual office paraphernalia.

Min and the Baron had followed her out. She glanced up to see them standing in front of Sammy's desk. Both of them were staring at the leather-bound folder with the bold title *Merry-Go-Round* on the cover.

"Leila's play?" Min asked.

"Yes. Sammy kept Leila's copy. I'll take it now."

Craig, Bartlett and the sheriff came out of the private office. Henry Bartlett was smiling—a self-satisfied, smug, chilly smile. "Miss Lange, you've been a great help to us today. But I think I should warn you that the jury won't take kindly to the fact that as a woman scorned, you put Ted Winters through this hellish nightmare."

Elizabeth stood up, her lips white. "What are you talking about?"

"I'm talking about the fact that in her own handwriting, your sister made the connection between you and Ted 'happening' to be in the same city so often. I'm talking about the fact that someone else also made that connection and tried to warn her with those letters. I'm talking about the look on your face when Ted put his arms around you at the memorial service. Surely you've seen this morning's paper? Apparently what may have been a mild flirtation for Ted was serious to you, and so when he dropped you, you discovered a way to take your revenge."

"You filthy liar!" Elizabeth did not know she had thrown the copy of the play at Henry Bartlett until it struck him in the chest.

His expression was impassive, even pleased. Bending, he picked up the script and handed it back to her. "Do me a favor, young lady, and stage that kind of outburst in front of the jury next week," he said. "They'll *exonerate* Ted."

# 2

While Craig and Bartlett went to confront the sheriff, Ted worked out with the Nautilus equipment in the men's spa. Each piece of equipment he used seemed to emphasize his own situation. The rowboat that went nowhere; the bicycle that no matter how furiously pedaled, stayed in place. On the surface he managed to exchange pleasantries with some of the other men in the gym—the head of the Chicago stock exchange, the president of Atlantic Banks, a retired admiral.

He sensed in all of them a wariness: they didn't know what to say to him, didn't want to say "Good luck." It was easier for them—and for him—when they got busy with the machines and concentrated on building muscles.

Men in prison tended to get pretty soft. Not enough exercise. Boredom. Pallid skin. Ted studied his own tan. It wouldn't last long behind bars.

He was supposed to meet Bartlett and Craig in his bungalow at ten o'clock. Instead, he went for a swim in the indoor pool. He'd have preferred the

Olympic pool, but there was always the chance Elizabeth might be there. He didn't want to run into her.

He had swum about ten laps when he saw Syd dive in at the opposite end of the pool. They were six lanes apart, and after a brief wave, he ignored Syd. But after twenty minutes, when the three swimmers between them had left, he was surprised to see that Syd was keeping pace with him. He had a powerful backstroke and moved with swift precision from one end of the pool to the other. Ted deliberately set out to beat him. Syd obviously caught on. After six laps they were in a dead heat.

They left the water at the same time. Syd slung a towel over his shoulders and came around the pool. "Nice workout. You're in good shape."

"I've been swimming every day in Hawaii for nearly a year and a half. I should be."

"The pool at my health club isn't like Hawaii, but it keeps me fit." Syd looked around. There were Jacuzzis in two corners of the glass-enclosed room. "Ted, I have to talk to you privately."

They went to the opposite end. There were three new swimmers in the pool, but they were well out of earshot. Ted watched as Syd rubbed the towel through his dark brown hair. He noticed that the hair on Syd's chest was completely gray. That'll be the next thing, he decided. He would grow old and gray in prison.

\* \* \*

Syd did not hedge. "Ted, I'm in trouble. Big trouble. With guys who play rough. It all began with that damn play. I borrowed too much. I thought I could sweat it out. If Cheryl gets this part, I'm on my way up again. But I can't stall them anymore. I need a loan. Ted, I mean a *loan.* But I need it now."

"How much?"

"Six hundred thousand dollars. Ted, it's small change for you, and it's a loan. But you owe it to me."

"I owe it to you?"

Syd looked around and then stepped closer. His mouth was within inches of Ted's ear. "I'd never have said this . . . never even told you I knew . . . But Ted, I *saw* you that night. You ran past me, a block from Leila's apartment. Your face was bleeding. Your hands were scratched. You were in shock. You don't remember, do you? You didn't even hear me when I called you. You just kept running." Syd's voice dropped to a whisper. "Ted, I caught up with you. I asked what had happened and you told me Leila was dead, that she had fallen off the terrace. Ted, then you said to me . . . I swear to God . . . you said to me, 'My father pushed her, my father pushed her.' You were like a little kid, trying to blame what you did on someone else. You even *sounded* like a little kid."

Ted felt waves of nausea. "I don't believe you."

"Why would I lie? Ted, you ran into the street. A cab came along. You nearly got run over stopping it.

Ask that cabbie who took you to Connecticut. He's going to be a witness, isn't he? Ask him if he didn't almost sideswipe you. Ted, I'm your *friend*. I know how you felt when Leila went nuts in Elaine's. I know how *I* felt. When I saw you, I was on my way to try to talk sense to Leila. I was mad enough to kill her myself. Have I mentioned this once to you, to anyone? I wouldn't do it now, except I'm desperate. You've got to help me! If I don't come up with that money in forty-eight hours—I'm finished."

"You'll have the money."

"Oh, Christ, Ted, I *knew* I could count on you. God, thanks, Ted." Syd put his hands on Ted's shoulders.

"Get away from me." Ted's voice was almost a shout. The swimmers looked at them curiously. Ted shook himself free, grabbed his towel and ran blindly out of the pool area.

# 3

Scott questioned Cheryl in her bungalow. This one was furnished in a splashy yellow-and-green-and-white print, with white carpeting and white walls. Scott felt the thickness of the carpet under his feet. All wool. Top quality. Sixty . . . seventy dollars a yard? No wonder Min had that haunted look! Scott knew exactly how much old Samuel had left her. There couldn't be much left, after what she'd poured into this place. . . .

Cheryl was not happy about having been paged in the spa to meet him. She was wearing her own version of the standard tank suit, a skimpy scrap of material which did not quite cover her breasts and arched up on either side of her hipbones. The terrycloth robe was slung on her shoulders. She did not attempt to conceal her impatience. "I'm due in a calisthenics class in ten minutes," she told him.

"Well, let's hope you make it," he said. His throat muscles tightened as the active dislike he felt for Cheryl swelled within him. "Your chances will improve a lot if you give me some straight answers. Like did you write some pretty nasty letters to Leila before she died?"

As he had anticipated, the interrogation was, at first, fruitless. Cheryl cleverly dodged his questions. Anonymous letters? Why would she be interested in sending them? Break up Ted and Leila? What difference would it have made if they *had* ended up married? It wouldn't have lasted. Leila didn't have it in her to stick with one man. She had to hurt men before they hurt her. The play? She had no idea of how the rehearsals for Leila's play had gone. Frankly, she hadn't been that interested.

Finally Scott had had enough. "Listen, Cheryl, I think there's something you'd better realize. I'm not satisfied that Sammy's death was from natural causes. The second anonymous letter she was carrying is missing.

"You went to Sammy's desk. You left a bill marked *Paid in full.* An anonymous letter was on top of the desk with other fan mail. And then the letter disappeared. Granted someone else *may* have entered the reception area so quietly that even though the door was open, neither Min nor the Baron nor Sammy heard anyone come in. But that's a bit unlikely, isn't it?" He did not share with Cheryl the fact that Min and the Baron both had had access to the desk, out of Sammy's presence. He was rewarded by a faint glow of alarm in Cheryl's eyes. She licked her lips nervously.

"You're not suggesting I had anything to do with Sammy's death?"

"I'm suggesting that you took that first letter from Sammy's desk, and I want it now. That is state's evidence in a murder trial."

She looked away, and as Scott studied her, he saw an expression of naked panic come over her face. He followed her gaze and saw a sliver of charred paper wedged under the baseboard. Cheryl lunged from the couch to pick it up, but he was too quick for her.

On the ragged piece of cheap paper were pasted three words:

*Learn your lines.*

Scott took out his wallet and carefully inserted the tiny scrap in it. "So you did steal that letter," he said. "Destroying evidence is a felony, punishable by imprisonment. What about the second letter? The one Sammy was carrying? Did you destroy that one too? And how did you get it from her? You'd better get yourself a lawyer, lady."

Cheryl clutched his arm. "Scott, my God, please. I swear I didn't write those letters. I swear the only time I saw Sammy was in Min's office. All right. I took this letter from Sammy's desk. I thought it might help Ted. I showed it to Syd. He said people would think I wrote it. He tore it up; I didn't. I swear that's as much as I know." Tears were spilling down her cheeks. "Scott, any publicity, *any publicity about this at all* could kill my chances of being Amanda. Scott, please."

Scott heard the contempt in his voice. "I really don't give a damn how publicity affects your career, Cheryl. Why don't we make a bargain? I'll hold off bringing you in for formal questioning and you do some hard thinking. Maybe your memory will suddenly get better. For your sake, I hope so."

# 4

In a state of dazed relief, Syd headed back to his bungalow. *Ted was going to lend him the money.* It had been so tempting to make the story stronger, to say that Ted had outright admitted killing Leila. But at the last instant, he'd changed his mind and quoted Ted exactly. God, Ted had sounded creepy when he'd rambled about his father that night. Syd still felt a violent wrench in his gut whenever he thought of running after Ted. It had been immediately obvious that Ted had been in some sort of psychotic state. After Leila's death, he'd waited to see whether Ted would ever sound him out about that meeting. His reaction today proved he had no memory of it.

He cut across the lawn, deliberately avoiding the path. He didn't want to make small talk with anyone. There'd been some new arrivals yesterday. One of them he recognized as a young actor who'd been leaving his photos at the agency and phoning constantly. He wondered what old broad was paying his way. Today of all days, Syd didn't want to spend his time dodging eager would-be clients.

His first move when he reached the privacy of his own place was to make a drink. He needed one. He *deserved* one. His second was to phone his early-morning caller. "I'll have the money to you by the weekend," he said, with newfound confidence.

Now if he could just hear from Bob Koenig. The phone rang before he could complete the thought. The operator asked him to hold on for Mr. Koenig. Syd felt his hands begin to tremble. He caught a look at his reflection in the mirror. The expression wasn't of the kind that inspired confidence in Los Angeles.

Bob's first words were "Congratulations, Syd."

*Cheryl had the part!* Syd's mind began clicking percentages. With two words, Bob had put him in the big time again.

"I don't know what to say." His voice became stronger, more confident. "Bob, I'm telling you, you've made the right choice. Cheryl's going to be fantastic."

"I know all that, Syd. The bottom line is that rather than risk any bad press with Margo, we're going with Cheryl. I talked her up. So what if she's box-office poison now? That's what they said about Joan Collins and look what she's done."

"Bob, that's what I've been telling you all along."

"We'd better both be right. I'll arrange a press reception for Cheryl at the Beverly Hilton for Friday afternoon about five o'clock."

"We'll be there!"

"Syd, this is very important. From now on, we treat Cheryl as a superstar. And by the way, tell Cheryl to plaster a smile on her face. Amanda is a strong, but *likable* character. I don't want to read

about any more outbursts at waiters or limo drivers.
And I mean it."

Five minutes later, Syd was confronting a hysterical Cheryl Manning. "You mean you *admitted* to
Scott that you took that letter, you dumb bitch?" He
grabbed her shoulders. "Shut up and listen to me.
*Are there any more letters?*"

"Let go. You're hurting me. I don't know." Cheryl
tried to shrink away from him. "I can't lose that
part. I can't. I *am* Amanda."

"You bet you can't lose that part!" Syd shoved her
backward, and she toppled against the couch.

Fury replaced fear. Cheryl brushed back her hair
and clenched her teeth. Her mouth became a thin,
menacing slash. "Do you always push when you're
angry, Syd? You'd better get something straight.
*You* tore up that letter. *I* didn't. And I didn't *write*
that letter, or any others. Scott doesn't believe me.
So you march yourself over to him and tell him the
truth: that I planned to give that letter to Ted to
help his defense. You convince Scott, do you hear
me, Syd? Because on Friday I'm not going to be
here. I'm going to be at my press reception, and
there isn't going to be a whisper to connect me to
any poison-pen letters or destroyed evidence."

They glared at each other. In a frenzy of frustration, Syd realized that she might be telling the truth
and that by destroying the letter he might have
thrown away the series. If one hint of unfavorable

publicity hit the papers before Friday . . . If Scott refused to let Cheryl leave the Spa . . .

"I've got to think," he said. "I'll figure something out."

He had one last card to play.

The question was how to play it.

# 5

When Ted returned to his bungalow, he found Henry Bartlett and Craig waiting for him. A jubilant Bartlett did not seem to notice his silence. "I think we've had a break," he announced. As Ted took his place at the table, Bartlett told him about the discovery of Leila's diary. "In her own hand, she'd checked off when you and Elizabeth Lange were in the same cities. Did you see her every time you were there?"

Ted leaned back and folded his arms behind his head and closed his eyes. It seemed so long ago.

"Ted, at least here I can *help* you." Craig's enthusiasm was a quality that had for a long time been missing from his voice and demeanor. "You kept Elizabeth's schedule on your desk. I can swear that you adjusted your travel plans so that you'd be able to see her."

Ted did not open his eyes. "Will you kindly explain that?"

Henry Bartlett had been driven past irritation. "Listen, Mr. Winters. I wasn't hired to take on this case so that you could wipe your feet on me. It's the rest of your life; but it's also my professional reputation. If you can't or won't cooperate in your own defense, maybe it's not too late for you to get another attorney." He shoved his files across the table and watched as papers spilled from them. "You insisted on coming here when it would have been much better to have ready access to my staff. You disappeared for a long walk yesterday when we were supposed to work. You were supposed to be here an hour ago and we're twiddling our thumbs waiting for you. You've blackballed one line of defense that might work. Now we have a decent shot at destroying Elizabeth Lange's credibility as a witness and you're not interested."

Ted opened his eyes. Slowly he lowered his arms until they rested on the table. "Oh, but I *am* interested. Tell me about it."

Bartlett chose to ignore the sarcasm. "Listen, we're going to be able to produce a facsimile of two letters Leila received that suggest you were involved with someone else. Cheryl is one possibility as that someone else. We know she'd say anything. But there's a better way. You did try to coordinate your schedule with Elizabeth's—"

Ted interrupted him. "Elizabeth and I were very good friends. We liked each other. We enjoyed each other's company. If I had my choice of being in Chicago on Wednesday and Dallas on Friday or the other way around, and found that a good friend with whom I could enjoy a late supper and relax was in those same cities, yes, I would arrange my schedule to do that. So what?"

"Come off it, Ted. You did it half a dozen times in the same weeks that Leila started to fall apart— *when she was receiving those letters.*"

Ted shrugged.

"Ted, Henry is trying to plan your defense," Craig snapped. "At least pay attention to him."

Bartlett continued. "What we are trying to show you is this: Step One. Leila was receiving letters saying that you were involved with someone else. Step Two. Craig is witness to the fact that you synchronized your schedule with Elizabeth's. Step Three. In her own handwriting, Leila made the obvious connection between you two in her diary. Step Four. You had no reason to kill Leila if you were no longer interested in her. Step Five. What to you was a mild flirtation was very, very different to Elizabeth. She was head over heels in love with you." Triumphantly Henry threw the copy of the *Globe* at Ted. "Look at that picture."

Ted studied it. He remembered the moment at the end of the service when some fool had asked the organist to play "My Old Kentucky Home." Leila had told him about singing that to Elizabeth when they took off for New York. Beside him, Elizabeth had gasped; then the tears that she'd held back flooded her face. He'd put his arms around her, turned her to him and whispered, "Don't, Sparrow."

"She was in love with you," Henry continued. "When she realized that for you it was simply a flirtation, she turned on you. She took advantage of that wacko's crazy accusation to destroy you. I'm telling you, Teddy, we may be able to make this stick."

Ted tore the paper in half. "Apparently, my job is to be the devil's advocate. Let's suppose your scenario is true. Elizabeth was in love with me. But let's carry it one step further. Suppose I had come to realize that life with Leila would be a succession of constant ups and downs, of tantrums, of an insecurity that resulted in jealous accusations every time I spoke pleasantly to another woman. Suppose I'd come to realize that Leila was an actress first, last and always, that she didn't want a child. Suppose I'd realized that in Elizabeth I had found something I'd been looking for all my life."

Ted slammed his fist on the table. "Don't you know that you have just given me the very best reason in the world for killing Leila? Because do you think that Elizabeth would have looked at me twice while her sister was alive?" He pushed back his chair with a vehemence that caused it to topple over. "Why don't you two play golf or go for a swim or do anything that makes you feel good? Don't waste your time here. *I* don't plan to."

Bartlett's face turned crimson. "I've had

enough," he snapped. "Listen, *Mr.* Winters, you may know how to run hotels, but you don't know a damn thing about what goes on in a criminal courtroom. You hired me to keep you out of prison, but I can't do it alone. What's more, I don't intend to. Either you start cooperating with me or get yourself another lawyer."

"Calm down, Henry," Craig said.

"No, I won't calm down. I don't need this case. I can *possibly* win it, but not the way it's going now." He pointed at Ted. "If you are so sure that any defense I raise won't work, why don't you pleabargain right now? I might get you a maximum of seven to ten years. Is that what you want? Say so. Or else sit down at that table."

Ted picked up the chair he had knocked over. "Let's get to work," he said tonelessly. "I probably owe you an apology. I realize you're the best in your field, but I guess you can understand how trapped I feel. Do you really think there *is* a chance for an acquittal?"

"I've gotten acquittals in cases as rough as this," Bartlett told him. "What you don't seem to fathom," he added, "is that being guilty has nothing to do with the verdict."

# 6

Somehow Min managed to get through the rest of the morning. She was too busy fielding phone calls from the media to even think of the scene in the office between Elizabeth and Ted's lawyer. They had all left immediately after the blowup: Bartlett and Elizabeth furious, Craig distressed, Scott grim-faced. Helmut had escaped to the clinic. He had known she wanted to talk to him. He had avoided her this morning as he'd avoided her last night, when after telling her that he'd heard Ted attacking Leila, he'd locked himself in his study.

Who in hell had tipped off the press that Elizabeth and Ted were here? She answered the persistent inquiries with her standard reply: "We never release the names of our guests." She was told that both Elizabeth and Ted had been spotted in Carmel. "No comment."

Any other time she'd have loved the publicity. But now? She was asked if there was anything unusual about her secretary's death. "Certainly not."

At noon she told the operator to hold all calls and went to the women's spa. She was relieved to see that the atmosphere there was normal. There seemed to be no more talk about Sammy's death. She made it a point to chat with the guests lunching around the pool. Alvirah Meehan was there. She had spotted Scott's car and tried to pepper Min with questions about his presence.

When Min got back to the main house she went directly up to the apartment. Helmut was sitting on the couch, sipping a cup of tea. His face was a sickly gray. "Ah, Minna." He attempted a smile.

She did not return it. "We have got to talk," she told him abruptly. "What is the real reason you went to Leila's apartment that night? Were you having an affair with her? Tell me the truth!"

The cup rattled in the saucer as he put it down. "An affair! Minna, I hated that woman!"

Min watched as his face blotched and his hands clenched. "Do you think I was amused at the way she ridiculed me? An affair with her?" He slammed his fist on the cocktail table. "Minna, you are the only woman in my life. There has never been another woman since I met you. I swear that to you."

"Liar!" Min rushed over to him, bent down and grabbed his lapels. "Look at me. I tell you, look at me. Stop the phony aristocratic crap and the dramatics. You were dazzled by Leila. What man wasn't? Every time you looked at her, you raped her with your eyes. You were all like that, the pack of you. Ted. Syd. Even that clod, Craig. But you were the worst. Love. Hate. It's all one. And in your entire life, you've never put yourself out for anyone. I want the truth. *Why did you go to her that night?*" She released him, suddenly drained and exhausted.

He jumped to his feet. His hand brushed the teacup and it tipped over, sending splatters of tea onto the table and carpet. "Minna, this is impossible. I will not have you treating me like a germ under a microscope." Disdainfully he glanced at the mess. "Send for someone to clean this up," he ordered. "*I* have to get to the clinic. Mrs. Meehan is due for her collagen injections this afternoon." His tone became sarcastic. "Take heart, my dear. As you know, that's another outrageous fee in the till."

"I saw that dreary woman an hour ago," Min said. "You've made yet another conquest. She was gushing about how talented you are and how you are going to make her feel like a butterfly floating on a cloud. If I hear that idiotic expression from her once more . . ."

She broke off. Helmut's knees had begun to sag. She grabbed him before he could fall. "Tell me what is wrong!" she shrieked. "Tell me what you've done!"

# 7

When she left Min's office, Elizabeth rushed back to her bungalow, furious at herself for allowing Bartlett to goad her. He would say anything, do anything to discredit her testimony, and she was playing into his hands.

To distract herself, she opened the script of Leila's play. But the words were a jumble. She could not focus on them.

*Was there the ring of truth to Bartlett's accusations? Had Ted deliberately sought her out?*

She thumbed through the script restlessly, deciding to read it later. Then her glance fell on one of Leila's marginal notes. Shocked, she sank down on the couch and turned back to the first page.

*Merry-Go-Round.* A comedy by Clayton Anderson.

She read the play through rapidly, then sat for a long time totally absorbed in her thoughts. Finally she reached for a pen and pad and began rereading slowly, making her own notations.

At two thirty she laid the pen down. Pages of the pad were filled with her jottings. She became aware that she had skipped lunch, that her head ached dully. Some of Leila's markings in the margin had been almost indecipherable, but eventually she'd made them all out.

Clayton Anderson. The playwright of *Merry-Go-Round.* The wealthy college professor who had invested one million dollars of his own money in the play, but whose true identity was known to no one. Who was he? He had known Leila intimately.

She phoned the main house. The operator told her that Baroness von Schreiber was in her apartment but was not to be disturbed. "I'll be right there," Elizabeth told her crisply. "Tell the Baroness I have to see her."

\* \* \*

Min was in bed. She did look ill. There was no bravado, no bossiness in her demeanor or voice. "Well, Elizabeth?"

She's afraid of me, Elizabeth thought. With a rush of her old affection she sat by the bed. "Min, why did you bring me here?"

Min shrugged. "Because believe it or not, I was worried about you, because I love you."

"I believe that. And the other reason?"

"Because I am appalled at the idea that Ted may spend the rest of his life in prison. Sometimes people do terrible things in anger, because they are out of control, things they might never do if they were not goaded beyond their ability to stop themselves. I believe that happened. I *know* that happened to Ted."

"What do you mean you *know* that happened?"

"Nothing . . . nothing." Min closed her eyes. "Elizabeth, you do what you must. But I warn you. You will have to live with destroying Ted for the rest of your life. Someday you will again face Leila. I think she will not thank you. You know how she was after she had been utterly outrageous. Contrite. Loving. Generous. All of it."

"Min, isn't there another reason why you want Ted to be acquitted? It has to do with this place, doesn't it?"

"What do you mean?"

"I mean that just before Leila died, Ted was considering putting a Cypress Point Spa in all his new hotels. What happened to that plan?"

"Ted has not gone ahead with plans for new hotels since his indictment."

"Exactly. So there are a couple of reasons why you want Ted acquitted. Min, who is Clayton Anderson?"

"I have no idea. Elizabeth, I am very tired. Perhaps we can talk later."

"Min, come on. You're not that tired." The sharper tone in her voice made Min open her eyes and pull herself up on the pillows. I was right, Elizabeth thought. She's not so much sick as *afraid*. "Min, I just read and re-read that play Leila was in. I saw it with all of you that last preview, but I didn't pay attention to it. I was too worried about Leila. Min, someone who knew Leila inside and out wrote that play. That's why it was so perfect for her. Someone even used Helmut's expressions in it—'a butterfly floating on a cloud.' Leila noticed it too. She had a notation in the margin: *'Tell the Baron someone is stealing his thunder.'* Min . . ."

They stared at each other as the same thought struck them. "Helmut wrote the ads for this place," Elizabeth whispered. "He writes the daily bulletins. Maybe there *is* no wealthy college professor. Min, did Helmut write the play?"

"I . . . don't . . . know." Min struggled out of bed. She was wearing a loose caftan that suddenly seemed too large, as if she were shriveling inside it. "Elizabeth, will you excuse me? I have to make a call to Switzerland."

# 8

With an unfamiliar sense of worry, Alvirah walked reluctantly down the hedged path that led to treatment room C. The instructions the nurse had given her were re-confirmed by the note that had been on her breakfast tray this morning. The note was friendly and reassuring, but even so, now that the time had come, Alvirah still felt squeamish.

To ensure absolute privacy, the note said, patients entered the treatment rooms by the individual outside doors. Alvirah was to go to treatment room C at three P.M. and settle herself on the table. In view of the fact that Mrs. Meehan had an aversion to needles, she would be given a special-strength Valium and allowed to rest until three thirty, at which time Dr. von Schreiber would perform the treatment. She would continue to rest for an additional half-hour to allow the Valium to wear off.

The flowering hedges were over six feet high, and walking between them made her feel like a young girl in a bower. The day had become really warm, but in here the hedges held moisture, and the azaleas made her think of her own azalea plants in front of the house. They'd been really pretty last spring.

She was at the treatment-room door. It was

painted a pale blue, and a tiny gold *C* confirmed that she was in the right place. Hesitantly, she turned the handle and went in.

The room looked like a lady's boudoir. It had flowered wallpaper and a pale green carpet, a little dressing table and a love seat. The treatment table was made up like a bed, with sheets that matched the wallpaper, a pale pink comforter and a lace-edged pillow. On the closet door was a gilt-framed mirror with beveled edges. Only the presence of a cabinet with medical supplies suggested the real purpose of the room, and even that was finished in white wood with leaded glass doors.

Alvirah removed her sandals and placed them, neatly, side by side under the table. She had a size nine foot and didn't want the doctor tripping when he was giving the collagen injections. She lay down on the table, pulled up the comforter and closed her eyes.

They sprang open a moment later when the nurse came in. She was Regina Owens, the chief assistant, the one who had taken her medical history. "Don't look so worried," Miss Owens said. Alvirah liked her. She reminded her of one of the women whose houses she cleaned. She was about forty, with dark short hair, nice wide eyes and a pleasant smile.

She brought a glass of water and a couple of pills to Alvirah. "These will make you feel nice and drowsy, and you won't even know you're getting made gorgeous."

Obediently Alvirah put them into her mouth and swallowed the water. "I feel like a baby," she apologized.

"Not at all. You'd be amazed how many people are terrified of needles." Miss Owens came behind her and began massaging her temples. "You *are* tense. Now, I'm going to put a nice, cool cloth over your eyes and you just let yourself drift off to sleep. The doctor and I will be back in about a half-hour. By then you probably won't even know we're here."

Alvirah felt the strong fingers press against her temples. "That feels good," she murmured.

"I'll bet it does." For a few minutes Miss Owens continued to knead Alvirah's forehead, the back of her neck. Alvirah felt herself drifting into a pleasantly dreamy state. Then a cool cloth was placed over her eyes. She barely heard the click of the door when Miss Owens tiptoed out.

There were so many thoughts running through her head, like loose threads that she couldn't quite pull together.

*A butterfly floating on a cloud . . .*

She was beginning to remember why that seemed familiar. It was almost there.

"Can you hear me, Mrs. Meehan?"

She hadn't realized that Baron von Schreiber had come in. His voice sounded low and a little hoarse. She hoped the microphone would pick it up. She wanted everything on record.

"Yes." Her own voice sounded far away.

"Don't be afraid. You'll barely feel a pinprick."

He was right. She felt hardly anything, just a tiny sensation like a mosquito bite. And to think, she'd been worried! She waited. The doctor had told her he'd be injecting the collagen in ten or twelve spots on each side of her mouth. What was he waiting for?

It was getting hard to breathe. She *couldn't* breathe. "Help!" she cried, but the word wouldn't come out. She opened her mouth, gasping desperately. She was slipping away. Her arms, her chest, nothing moved. Oh, God, help me, help me, she thought.

Then darkness overcame her as the door opened and Nurse Owens said briskly, "Well, here we are, Mrs. Meehan. All set for your beauty treatment?"

# 9

What does it prove? Elizabeth asked herself as she walked from the main house along the path to the clinic. If Helmut wrote that play, he must be going through hell. The author had put one million dollars into the production. That was why Min was calling Switzerland. Her nest egg in a numbered account was a standing joke. "I'll never be broke," she had always bragged.

Min had wanted Ted acquitted so that she could

license Cypress Point Spas in all his new hotels. Helmut had a much more compelling reason. If he was "Clayton Anderson," he knew that even the nest egg was gone.

She would force him to tell her the truth, Elizabeth decided.

The foyer of the clinic was hushed and quiet, but the receptionist was not at her desk. From down the hall, Elizabeth heard running feet, raised voices. She hurried toward the sounds. Doors were open on the corridor as guests in the process of treatment peeked out. The room at the end of the hall was open. It was from there that the sounds were coming.

Room C. Dear God, that was where Mrs. Meehan was going to have the collagen treatment. There wasn't anyone in the Spa who hadn't heard about it. Had something gone wrong? Elizabeth almost collided with a nurse coming out of the room.

"You can't go in there!" The nurse was trembling.

Elizabeth pushed her aside.

Helmut was bent over the treatment table. He was compressing Alvirah Mechan's chest. An oxygen mask was on Alvirah's face. The noise of a respirator dominated the room. The coverlet had been pulled back; her robe was crumpled under her, the incongruous sunburst pin gleaming upward. As Elizabeth watched, too horrified to speak, a nurse handed Helmut a needle. He attached it to tubing and started an intravenous in Alvirah's arm. A male nurse took over compressing her chest.

From the distance Elizabeth could hear the wail of an ambulance siren screeching through the gates of the Spa.

It was four fifteen when Scott was notified that Alvirah Meehan, the forty-million-dollar lottery winner, was in the Monterey Peninsula hospital, a possible victim of an attempted homicide. The deputy who phoned had responded to the emergency call and accompanied the ambulance to the Spa. The attendants suspected foul play, and the emergency-room doctor agreed with them. Dr. von Schreiber claimed that she had not yet received a collagen treatment; but a drop of blood on her face seemed to indicate a very recent injection.

Alvirah Meehan! Scott rubbed his hands over suddenly weary eyes. That woman was bright. He thought of her comments at dinner. She was like the child in the fable *The Emperor's New Clothes* who says, "But he has no clothes on!"

Why would anyone want to hurt Alvirah Meehan? Scott had hoped she wouldn't get caught up with charlatans trying to invest her money for her, but the thought that anyone might deliberately try to kill her was incredible. "I'll be right there," he said as he slammed down the phone.

The waiting room of the community hospital was open and pleasant, with greenery and an indoor pond, not unlike the lobby of a small hotel. He never saw it without remembering the hours he had sat here, when Jeanie was a patient . . .

He was informed that the doctors were working on Mrs. Meehan, that Dr. Whitley would be available to see him shortly. Elizabeth came in while he was waiting.

"How is she?"

"I don't know."

"She shouldn't have had those injections. She really *was* afraid. She had a heart attack, didn't she?"

"We don't know yet. How did you get here?"

"Min. We came in her car. She's parking it now. Helmut rode in the ambulance with Mrs. Meehan. This can't be happening." Her voice rose. People in nearby chairs turned to stare at her.

Scott forced her to sit on the sofa beside him. "Elizabeth, get hold of yourself. You only met Mrs. Meehan a few days ago. You can't let yourself get this upset."

"Where's Helmut?" Min's voice, coming from behind them, was as flat as though there were no emotion left in her. She too seemed to be in a state of disbelief and shock. She came around the couch and sank into the chair facing them. "He must be so distraught . . ." She broke off. "Here he is."

To Scott's practiced eye, the Baron looked as though he had seen a ghost. He was still wearing the exquisitely tailored blue smock that was his surgical costume. He sank heavily into the chair beside Min and groped for her hand. "She is in a coma. They say she had some sort of injection. Min, it is impossible, I swear to you, impossible."

"Stay here." Scott's look included the three of

them. From the long corridor that led to the emergency area, he had seen the chief of the hospital beckon to him.

They spoke in the private office. "She was injected with something that brought on shock," Dr. Whitley said flatly. He was a tall, lean sixty-three-year-old whose usual expression was affable and sympathetic. Now it was steely, and Scott remembered that his longtime friend had been an Army fighter pilot in World War II.

"Will she live?"

"Absolutely impossible to say. She's in a coma which may become irreversible. She tried to say something before she went totally under."

"What was it?"

"It sounded like 'voy.' That's as much as she got out."

"That's no help. What does the Baron have to say? Does he have any idea how this could have happened?"

"We didn't let him near her, Scott, frankly."

"I gather you don't think much of the good doctor?"

"I have no reason to doubt his medical capabilities. But there's something about him that shouts 'phony' at me every time I see him. And if *he* didn't inject Mrs. Meehan, then who the hell did?"

Scott pushed back his chair. "That's just what I intend to find out."

As he left the office, Whitley called him back.

"Scott, something that might help us—could someone check Mrs. Meehan's rooms and bring in any medication she may have been taking? Until we reach her husband and get her medical history, we don't know what we may be dealing with."

"I'll take care of it myself."

Elizabeth drove back to the Spa with Scott. On the way he told her about finding the shred of paper in Cheryl's bungalow. "Then she did write those letters!" Elizabeth exclaimed.

Scott shook his head. "I know it sounds crazy, and I know Cheryl can lie as easily as most of us can breathe, but I've been thinking about this all day, and my gut feeling is she's telling the truth."

"What about Syd? Did you talk to him?"

"Not yet. She's bound to tell him she admitted that she stole the letter and that he tore it up. I decided to let him stew before I question him. That sometimes works. But I'm telling you, I'm inclined to believe her story."

"But if *she* didn't write the letters, who did?"

Scott shot a glance at her. "I don't know." He paused, then said, "What I mean is, I don't know *yet*."

Min and the Baron followed Scott's car in her convertible. Min drove. "The only way I can help you is to know the truth," she told her husband. "Did you do something to that woman?"

The Baron lit a cigarette and inhaled deeply. His

china-blue eyes watered. The reddish tint in his hair seemed brassy under the late-afternoon sun. The top of the convertible was down. A cool land breeze had dispelled the last of the daytime warmth. A sense of autumn was in the air.

"Minna, what crazy talk is that? I went into the room. She wasn't breathing. I saved her life. What reason would I have to hurt her?"

"Helmut, who is Clayton Anderson?"

He dropped the cigarette. It fell on the leather seat beside him. Min reached over and picked it up. "You'd better not ruin this car. There won't be a replacement. I repeat: Who is Clayton Anderson?"

"I don't know what you're talking about," he whispered.

"Oh, I think you do. Elizabeth came to see me. She read the play. That's why you were so upset this morning, isn't it? It wasn't the appointment book. It was the *play*. Leila had made notes in the margin. She picked up that idiotic phrase you use in the ads. Elizabeth caught it too. So did Mrs. Meehan. She saw one of the previews. That's why you tried to kill her, isn't it? You were still hoping to conceal the fact *you* wrote that play."

"Minna, I am telling you—you are *crazy*! For all we know that woman was self-injecting."

"That's nonsense. She talked constantly about her fear of needles."

"That could have been a cover-up."

"The playwright put over a million dollars in that

play. If you *are* that playwright, where would you have gotten the money?"

They were at the gates of the Spa. Min slowed down and glanced at him, unsmiling. "I tried to phone Switzerland to check on my balance. Of course, it was after business hours there. I will call tomorrow, Helmut. I hope—for your sake—that money is in my account."

His expression was as bland as ever, but his eyes were those of a man about to be hanged.

They met on the porch of Alvirah Meehan's bungalow. The Baron opened the door and they went in. Scott saw that Min had clearly taken advantage of Alvirah's naïveté. This was the most expensive of their accommodations—the rooms the First Lady used when she saw fit to seek R-and-R at the Spa. There were a living room, a dining room, a library, a huge master bedroom, two full baths on the first floor. *You sure socked it to her,* Scott thought.

His inspection of the premises was relatively brief. The medicine chest in the bathroom Alvirah used contained only over-the-counter drugs—maximum-strength Bufferin, Allerest, a nasal spray, a jar of Vicks VapoRub, Ben-Gay. *A nice lady whose nasal passages get stuffed up at night and who probably has a few twinges of arthritis.*

It seemed to him that the Baron was disappointed. Under Scott's careful scrutiny, he insisted on opening all the bottles, spilling out the contents, examining them to see if any extra medication was mixed with the ordinary tablets and pills. Was it an act? How good an actor was the Toy Soldier?

Alvirah's closet revealed well-worn brushed flannel nightgowns side by side with expensive dresses and caftans, most of them carrying labels from Martha Park Avenue and Cypress Point Spa Boutique.

An incongruous note was the expensive Japanese recorder in the carry-on bag that was part of the Louis Vuitton matching luggage. Scott raised his eyes. Sophisticated, professional equipment! He wouldn't have expected it of Alvirah Meehan.

Elizabeth watched as he thumbed through the cassettes. Three of them were marked in numerical sequence. The rest were blank. Scott shrugged, put them back and closed the bag. He left a few minutes later. Elizabeth walked with him to his car. On the ride over, she had not told him her suspicion that Helmut might have written the play. She wanted to be sure first, to demand the truth from Helmut himself. It was still possible that Clayton Anderson existed, she told herself.

It was exactly six o'clock when Scott's car disappeared past the gates. It was getting cool. Elizabeth shoved her hands into her pockets and felt the sunburst pin. She had taken it off Alvirah's robe after the ambulance left. Obviously it had great sentimental value.

They had sent for Alvirah's husband. She would give the pin to him tomorrow.

# 10

Ted returned to his bungalow from town at six thirty P.M. He had come back the long way, through the Crocker Woodland, to the service entrance of the Spa. He hadn't missed the cars, half-hidden in the brush beside the road leading to the Cypress Point grounds. Reporters. Like dogs on a scent, following the lead that the *Globe* article suggested. . . .

He peeled off his sweater. It had been too hot to wear—but on the other hand, at this time of year you could be surprised on the Peninsula. The winds could shift and become favorable or unfavorable at a moment's notice.

He drew the shades, switched on the lights and was startled to see the gleam of dark hair that rose over the back of the couch. It was Min. "It is important that I speak with you." The tone was the same he'd always known. Warm and authoritative, a curious blend that at one time had inspired confidence. She was wearing a long, sleeveless jacket over some sort of glittery one-piece outfit.

Ted sat opposite her and lit a cigarette. "I gave these up years ago, but it's amazing how many bad habits you can take on again when you're faced with a lifetime in prison. So much for discipline. I'm not very presentable, Min—but then, I'm not used to having unexpected guests in quite this way."

"Unexpected and uninvited." Min's eyes swept over him. "You've been jogging?"

"No. I've been walking. Quite a long distance. It gives one time to think."

"Your thoughts can't be very pleasant these days."

"No. They're not." Ted waited.

"May I have one of those?" Min indicated the pack of cigarettes he had tossed on the table.

Ted offered her one and lit it for her.

"I too gave them up, but in times of stress . . ." Min shrugged. "I gave up many things in my life while I was clawing my way up. Well, you know how it is . . . launching a model agency and trying to keep it going when there was no money coming in . . . marrying a sick old man and being his nurse, his mistress, his companion for five endless years . . . Oh, I thought I had reached a point of certain security. I thought I had earned it."

"And you haven't?"

Min waved a hand. "It's lovely here, isn't it? This spot is ideal. The Pacific at our feet, the magnificent coastline, the weather, the comfort and beauty of these accommodations, the unparalleled facilities of the Spa . . . Even Helmut's monstrosity of a Roman bath could be a stunning draw. Nobody else would be fool enough to try to build one; nobody else would have the flair to run it."

No wonder she's here, Ted thought. She couldn't risk talking to me with Craig around.

It was as though Min read his mind. "I know what Craig would advise. But Ted, *you're* the entrepreneur, the daring businessman. You and I think alike. Helmut is utterly impractical—I know that; but he also has vision. What he needs, and has always needed, is the money to bring his dreams to fruition. Do you remember a conversation we had— the three of us—when your damn bulldog Craig wasn't around? We talked about your putting a Cypress Point Spa in all your new hotels. It's a fabulous idea. It would work."

"Min, if I'm in prison, there won't *be* new hotels. We've stopped building since the indictment. You know that."

"Then lend me money now." Min's mask dropped. "Ted, I am desperate. I will be bankrupt in weeks. *It need not be!* This place lost something in these past few years. Helmut has not been bringing in new guests. I think I know now why he's been in a terrible state. But it could change. Why do you think I brought Elizabeth here? To help *you*."

"Min, you saw her reaction to me. If anything, you've made things worse."

"I'm not sure about that. This afternoon I begged her to reconsider. I told her she would never forgive herself if she destroyed you." Min crushed the cigarette into the ashtray. "Ted, I know what I'm saying. Elizabeth is in love with you. She always has been. Make it work for you. It's not too late." She grasped his arm.

He shook off her grip. "Min, you don't know what you're talking about."

"I'm telling you what I *know*. It's something I sensed from the first time she laid eyes on you. Don't you know how difficult it was for her to be around you and Leila, wanting Leila to be happy, loving you both? She was torn in two. That's why she took that play before Leila died. It wasn't a role she wanted. Sammy talked to me about it. She saw it too. Ted, Elizabeth is fighting you because she feels guilty. She knows Leila goaded you beyond endurance. *Make it work for you!* And Ted, I beg you— *help me now*! Please! I beg you."

With naked appeal she looked at him. He had been perspiring, and his dark brown hair was matted in ringlets and waves. A woman would kill for that head of hair, Min thought. His high cheekbones accentuated the narrow, perfectly shaped nose. His lips were even, his jaw just square enough to impart a look of strength to his face. His shirt was clinging to his body. His limbs were tanned and muscular. She wondered where he had been and realized he might not have heard yet about Alvirah Meehan. She did not want to talk about that now.

"Min, I can't go ahead with spas in hotels that won't be built if I go to prison. I can bail you out now, and I will. But let me ask you something: has it ever occurred to you that Elizabeth might be *wrong*, might be mistaken about the time? Has it even occurred to you that I'm telling the truth, when I say I did *not* go back upstairs?"

Min's smile of relief turned to astonishment. "Ted, you can trust me. You can trust Helmut. He hasn't told a soul except me. . . . He never will tell a soul. . . . He *heard* you shouting at Leila. He *heard* her begging for her life."

# 11

Should she have told Scott what she suspected about the Baron? Elizabeth wondered as she went into the welcome calm of her bungalow. Her senses absorbed the emerald-and-white color scheme. Splashy print on thick white carpeting. She could almost imagine there was a lingering hint of Joy mixed with the salty sea air.

Leila.

Red hair. Emerald eyes. The pale skin of the natural redhead. The billowing white satin pajamas that she'd been wearing when she died. Those yards of material must have floated around her as she fell.

My God. My God. Elizabeth slipped the double lock and huddled on the couch, her head in her hands, appalled at the vision of Leila, floating down through the night to her death. . . .

Helmut. Had he written *Merry-Go-Round* ? If so, had he cleaned out Min's untouchable Swiss account to finance it? He would have been frantic when Leila said she was quitting the show. How frantic?

Alvirah Meehan. The ambulance attendants. The speck of blood on Alvirah's face. The incredulous tone when the paramedic spoke to Helmut: "What do you mean you hadn't started the injections? Who do you think you're kidding?"

Helmut's hands compressing Alvirah's chest . . . Helmut starting the intravenous . . . But Helmut must have been frantic hearing Alvirah talk about "a butterfly floating on a cloud." Alvirah had seen a preview of the play. Leila had made the connection to Helmut. Had Alvirah Meehan made it as well?

She thought about Min's speech to her this afternoon, about Ted. She had virtually acknowledged Ted's guilt, then tried to persuade her that Leila had provoked him over and over again. Was that true?

Was Min right—that Leila would never want to see Ted behind bars for the rest of his life? And why did Min sound so positive about Ted's guilt? Two days ago she'd been saying it must have been an accident.

Elizabeth locked her arms around her knees and laid her head on her hands.

"I don't know what to do," she whispered to herself. She had never felt lonelier in her life.

\* \* \*

At seven o'clock she heard the faint chimes that indicated "cocktail" hour had begun. She decided to have dinner served in the bungalow. It was impossible to envision going through the motions of socializing with any of those people, knowing that Sammy's body was in the morgue awaiting shipment to Ohio, that Alvirah Meehan was fighting for her life in Monterey Hospital. Two nights ago she had been at the table with Alvirah Meehan. Two nights ago Sammy had been in this room with her. Who would be next?

At quarter of eight Min called. "Elizabeth, everyone is inquiring about you. Are you all right?"

"Of course. I just need to be quiet."

"You're sure you're not ill? You should know—Ted especially is very concerned."

*Hand it to Min. She never gives up.* "I'm really fine, Min. Would you have them send a tray? I'll take it a bit easy and go for a swim later. Don't worry about me."

She hung up the phone. Walked around the room restlessly, already longing to be in the water.

"IN AQUA SANITAS," the inscription read. For once Helmut was right. Water would soothe her, turn off her mind.

# 12

He was reaching for the tank when there was a sharp knock on the door. Frantically he yanked the mask from his face and pulled his arms out of the cumbersome wet suit. He jammed the tank and the mask into the closet, then rushed into the bathroom and turned on the shower.

The knocking was repeated, an impatient staccato. He managed to get free of the suit, dropped it behind the couch and grabbed his robe.

Making his voice sound annoyed, he shouted, "All right, all right" and opened the door.

The door was pushed open. "What took you so long? We've got to talk."


It was nearly ten o'clock when he was at last able to go to the pool. He reached it just in time to see Elizabeth walking down the path to her bungalow. In his hurry, he brushed against a chair at the edge of the patio. She turned around, and he barely had time to step back into the bushes.

Tomorrow night. There was still a chance to get to her here. If not, a different kind of accident would have to be arranged.

Like Alvirah Meehan, she had picked up the scent and was leading Scott Alshorne along the trail.

* * *

That scraping noise. It had been the sound of a chair grating against the patio tiles. The air had become cool but was very still. There was no breeze to set anything in motion. She'd turned quickly and for just an instant had thought she'd seen someone moving. But that was foolish. Why would anyone bother to stand in the shadows of the trees?

Even so, Elizabeth quickened her steps and was glad to be back in the bungalow with the door locked. She phoned the hospital. There was no change in Mrs. Meehan's condition.

It took a long time to fall asleep. What was eluding her? Something that had been said, something she ought to have seized on. Finally she drifted off. . . .

She was searching for someone. . . . She was in an empty building with long, dark halls. . . . Her body was aching with need. . . . Her arms were outstretched. . . . What was that poem she'd read somewhere? "Is there yet one, oh eyes and lips remembered, who turns and reaches for me in the night?" She whispered it over and over. . . . She saw a staircase. . . . She hurried down it. . . . He was there. His back to her. She threw her arms around him. He turned and caught her and held her. His mouth was on hers. "Ted, I love you, I love you," she said, over and over again. . . .

Somehow she managed to wake up. For the rest

of the night, miserable and despairing, she lay numbly in the bed where Leila and Ted had so often slept together, determined not to sleep.

Not to dream.

# Thursday,
## September 3

Dear Cypress Point Spa guest,

A cheery good morning to you. I hope as you read this you are sipping one of our delicious fruit-juice eye-openers. As some of you know, all the oranges and grapefruits are specially grown for the Spa.

Have you shopped in our boutique this week? If not, you must come and see the stunning fashions we have just received for both men and women. One-of-a-kind only, of course. Each of our guests is unique.

A health reminder. By now you may be feeling muscles you'd forgotten you had. Remember, exercise is never pain. Mild discomfort shows you are achieving the stretch. And whenever you exercise, keep your knees relaxed.

Are you looking your very best? For those tiny lines that time and life's experience trace on our face, remember, collagen, like a gentle hand, is waiting to smooth them away.

Be serene. Be tranquil. Be merry. And have a pretty day.

**Baron and Baroness Helmut von Schreiber**

# 1

Long before the first rays of the sun proclaimed yet another brilliant day on the Monterey Peninsula, Ted lay awake thinking about the weeks ahead. The courtroom. The defendant's table where he would sit, feeling the eyes of the spectators on him, trying to get a sense of the impact of the testimony on the jurors. The verdict: Guilty of Murder in the Second Degree. Why Second Degree? he had asked his first lawyer. "Because in New York State, First Degree is reserved for killing a peace officer. For what it's worth, it amounts to about the same, as far as sentencing goes." Life, he told himself. A life in prison.

At six o'clock he got up to jog. The morning was cool and clear, but it would be a hot day. Without a sense of where he wanted to run, he let his feet follow whatever roads they chose and was not surprised to find himself after forty minutes in front of his grandfather's house in Carmel. It was on the ocean block. It used to be white, but the present owners had painted it a moss green—attractive enough, but he preferred the way the white paint used to gleam in the afternoon sun. One of his earliest memories was of this beach. His mother helped him to build a castle; laughing, her dark hair swirling around her face, so happy to be here instead of New York, so grateful for the reprieve. That bloody bastard who was his father! The way he'd ridiculed her, mimicked her, hammered at her. *Why?* What gives anyone a streak of cruelty like that? Or was it simply alcohol that brought out something savage and evil in his father, until he was drinking so much that the savage streak became his personality, all there was, the bottle and the fists? *And had he inherited the same savage streak?*

Ted stood on the beach, staring at the house, seeing his mother and grandmother on the porch, seeing his grandparents at his mother's funeral, hearing his grandfather say, "We should have made her leave him."

His grandmother whispered, "She wouldn't leave him—it would have meant giving up Ted."

Had it been his fault? he wondered as a child. He still asked himself the same question. There was still no answer.

There was someone watching him from a window. Quickly he continued to jog down the beach.

Bartlett and Craig were waiting in his bungalow. They'd already had breakfast. He went to the phone and ordered juice, toast, coffee. "I'll be right back," he told them. He showered and put on shorts and a T-shirt. The tray was waiting when he came out. "Quick service here, isn't it? Min really knows how to run a spa! It would have been a good idea to franchise this place for new hotels."

Neither man answered him. They sat at the library table watching him, seeming to know that he neither expected nor wanted comment. He swallowed the orange juice in one gulp and reached for the coffee. "I'm going to the spa for the morning," he said. "I might as well have a decent workout. We'll leave for New York tomorrow. Craig, call an emergency board meeting for Saturday morning. I'm resigning as president and chairman of the company, and appointing you in my place."

His expression warned Craig not to argue. He turned to Bartlett, his eyes ice-cold. "I've decided to plea-bargain, Henry. Give me the best and worst possible scenarios of what kind of sentence I can expect to get."

# 2

Elizabeth was still in bed when Vicky brought in her breakfast tray. She set it down next to the bed and studied Elizabeth. "You're not feeling well."

Elizabeth propped her pillows against the headboard and sat up. "Oh, I guess I'll survive." She attempted a smile. "One way or another, we have to, don't we?" She reached over and picked up the vase with the single flower from the tray. "What's that you always say about carrying roses to fading flowers?"

"I don't mean you." Vicky's angular face softened. "I was off the last two days. I just heard about Miss Samuels. What a nice lady she was. But will you tell me what she was doing in the bathhouse? She once told me just *looking* at that place gave her the creeps. She said it reminded her of a tomb. Even if she wasn't feeling well, that would be the last place she'd go . . ."

After Vicky left, Elizabeth picked up the schedule that was on the breakfast tray. She hadn't intended to go to the Spa for either treatments or exercise, but changed her mind. She was slated for a massage with Gina at ten o'clock. Employees talk. Just now Vicky had underscored her own belief that Sammy would never have gone into the bathhouse on her own. When she had arrived on Sunday and had the massage, Gina had gossiped about the financial problems of the Spa. She might be able to hear more gossip if she asked the right questions.

As long as she was going there, Elizabeth decided to go through the full schedule. The first exercise class helped her to limber up, but it was hard not to look across the room to the place in the front row where Alvirah Meehan had been the other day. She had labored so hard to bend and twist that at the end of the class she had been puffing furiously, her face bright red. "But I kept up!" she had told Elizabeth proudly.

She ran into Cheryl in the corridor leading to the facial rooms. Cheryl was wrapped in a terry-cloth robe. Her finger- and toenails were painted a brilliant bluish-pink. Elizabeth would have passed her without speaking, but Cheryl grasped her arm. "Elizabeth, I've got to talk to you."

"About what?"

"Those poison-pen letters. Is there any chance of finding any more of them?" Without waiting for an answer, she rushed on: "Because if you *have* any more, or *find* any more, I want them analyzed, or tested, or fingerprinted, or whatever you and the world of science can do to trace them back to the sender. *I did not send them!* Got it?"

Elizabeth watched her sweep down the corridor. As Scott had commented, she *sounded* convincing. On the other hand, if she was reasonably sure that those last two letters were the only ones likely to be found, it would be the perfect attitude for her to take. How good an actress was Cheryl?

At ten o'clock Elizabeth was on the massage table. Gina came into the room. "Pretty big excitement around this place," she commented.

"I would say so."

Gina wrapped Elizabeth's hair in a plastic cap. "I know. First Miss Samuels, then Mrs. Meehan. It's crazy." She poured cream on her hands and began to massage Elizabeth's neck. "The tension's there again. This has been a lousy time for you. I know you and Miss Samuels were close."

It was easier not to talk about Sammy. She managed to murmur, "Yes, we were," then asked, "Gina, did you ever have Mrs. Meehan for a treatment?"

"Sure did. Monday and Tuesday. She's some character. What happened to her?"

"They're not sure. They're trying to check her medical history."

"I'd have thought she was sound as a dollar. A little chunky, but good skin tone, good heartbeat, good breathing. She was scared of needles, but that doesn't give anyone cardiac arrest."

Elizabeth felt the soreness in her shoulders as Gina's fingers kneaded the tight muscles.

Gina laughed ruefully. "Do you think there was anyone in the Spa who didn't know Mrs. Meehan was having a collagen injection in treatment room C? One of the girls overheard her ask Cheryl Manning if she'd ever had collagen there. Can you imagine?"

"No, I can't. Gina, the other day you told me the Spa hasn't been the same since Leila died. I know she attracted the celebrity-watchers, but the Baron used to bring in a pretty healthy bunch of new faces every year."

Gina poured more cream into her palms. "It's funny. About two years ago that dried up. Nobody can figure out why. He was making enough trips, but most of them were in the New York area. Remember, he used to work the charity balls in a dozen major cities, personally present the certificate for a week at the Spa to whoever came up with the winning ticket, and by the time he got finished talking, the lucky winner had three of her friends going along for the ride—as paying guests."

"Why do you think it stopped?"

Gina lowered her voice. "He was up to something. No one could figure out what—including Min, I guess. . . . She started to travel with him a lot. She was getting plenty worried that His Royal Highness, or whatever he calls himself, had something going in New York. . . ."

*Something going?* As Gina kneaded and pounded her body, Elizabeth fell silent. Was that something a play called *Merry-Go-Round*? And if so, had Min guessed the truth long ago?

# 3

Ted left the Spa at eleven o'clock. After two hours of using the Nautilus equipment and swimming laps, he'd had a massage and then sat in one of the private open-air Jacuzzis that dotted the enclosure of the men's spa. The sun was warm; there was no breeze; a flock of cormorants drifted overhead, like a floating black cloud in an otherwise cloudless sky.

Waiters were setting up for lunch service on the patio. The striped umbrellas in soft tones of lime green and yellow that shaded the tables complemented the colorful slates on the ground.

Again Ted was aware of how well the place was run. If things were different, he'd put Min and the Baron in charge of creating a dozen Cypress Point Spas all over the world. He almost smiled. Not *completely* in charge—all the Baron's proposed expenditures would be monitored by a hawk-eyed accountant.

Bartlett had probably been on the phone with the district attorney. By now he would have some idea of the kind of sentence he might expect. It still seemed absolutely incredible. Something he had no memory of doing had forced him to become a totally different person, had forced him to lead a totally different life.

He walked slowly to his bungalow, nodding distantly to the guests who'd cut the last exercise class and were lazing by the Olympic pool. He didn't want to get into a conversation with them. He didn't want to face the discussions he would have with Henry Bartlett.

Memory. A word that haunted him. Bits and pieces. Going back up in the elevator. Being in the hall. Swaying. He'd been so goddamn drunk. And then what? Why had he blotted it out? Because he didn't want to remember what he had done?

Prison. Confinement in a cell. It might be better to . . .

There was no one in his bungalow. That, at least, was a break. He'd expected to find them again around the library table. He should have given Bartlett this unit and taken the smaller one himself. At least then he'd have more peace. The odds were they'd be back for lunch.

Craig. He was a good detail man. The company wouldn't grow with him at the helm, but he might be able to keep it on a holding course. He should be grateful for Craig. Craig had stepped in when the plane with eight top company executives had crashed in Paris. Craig had been indispensable when Kathy and Teddy died. Craig was indispensable now. And to think . . .

How many years would he have to serve? Seven? Ten? Fifteen?

There was one more job he needed to do. He took personal stationery from his briefcase and began to write. When he had finished he sealed the envelope, rang for a maid and asked her to deliver it to Elizabeth's bungalow.

He would have preferred to wait until just before he left tomorrow; but perhaps if she knew there wouldn't be any trial, she might stay here a little longer.

When she returned to her bungalow at noon, Elizabeth found the note propped on the table. The sight of the envelope, white bordered in cerise, the flag colors of Winters Enterprises, with her name written in the firm, straight hand that was so familiar, made her mouth go dry. How many times in her dressing room had a note on that paper, in that handwriting, been delivered between acts? *"Hi, Elizabeth. Just got into town. How about late supper—unless you're tied up? First act was great. Love, Ted."* They'd have supper and call Leila from the restaurant. "Watch my guy for me, Sparrow. Don't let some painted bitch try to stake him out."

They'd both have their ears pressed to the phone. "You staked me out, Star," Ted would say.

*And she would be aware of his nearness, of his cheek grazing hers, and dig her fingers into the phone, always wishing she'd had the courage not to see him.*

She opened the envelope. She read two sentences before she let out a stifled cry and then had to wait before she could force herself to go back to finishing Ted's letter.

Dear Elizabeth,

I can only tell you that I am sorry, and that word is meaningless. You were right. The Baron heard me struggling with Leila that night. Syd saw me on the street. I told him Leila was dead. There's no use any longer in trying to pretend I wasn't there. Believe me, I have absolutely no memory of those moments, but in light of all the facts, I am going to enter a plea of guilty to manslaughter when I return to New York.

At least, this will bring this terrible affair to a conclusion and spare you the agony of testifying at my trial and being forced to relive the circumstances of Leila's death.

God bless and keep you. Long ago Leila told me that when you were a little girl and leaving Kentucky to come to New York, you were frightened and she sang that lovely song to you . . . *"Weep no more, my lady."*

Think of her as singing that song to you now, and try to begin a new and happier chapter in your life.

Ted

For the next two hours Elizabeth sat hunched up on the couch, her arms locked around her knees, her eyes staring ahead unseeingly. This was what you wanted, she tried to tell herself. He's going to pay for what he did to Leila. But the pain was so intense it gradually retreated into numbness.

When she got up, her legs were stiff, and she moved with the cautious hesitancy of the old. There was still the matter of the anonymous letters.

Now she would not rest until she had found out who had sent them and precipitated this tragedy.

It was past one o'clock when Bartlett phoned Ted. "We have to talk right away," Henry said shortly. "Get over as soon as you can."

"Is there any reason we can't meet here?"

"I've got some calls from New York coming in. I don't want to risk missing them."

When Craig opened the door for him, Ted did not
waste time on preliminaries. "What's up?"

"Something you won't like."

Bartlett was not at the oval dinette table he used
as a desk in this suite. Instead, he was leaning back
in an armchair, one hand on the phone as though
expecting it to leap into his hand. He had a medita-
tive expression, Ted decided, not unlike that of a
philosopher confronted with a problem too difficult
to solve.

"How bad is it?" Ted asked. "Ten years? Fifteen
years?"

"Worse. They won't take a plea. A new eyewitness has come forward."

Briefly, even brusquely, he explained. "As you
know, we put private investigators on Sally Ross. We
wanted to discredit her in every way possible. One
of the investigators was in her apartment building
night before last. A thief was caught red-handed
trying to rob the apartment one floor above Mrs.
Ross's. He's been making a deal of his own with the
district attorney. He was in that apartment once
before. The night of March twenty-ninth. *He claims
he saw you push Leila off the terrace!*"

He watched the sickly pallor that stole over Ted's
face change his deep tan to a muddy beige. "No
plea bargain," Ted whispered. His voice was so low
that Henry had to lean forward to catch the words.

"Why should they, with a witness like that? From
what my people tell me, there's no question that his
view was unobstructed. Sally Ross had that eucalyp-

tus tree on the terrace, obscuring her line of vision. One floor higher up, and the tree wasn't in the way."

"I don't care how many people saw Ted that night," Craig blurted. "He was drunk. He didn't know what he was doing. I'll perjure myself. I'll say he was on the phone with me at nine thirty."

"You *can't* perjure yourself," Bartlett snapped. "You're already on record as saying you heard the phone ring and didn't pick it up. Don't even think of it."

Ted jammed clenched fists into his pockets. "Forget the goddamned phone. What exactly does this witness claim he saw?"

"So far the district attorney has refused to take my calls. I've got a few inside connections there, and from what they've been able to find out, this guy claims Leila was struggling to save herself."

"Then I could be facing the maximum?"

"The judge assigned to this case is an imbecile. He'll let a throat-slasher from the ghetto off with a slap on the wrist, but he likes to show how tough he is when he deals with important people. And you're important."

The phone rang. Bartlett had it at his ear before the second ring. Ted and Craig watched as his frown deepened; he moistened his lips with his tongue, then bit his lower lip. They listened as he barked out instructions: "I want a rap sheet on that guy. I want to know what kind of deal he was offered. I want pictures taken from that woman's terrace on a rainy night. Get on with it."

When he put down the receiver, he studied Ted and Craig, noticing how Ted had slumped in his chair and Craig had straightened in his. "We go to trial," he said. "That new eyewitness has been in the apartment before. He described the inside of several of the closets. This time they caught him when he barely got his feet in the entrance hall. He says he *saw* you, Teddy. Leila was clawing at you, trying to save herself. You picked her up, you held her over that railing and you shook her until she let go of your arms. It won't be a pretty scene when it's described in court."

"I . . . held . . . her . . . over . . . the . . . railing . . . before . . . I . . . dropped . . . her. . . ." Ted picked up a vase from the table and threw it across the room at the marble fireplace. It smashed, and sprays of delicate crystal cascaded across the carpet. "No! It's not possible!" He turned and ran blindly for the door. He slammed it behind him with a force that shattered the window panel.

They watched as he ran across the lawn to the trees that separated the Spa grounds from the Crocker Woodland.

"He's guilty," Bartlett said. "There's no way I can get him off now. Give me a clean-cut liar and I can work with him. If I put him on the stand, the jury will find Teddy arrogant. If I *don't*, we'll have Elizabeth describing how he shouted at Leila, and two eyewitnesses to tell how he killed her. And I'm supposed to work with that?" He closed his eyes. "By the way, he's just proved to us that he has a violent temper."

"There was a special reason for that outburst," Craig said quietly. "When Ted was eight years old, he saw his father in a drunken rage hold his mother over the terrace of their penthouse."

He paused to catch his breath. "The difference is his father decided not to drop her."

# 4

At two o'clock, Elizabeth phoned Syd and asked him to meet her at the Olympic pool. When she got there, a mixed water-aerobics class was starting. Men and women holding beach balls were studiously following the directions of the instructor. "Hold the ball between your palms; swing from side to side . . . no, keep it underwater . . . that's where we get the pull." Music was turned on.

She chose to sit at a table at the far end of the patio. There was no one nearby. Ten minutes later, she heard a scraping sound behind her and gasped. It was Syd. He had cut through the bushes and pushed aside a chair to get onto the patio. He nodded in the direction of the pool. "We had the janitor's apartment in Brooklyn when I was growing up. It's amazing how much muscle tone my mother got swinging a broom."

His tone was pleasant enough, but his manner was guarded. The polo shirt and shorts he was wearing revealed the wiry strength of his arms and the taut muscles in his legs. Funny, Elizabeth thought, I always considered Syd soft-looking, maybe because he has such a poor carriage. That's a mistake.

The scraping sound. Had she heard a chair being moved last night when she was leaving the pool? And Monday night, she thought she had seen something or someone moving. Was it possible she'd been watched while she was swimming? It was a fleeting but upsetting thought.

"For a place that costs so much to relax in, there are quite a few uptight people around here," Syd said. He sat down across from her.

"And I'm the most uptight, I suppose. Syd, you had your own money in *Merry-Go-Round*. You brought the script to Leila. You handled some of the script revisions. I have to talk to the playwright, Clayton Anderson. Where can I get in touch with him?"

"I have no idea. I never met him. The contract was negotiated through his lawyer."

"Tell me the lawyer's name."

"No."

"That's because there *is* no lawyer, right, Syd? Helmut wrote that play, didn't he? He brought it to you, and you brought it to Leila. Helmut knew Min would throw a fit if she found out about it. That play was written by a man obsessed—by Leila. That's why for Leila the play would have worked."

His face turned a dull red. "You don't know what you're talking about."

She handed him the note Ted had written to her. "Don't I? Tell me about meeting Ted the night Leila died. Why didn't you come forward with that information months ago."

Syd scanned the note. "He put that in writing! He's a bigger fool than I realized."

Elizabeth leaned forward. "According to this, the Baron heard Ted struggling with Leila, and Ted told *you* that Leila was dead. Did it ever occur to either of you to see what had happened, if there was any chance to help her?"

Syd shoved his chair back. "I've listened to you long enough."

"No, you haven't. Syd, why did you go to Leila's apartment that night? Why did the Baron go there? She didn't expect either one of you."

Syd stood up. Anger made his face ugly. "Listen, Elizabeth, your sister wiped me out when she quit that play. I went to ask her to reconsider. I never got inside that apartment building. Ted ran past me on the street. I chased him. He told me she was dead. Who lives after a fall like that? I stayed out of it. I never saw the Baron that night." He threw Ted's letter back at her. "Aren't you satisfied? Ted's going to jail. That's what you want, isn't it?"

"Don't leave, Syd. I've still got lots of questions.

The letter Cheryl stole. Why did you destroy it? It might have helped Ted. I thought you were so anxious to help him."

Syd sat down heavily. "Look, Elizabeth, I'll make a deal with you. Tearing up that letter was my mistake. Cheryl swears she didn't write that one or any like it. I believe her."

Elizabeth waited. She was not going to concede that Scott believed Cheryl as well.

"You're right about the Baron," Syd continued. "He wrote the play. You know how Leila put him down. He wanted to have power over her, make her indebted to him. Another guy would want to drag her into bed." He waited. "Elizabeth, if Cheryl can't leave tomorrow and be at her press reception, she'll lose this series. The studio will drop her if they find out she's being detained. You've got Scott's ear. Persuade him to leave Cheryl out of this, and I'll give you a hint about those letters."

Elizabeth stared at him. Syd seemed to take her silence for assent. As he spoke, he tapped the table with his fingertips. "The Baron wrote *Merry-Go-Round*. I've got his handwritten changes on the early scripts. Let's play 'Suppose,' Elizabeth. *Suppose* the play is a hit. The Baron doesn't need Min anymore. He's tired of the Spa game. Now he's a Broadway playwright, and constantly with Leila. How could Min prevent that from happening? By making sure the play is a flop. How does she do that? By destroying Leila. And she was just the one who knew how. Ted and Leila were together for three years. If Cheryl wanted to get on their case, why would she have waited that long?"

He did not wait for her response. The chair made the same grating sound as it had when he'd arrived. Elizabeth stared after him. It was possible. It made sense. She could hear Leila say, "God, Sparrow, Min's really got the hots for the Toy Soldier, hasn't she? I'd hate to be the one who got cozy with him. Min would be on the warpath with a hatchet."

Or with scissors and paste?

Syd disappeared through the hedges. Watching him, Elizabeth could not see the grim smile he allowed himself as he passed from her vision.

It might work, Syd thought. He'd been wondering how to play this card, and she had made it easy for him. If she fell for it, Cheryl might be in the clear. The smile disappeared. *Might be.*

But what about himself?

# 5

Unseeing and motionless, Elizabeth sat at the pool until the brisk voice of the water-aerobics instructor cut through the increasing shock she felt as her mind analyzed the enormity of Min's possible betrayal. She got up and followed the path to the main house.

The afternoon had fulfilled the morning's promise. The sun was golden warm; there was no breeze; even the cypress trees looked mellow, their dark leaves shimmering, the craggy shapes unthreatening. The cheerful clusters of petunias, geraniums and azaleas, perky from recent watering, were now straining toward the warmth, the blossoms open and radiant.

In the office she found a temporary receptionist, a thirtyish, pleasant-faced woman. The Baron and Baroness had gone to the Monterey Peninsula hospital to offer their assistance to Mrs. Meehan's husband. "They're just heartsick about her." The receptionist seemed deeply impressed by their concern.

They'd been heartsick when Leila died, Elizabeth remembered. Now she wondered how much of Min's grief had resulted from guilt. She scribbled a note to Helmut and sealed it. "Please give this to the Baron as soon as he comes back."

She glanced at the copy machine. Sammy had been using that machine when for some reason she'd wandered into the bathhouse. Suppose she really had had some sort of attack that disoriented her. Suppose she had left that letter in the copier. Min had come down early the next morning. Min might have found it and destroyed it.

Wearily, Elizabeth went back to her bungalow. She'd never know who had sent those letters. No one would ever admit it. Why was she staying here now? It was all over. And what was she going to do with the rest of her life? In his note, Ted had told her to start a new and happier chapter. Where? How?

Her head was aching—a dull, steady pounding. She realized that she had skipped lunch again. She'd call and inquire after Alvirah Meehan and then start packing. Funny, how awful it is when there's no place in the world you want to go, no single human being you want to see. She pulled a suitcase out of the closet, opened it, then stopped abruptly.

She still had Alvirah's sunburst pin. It was in the pocket of the slacks she'd been wearing when she'd gone to the clinic. When she took it out and held it, she realized it was heavier than it looked. She was no expert on jewelry, but clearly this was not a valuable piece. Turning it over, she began to study the back. It didn't have the usual safety catch. Instead, there was an enclosed device of some sort. She turned the pin again and studied the face. The small opening in the center was a microphone!

The impact of her discovery left her weak. The seemingly artless questions, the way Alvirah Meehan had fiddled with that pin—she'd been pointing the microphone to catch the voices of the people she was with. The suitcase in her bungalow with the expensive recording equipment, the cassettes there . . . Elizabeth knew she had to get them before anyone else did.

She rang for Vicky.

* * *

Fifteen minutes later she was back in her own bungalow, the cassettes and recorder from Alvirah Meehan's suitcase in her possession. Vicky looked flustered and somewhat apprehensive. "I hope no one saw us go in there," she told Elizabeth.

"I'm giving everything to Sheriff Alshorne," Elizabeth assured her. "I just want to be certain they won't disappear if Mrs. Meehan's husband tells anyone about them." She agreed that tea and a sandwich would taste good. When Vicky returned with the tray, she found Elizabeth, earphones on her head, her notebook in her lap, a pen in her hands, listening to the tapes.

# 6

Scott Alshorne did not like having a suspicious death and a suspicious near-death unresolved. Dora Samuels had suffered a stroke just before her death. How long before? Alvirah Meehan had had a drop of blood on her face which suggested an injection. The lab report showed a very low blood sugar, possibly the result of an injection. The Baron's efforts had fortunately saved her life. So where did that leave him?

Mrs. Meehan's husband had not been located last

night until late evening—one A.M. New York time.
He'd chartered a plane and arrived at the hospital
at seven A.M. local time. Early in the afternoon,
Scott went there to talk to him.

The sight of Alvirah Meehan, ghostly pale, barely
breathing, hooked to machines, was incredible to
Scott. People like Mrs. Meehan weren't *supposed* to
be sick. They were too hearty, too filled with life.
The burly man whose back was to him didn't seem
to notice his presence. He was bending over, whis-
pering to Alvirah Meehan.

Scott touched his shoulder. "Mr. Meehan, I'm
Scott Alshorne, the sheriff of Monterey County. I'm
sorry about your wife."

Willy Meehan jerked his head toward the nurses'
station. "I know all about how they think she is. But
I'm telling you, she's going to be just fine. I told her
that if she up and died on me, I was going to take
that money and spend it on a blond floozy. She
won't let that happen—will you, honey?" Tears began to stream from his eyes.

"Mr. Meehan, I have to speak with you for just a
few minutes."

She could hear Willy talking to her, but she
couldn't reach him. Alvirah had never felt so weak.
She couldn't even move her hand, she was so tired.

And there was something she had to tell them.
She *knew* what had happened now. It was so clear.
She *had* to make herself talk. She tried moving her
lips, but she couldn't. She tried to wiggle her finger.

Willy's hand was covering hers, and she couldn't get up the strength to make him understand that she was trying to reach him.

If she could just move her lips, just get his attention. He was talking about the trips they were going to take. A tiny stab of irritation flared through her mind. Keep quiet and *listen* to me, she wanted to shout at him. . . . Oh, Willy, please listen. . . .

The conversation in the corridor outside the intensive-care unit was unsatisfactory. Alvirah was "healthy as a horse." She was never sick. She was on no medication. Scott did not bother to ask if there was a possibility that she used drugs. There wasn't, and he wouldn't insult this heartbroken man with the question.

"She was looking forward so much to this trip," Willy Meehan said as he put his hand on the door of the intensive-care unit. "She was even writing articles about it for the *Globe.* You should have seen how excited she was when they were showing her how to record people's conversations. . . ."

*"She was writing articles!"* Scott exclaimed. "She was recording people?"

He was interrupted. A nurse rushed out. "Mr. Meehan, will you come in? She's trying to talk again. We want you to speak to her."

Scott rushed in behind him. Alvirah was straining to move her lips. *"Voi . . . voi . . . ."*

Willy grasped her hand. "I'm here, honey, I'm here."

The effort was so much. She was getting so tired. She was going to fall asleep. If she could just get even one word out to warn them. With a terrible effort, Alvirah managed that word. She said it loud enough that she could hear it herself.

She said, "Voices."

# 7

The afternoon shadows deepened as, unmindful of time, Elizabeth listened to Alvirah Meehan's tapes. Sometimes she stopped and re-wound a segment of the tape and listened to it several times. Her lined pad was filled with notes.

Those questions that had seemed so tactless had actually been so clever. Elizabeth thought of how she had sat at the table with the Countess, wishing she could overhear the conversations at Min's table. Now she could. Some of the talk was muffled, but she could hear enough to detect stress, evasion, attempts to change the subject.

She began to systematize her notations, creating a separate page for everyone at the table. At the bottom of each page she scribbled questions as they came to mind. When she finished the third tape, it seemed to her that she merely had a jumble of confusing sentences.

*Leila, how I wish you were here. You were too cynical, but so many times you were right about people. You could see through their facades. Something is wrong, and I'm missing it. What is it?*

It seemed to her that she could hear Leila's answer, as if she were in the room. *For heaven's sake, Sparrow, open your eyes! Stop seeing what people want you to see. Start listening. Think for yourself. Didn't I teach you that much?*

She was just about to put the last cassette from Alvirah's sunburst pin into the recorder when the phone rang. It was Helmut. "You left a note for me."

"Yes, I did. Helmut, why did you go to Leila's apartment the night she died?"

She heard him gasp. "Elizabeth, do not talk on the phone. May I come to you now?"

While she waited, she hid the recording equipment and her pad. She had no intention of letting Helmut become aware of the tapes.

For once, his rigid military carriage seemed to have deserted him. He sat opposite her, his shoulders slumped. His voice low and hurried, his German accent more pronounced as he spoke, he told her what he had told Min. He had written the play. He had gone to plead with Leila to reconsider.

"You took the money out of Min's Swiss account."

He nodded. "Minna has guessed. What is the use?"

"Is it possible that she always knew? That she sent those letters because she wanted to upset Leila enough to destroy her performance? No one knew Leila's emotional state better than Min."

The Baron's eyes widened. "But how magnificent. It is just the sort of thing Minna *would* do. Then she may have known all along that there was no money left. Could she have been simply punishing me?"

Elizabeth did not care if her face showed the disgust she felt. "I don't share your admiration for that scheme, if it was Min's doing." She went to the desk and got a fresh pad. "You heard Ted struggling with Leila?"

"Yes, I did."

"Where were you? How did you get in? How long were you there? Exactly what did you hear?"

It helped to be writing, to concentrate on taking down word for word what he said. He had heard Leila pleading for her life, and he had not tried to help her.

When he had finished, perspiration was glistening on his smooth cheeks. She wanted to get him out of her sight, but she could not resist saying, "Suppose instead of running away, you had gone into that apartment? Leila might be alive right now. Ted might not be plea-bargaining for a lighter sentence if you hadn't been so worried about saving yourself."

"I don't believe that, Elizabeth. It happened in seconds." The Baron's eyes widened. "But haven't you heard? There is no plea bargain. It's been on the news all afternoon. A second eyewitness saw Ted hold Leila over the terrace before he dropped her. The district attorney wants Ted to get life."

Leila had not toppled over the railing in a struggle. He had held her, then deliberately dropped her. That Leila's death had taken a few seconds longer seemed to Elizabeth even more cruel than her worst fears. I should be *glad* they're going for the maximum penalty, she told herself. I should be *glad* to have the chance to testify against him.

She wanted desperately to be alone, but she managed to ask the Baron one more question: "Did you see Syd near Leila's apartment that night?"

Could she trust the look of astonishment on his face? "No, I did not," he said firmly. "Was he there?"

It is finished, Elizabeth told herself. She put in a call to Scott Alshorne. The sheriff was out on official business. Could someone else help her? No. She left a message for him to phone her. She would turn over Alvirah Meehan's recording equipment to him and get on the next plane to New York. No wonder they'd all sounded so on edge from Alvirah's relentless questioning. Most of them had something to hide.

The sunburst pin. She started to put it into a bag with the recorder and then realized she hadn't listened to the last cassette. It occurred to her that Alvirah had been wearing the pin in the clinic. . . . She managed to extract the cassette from the tiny container. If Alvirah was so concerned about the collagen injections, would she have left the recorder on during the treatment?

She had. Elizabeth turned up the volume and held the recorder to her ear. The cassette began with Alvirah in the treatment room talking with the nurse. The nurse reassuring her, talking about Valium; the click of the door, Alvirah's even breathing, the click of the door again . . . The Baron's somewhat muffled and indistinct voice, reassuring Alvirah, starting the injection; the click of the door, Alvirah's gasps, her attempt to call for help, her frenzied breath, a click of the door again, the nurse's cheerful voice, "Well, here we are, Mrs. Meehan. All set for your beauty treatment?" And then the nurse, upset, on the edge of panic, saying, "Mrs. Meehan, *what's the matter*? Doctor . . ."

There was a pause, then the voice of Helmut barking orders —"Open that robe!"—calling for oxygen. There was a pounding sound—that must have been when he was compressing her chest; then Helmut called for an intravenous. That was when I was there, Elizabeth thought. He tried to kill her. Whatever he gave her was meant to kill her. Alvirah's persistent references to that sentence about "a butterfly floating on a cloud," her constantly saying that that reminded her of something, her calling him a clever author—did he perceive that as her toying with him? Had he still hoped that somehow Min wouldn't learn the truth about the play, about her Swiss bank account?

She replayed the last tape again and again. There

was something about it she didn't understand. What was it? What was she missing?

Not knowing what she was looking for, she reread the notes she had taken when Helmut described Leila's death. Her eyes became riveted to one sentence. But that's *wrong*, she thought.

Unless.

Like an exhausted climber within inches of an icy summit, she reviewed the notes she had made from Alvirah Meehan's tapes.

And found the key.

It had always been there, waiting for her. Did he realize how close she had been to the truth?

Yes, he did.

She shivered, remembering the questions that had seemed so innocent, her own troubled answers that must have been so threatening to him.

Her hand flew to the phone. She would call Scott. And then she withdrew her fingers from the dial. Tell him what? There wasn't a shred of proof. There never would be.

Unless she could force his hand.

# 8

For over an hour, Scott sat by Alvirah's bedside, hoping she would say something else. Then, touching Willy Meehan's shoulder, he said, "I'll be right back." He had seen John Whitley at the nurses' station and followed him into his office.

"Have you anything more you can tell me, John?"

"No." The doctor looked both angry and perplexed. "I don't like not knowing what I'm dealing with. Her blood sugar was so low that without a history of severe hypoglycemia we have to suspect that somebody injected her with insulin. She sure as hell has a puncture mark where we found the spot of blood on her cheek. If Von Schreiber claims he didn't inject her face at all, something's screwy."

"What are her chances?" Scott asked.

John shrugged. "I don't know. It's too soon to tell if she has incurred any brain damage. If willpower can bring her back, that husband of hers will manage it. He's doing everything right. Talking to her about chartering a plane to get here, about fixing the house when they go home. If she can hear him, she'll want to stay around."

John's office overlooked the garden. Scott walked to the window, wishing he could spend some time alone, *think* this through. "We can't *prove* Mrs. Meehan was the victim of an attempted murder.

We can't prove Miss Samuels was the victim of murder."

"I don't think you can make either one stick, no."

"So that means even if we can make a stab at figuring who would want those women dead—and have the guts to attempt to kill them at a place like the Spa—we still may not be able to prove anything."

"That's more your line of work than mine, but I'd agree."

Scott had one parting question: "Mrs. Meehan has been trying to talk. She finally came out with a single word—*'voices.'* Is it likely that someone in her condition is really trying to communicate something that makes sense?"

Whitley shrugged. "My impression is that her coma is still too deep to be certain as to her recall. But I could be wrong. It wouldn't be the first time."

Again Scott conferred with Willy Meehan in the corridor. Alvirah was planning to write a series of articles. The editor of the *New York Globe* had told her to get all the inside information she could on celebrities. Scott remembered her endless questions the night he had been at the Spa for dinner. He wondered what Alvirah might unwittingly have learned. At least it gave some reason for the attack on her—if there had been an attack. And it explained the expensive recording equipment in her suitcase.

He was scheduled to meet with the mayor of Carmel at five o'clock. On his two-way car radio, he learned that Elizabeth had phoned him twice. The second call was urgent.

Some instinct made him cancel his appointment with the mayor for the second time in two days and go directly to the Spa.

Through the picture window, he could see Elizabeth on the phone. He waited until she put the receiver down before he knocked. In the thirty-second interval, he had a chance to study her. The afternoon sun was sending slanted rays into the room which created shadows on her face and revealed the high cheekbones, the wide, sensitive mouth, the luminous eyes. If I were a sculptor, I'd want her to model for me, he thought. She has an elegance that goes beyond beauty.

Eventually she would have surpassed Leila.

Elizabeth turned the tapes over to him. She indicated the writing pad with its lines of notations. "Do me a favor, Scott," she asked him. "Listen to these tapes very, very carefully. This one"—she indicated the cassette she had taken from the sunburst pin—"is going to shock you. Play it over and see if you don't catch what I think I've heard."

Now there was a determined thrust to her jaw, a glitter in her eyes. "Elizabeth, what are you up to?" he asked.

"Something that I have to do—that *only* I can do."

Despite Scott's increasingly stern demands for an explanation, she would not tell him more. He did remember to tell her that Alvirah Meehan had managed to utter one word. "Does 'voices' suggest anything to you?"

Elizabeth's smile was enigmatic.

"You bet it does," she said grimly.

# 9

Ted had bolted from the Spa grounds in early afternoon. By five o'clock he had still not returned. Henry Bartlett was visibly chafing to go back to New York. "We came here to prepare Ted's defense," he said. "I hope he realized his trial is scheduled to start in five days. If he won't meet with me, I'm not doing any good sitting around here."

The phone rang. Craig jumped to answer it. "Elizabeth. What a nice surprise. . . . Yes, it's true. I'd like to think we can still persuade the district attorney to accept a plea, but that's pretty unrealistic. . . . We hadn't talked about dinner yet, but of course it would be good to be with you. . . . Oh, that! I don't know. It just didn't seem funny anymore. And it always annoyed Ted. Fine. . . . See you at dinner."

Scott drove home with the windows of the car open, appreciating the cool breeze that had begun to blow in from the ocean. It felt good, but he could not shake the sense of apprehension that was overcoming him. Elizabeth was up to something, and every instinct told him that whatever it was, it might be dangerous.

A faint mist was setting in along the shoreline of Pacific Grove. It would develop into a heavy fog later on. He turned the corner and pulled into the driveway of a pleasant narrow house a block from the ocean. For six years now he had been coming home to this empty place and never once not felt that moment of nostalgia that Jeanie was no longer here waiting for him. He used to talk cases through with her. Tonight he would have asked her some hypothetical questions. Would you say that there is a connection between Dora Samuels' death and Alvirah Meehan's coma? Another question jumped into his mind. Would you say that there is a connection between those two women and Leila's death?

And finally: Jeanie, what the hell is Elizabeth up to?

To clear his head, Scott showered, changed into old slacks and a sweater. He made a pot of coffee and put a hamburger on the grill. When he was ready to eat, he turned on the first of Alvirah's tapes.

He began listening at quarter of five. At six o'clock, his notebook, like Elizabeth's, was filled with jottings. At quarter of seven, he heard the tape that documented the attack on Alvirah. "That son of a bitch, Von Schreiber!" he muttered. He *did* inject her with something. But with what? Suppose he had started the collagen and seen her go into some sort of attack? He had returned almost immediately with the nurse.

Scott replayed the tape, then played it a third time and finally realized what Elizabeth had wanted him to hear. There was something odd about the Baron's voice the first time he spoke to Mrs. Meehan. It was hoarse, guttural, startlingly different from his voice a moment or two later, when he was shouting orders to the nurse.

He phoned the hospital and asked for Dr. Whitley. He had one question for him. "Do you think an injection that drew blood is the kind that a doctor would have administered?"

"I've seen some sloppy injections given by top-flight surgeons. And if a doctor gave the shot that was meant to harm Mrs. Meehan—he may have had the grace to be nervous."

"Thanks, John."

"Don't mention it."

He was reheating the coffee when his bell rang. In quick strides he reached the door, flung it open to face Ted Winters.

His clothes were rumpled, his face smudged with dirt, his hair matted; vivid, fresh scratches covered his arms and legs. He stumbled forward and would have fallen if Scott had not reached out to grasp him.

"Scott, you've got to help me. Somebody's got to help me. It's a trap, I swear it is. Scott, I tried for hours and I couldn't do it. I couldn't make myself do it."

"Easy . . . easy." Scott put his arm around Ted and guided him to the couch. "You're ready to pass out." He poured a generous amount of brandy into a tumbler. "Come on, drink this."

After a few sips, Ted ran his hand over his face, as if trying to erase the naked panic he had shown. His attempt at a smile was a wan failure, and he slumped with weariness. He looked young, vulnerable, totally unlike the sophisticated head of a multi-million-dollar corporation. Twenty-five years vanished, and Scott felt that he was looking at the nine-year-old boy who used to go fishing with him.

"Have you eaten today?" he asked.

"Not that I remember."

"Then sip that brandy slowly, and I'll get you a sandwich and coffee."

He waited until Ted had finished the sandwich before he said, "All right, you'd better tell me all about it."

"Scott, I don't know what's happening, but I *do* know this: I could not have killed Leila the way they're trying to say I did. I don't care how many witnesses come out of the woodwork—something is wrong."

He leaned forward. Now his eyes were pleading. "Scott, you remember how terrified Mother was of heights?"

"She had good cause to be. That bastard of a father of yours—"

Ted interrupted him. "He was disgusted because he could see that I was developing that same phobia. One day when I was about eight, he made her stand out on the terrace of the penthouse and look down. She began to cry. She said, 'Come on, Teddy,' and we started to go inside. He grabbed her and picked her up, and that son of a bitch held her over the railing. It was thirty-eight floors up. She was screaming, begging. I was clawing at him. He didn't pull her in until she'd fainted. Then he just dropped her on the terrace floor and said to me, 'If I ever see you look frightened out here, I'll do the same thing to you.' "

Ted swallowed. His voice broke. "This new eyewitness says I did that to Leila. Today I tried to make myself walk down the cliffs at Point Sur. *I couldn't do it!* I couldn't make my legs go to the edge."

"People under stress can do some pretty funny things."

"No. No. If I'd killed Leila, I'd have done it some other way. I know that. To say that drunk or sober, I could hold her over the railing . . . Syd swears I told him that my *father* pushed Leila off the terrace; he may have known that story about my father. Maybe everybody's lying to me. Scott, I've *got* to remember what happened that night."

With compassionate eyes, Scott studied Ted, taking in the exhausted droop of his shoulders, the fatigue that emanated from his body. He'd been walking all afternoon, trying to make himself stand at the edge of a cliff, battling his own personal demon in search of the truth. "Did you tell them this when they began questioning you about Leila's death?"

"It would have sounded ridiculous. I build hotels where we make people *want* terraces. I've always been able to avoid going out on them without making an issue of it."

Darkness was setting in. Beads of perspiration like unchecked tears were running down Ted's cheeks. Scott switched on a light. The room with its comfortable overstuffed furniture, the pillows Jeanie had embroidered, the tall-backed rocking chair, the pine bookcase came to life. Ted did not seem to notice. He was in a world where he was trapped by other people's testimony, on the verge of being confined to prison for the next twenty or thirty years. He's right, Scott decided. His only hope is to go back to that night. "Are you willing to have hypnosis or sodium pentothal?" he asked.

"Either . . . both . . . it doesn't matter."

Scott went to the phone and called John Whitley at the hospital again. "Don't you ever go home?" he asked.

"I do get there, now and again. In fact, I'm on my way now."

"I'm afraid not, John. We have another emergency. . . ."

# 10

Craig and Bartlett walked together toward the main house. They had deliberately skipped the "cocktail" hour and could see the last of the guests leaving the veranda as the muted gong announced dinner. A cool breeze had come up from the ocean, and the webs of lichen hanging from the giant pines that formed the border of the north end of the property swayed in a rhythmic, solemn movement that was accentuated by the tinted lights scattered throughout the grounds.

"I don't like it," Bartlett told Craig. "Elizabeth Lange is up to something pretty strange when she asks to have dinner with us. I can tell you the district attorney isn't going to like it one damn bit if he hears his star witness is breaking bread with the enemy."

"Former star witness," Craig reminded him.

"Still star witness. That Ross woman is a total nut. The other one is a petty thief. I won't mind being the one to cross-examine those two on the stand."

Craig stopped and grabbed his arm. "You mean you think Ted may still have a chance?"

"Hell, of course not. He's guilty. And he's not a good enough liar to help himself."

There was a placard in the foyer. Tonight there would be a flute-and-harp recital. Bartlett read the names of the artists. "They're first-rate. I heard them in Carnegie Hall last year. You ever go there?"

"Sometimes."

"What kind of music do you like?"

"Bach fugues. And I suppose that surprises you."

"Frankly, I never thought about it one way or another," Bartlett said shortly. Christ, he thought, I'll be glad when this case is over. A guilty client who doesn't know how to lie and a second-in-command with a chip on his shoulder who would never get over his inferiority complex.

Min, the Baron, Syd, Cheryl and Elizabeth were already at the table. Only Elizabeth seemed perfectly relaxed. She, rather than Min, had somehow assumed the role of hostess. The place on either side of her was vacant. When she saw them approaching, she reached out her hands to them in a welcoming gesture. "I saved these seats specially for you."

And what the hell is that supposed to mean? Bartlett wondered sourly.

Elizabeth watched as the waiter filled their glasses with nonalcoholic wine. She said, "Min, I don't mind telling you that when I get home I'll enjoy a good, stiff drink."

"You should be like everyone else," Syd told her. "Where's your padlocked suitcase?"

"Its contents are much more interesting than liquor," she told him. Throughout dinner she led the conversation, reminiscing on the times they had been together at the Spa.

Once dessert was served, it was Bartlett who challenged her. "Miss Lange, I've had the distinct impression that you're playing some sort of game, and I for one don't believe in participating in games unless I know the rules."

Elizabeth was raising a spoonful of raspberries to her lips. She swallowed them, then put down the spoon. "You're quite right," she told him. "I wanted to be with all of you tonight for a very specific reason. You should all know that I no longer believe Ted is responsible for my sister's death."

They stared at her, their faces shocked.

"Let's talk about it," Elizabeth said. "Someone deliberately destroyed Leila by sending those poison-pen letters to her. I think it was you or you." She pointed at Cheryl, then at Min.

"You are absolutely wrong," Min said indignantly.

"I told you to come up with more letters and trace them." Cheryl spat out the words.

"I may do just that," Elizabeth told her. "Mr. Bartlett, did Ted tell you that both Syd and the Baron were around my sister's apartment house the night she died?" She seemed to enjoy his look of astonishment. "There is more to my sister's death than has come out. I know that. One, maybe *two* of you know that. You see, there's another possible scenario. Syd and Helmut had money in that play. Syd knew Helmut was the playwright. They went together to plead with Leila. Something went wrong and Leila died. It would have been considered an accident if it hadn't been for that woman who swore she saw Ted struggling with Leila. At that point, my testimony that Ted had come back trapped him."

The waiter was hovering over them. Min waved him away. Bartlett realized that people at the surrounding tables were watching them, sensing the tension. "Ted doesn't remember anything about going back to Leila's apartment," Elizabeth said, "but suppose he did go back; suppose he left immediately; suppose one of you struggled with Leila. You're all about the same size. It was raining. That Ross woman might have seen Leila struggling, and simply assumed it was Ted. You two agreed to let Ted take the blame for Leila's death and concocted the stories you told him. It's possible, isn't it?"

"Minna, this girl is crazy," the Baron sputtered. "You must know—"

"I deny absolutely that I was in that apartment that night," Syd said.

"You admit you ran after Ted. But from where? The apartment? Because he'd seen you pushing Leila? It would have been a stroke of luck if he was so traumatized that he blocked it out.

"The Baron claims he heard Leila and Ted quarreling. But I heard them too. I was on the telephone. *And I did not hear what he claims he heard!*"

Elizabeth leaned her elbows on the table and looked searchingly from one angry face to the next.

"I'm very grateful for this information," Henry

Bartlett told her. "But you seem to have forgotten there's a new witness."

"A very convenient new witness," Elizabeth said. "I spoke to the district attorney this afternoon. This witness turns out not to be very bright. The night he claims he was in that apartment watching Ted drop Leila off the terrace, he was in jail." She stood up. "Craig, would you walk me to my place? I've got to finish packing, and I want to get a swim in. It may be a long time before I'm here again . . . if ever."

Outside, the darkness was now absolute. The moon and stars were again covered with a misty fog; the Japanese lanterns in the trees and bushes were hazy dots of light. Craig put his arm around her shoulders. "That was quite a performance," he said.

"It was just that: a performance. I can't prove anything. If they stick together, there isn't a shred of evidence."

"Do you have any more of those letters that Leila was receiving?"

"No. I was bluffing about that."

"That's a shocker about the new witness."

"I was bluffing about that too. He *was* in jail that evening, but he was released on bond at eight o'clock. Leila died at nine thirty-one. The most they can do is cast doubt on his credibility."

She leaned against him as they reached her bungalow. "Oh, Craig, it's all so crazy, isn't it? I feel as if I'm digging and digging for the vein of truth the way the old prospectors dug for a vein of gold. . . .

The only trouble is I'm out of time, so I had to start blasting. But at the very least, I may have upset one of them enough so that he—or she—will make a slip."

His hand smoothed her hair. "You're going back tomorrow?"

"Yes. How about you?"

"Ted still hasn't turned up. He may be on a bender. I can't say I blame him. Though it wouldn't be like him. . . . Obviously, we'll wait for him. But when this is over, when you're ready—promise that you'll call me."

"And get your Japanese-houseboy imitation on the recorder? Oh, I forgot. You said you changed it. Why did you do that, Craig? I always thought it was pretty funny. So did Leila."

He looked embarrassed. She did not wait for him to answer.

"This place used to be such fun," Elizabeth murmured. "Remember when Leila invited you here that first time, before Ted came?"

"Of course I remember."

"How did you meet Leila? I forget."

"She was staying at the Beverly Winters. I sent flowers to her suite. She called to thank me, and we had a drink. She was on her way here, and she invited me along. . . ."

"And then she met Ted. . . ." Elizabeth kissed his cheek. "Pray that whatever I've done tonight works. If Ted is innocent, I want him off just as badly as you do."

"I know you do. You're in love with h m, aren't you?"

"I have been from that first day    u i roduced him to Leila and me."

Inside the bungalow, Elizabeth pu¹ on her swimsuit and robe. She went to the desk and wrc ⸱ a long letter addressed to Scott Alshorne. Then she   ng for the maid. It was a new girl, one she'd never see before, but she had to take the chance. She put the envelope for Scott inside a new one and scribbled a brief note. "Give this to Vicky in the morning," she instructed the girl. "No one else. Is that clear?"

"Of course." The girl was slightly offended.

"Thank you." Elizabeth watched the girl leave and wondered what she would say if she could have read the note to Vicky.

It read: *"In case of my death, deliver this to Sheriff Alshorne immediately."*

At eight o'clock, Ted walked into a private room in the Monterey Peninsula hospital. Dr. Whitley introduced a psychiatrist who was waiting to administer the injection. A video camera had already been set up. Scott and a deputy sheriff were to be witnesses to the statements given under sodium pentothal.

"I still think you ought to have your lawyer here," Scott told him.

Ted was grim-faced. "Bartlett has been the very one urging me not to undergo this test. I don't intend to waste any more time talking about it. Let the truth come out."

He slipped his feet out of his shoes and lay down on the contour couch.

A few minutes after the injection had taken effect he began to answer questions about the last hour he spent with Leila.

"She kept accusing me of cheating on her. Had pictures of me with other women. Group pictures. I told her that that was part of my job. The hotels. I was never with any woman alone. I tried to reason with her. She had been drinking all day. I was drinking with her. Sick of it. I warned her she had to trust me; I couldn't face those scenes the rest of my life. She told me she knew I was trying to break off with her. Leila. Leila. She went wild. I tried to calm her down. She scratched my hands. The phone rang. It was Elizabeth. Leila kept shouting at me. I got out. Went to my apartment downstairs. Looked at myself in the mirror. Blood on my cheek. On my hands. Tried to phone Craig. Knew I couldn't live like that anymore. Knew it was over. But thought maybe Leila would do something to herself. Better stay with her till I can get Elizabeth. God, I'm so drunk. The elevator. Leila's floor. Door open. Leila screaming."

Scott leaned forward intently. "What is she screaming, Ted?"

*"Don't. Don't."* Ted was trembling, shaking his head, his expression shocked and disbelieving.

"Ted, what do you see? What happened?"

"Push door open. Room is dark. The terrace. Leila. Hold on. Hold on. Help her. Christ, grab her! Don't let her fall! *Don't let Mommy fall!*"

Ted began to sob—deep, racking sounds that filled the room. His body twitched convulsively.

"Ted, who did that to her?"

"Hands. Just see hands. She's gone. *It's my father*." His words became broken. "Leila's dead. Daddy pushed her. Daddy killed her."

The psychiatrist looked at Scott. "You won't get any more now. Either that's all he knows or he still can't bring himself to face the entire truth."

"That's what I'm afraid of," Scott whispered. "How soon will he come out of it?"

"Pretty fast. He'd better rest awhile."

John Whitley stood up. "I want to look in on Mrs. Meehan. I'll be right back."

"I'd like to go with you." The cameraman was packing his equipment. "Drop the tape in my office," Scott told him. He turned to his deputy. "Stay here. Don't let Mr. Winters leave."

The head nurse in the ICU was visibly excited. "We were just about to send for you, Doctor. Mrs. Meehan seems to be coming out of the coma."

"She said 'voices' again." Willy Meehan's face was alive with hope. "Just as clear. I don't know what she meant, but she knew what she was trying to say."

"Does that mean she's out of danger?" Scott asked Dr. Whitley.

John Whitley studied the chart and reached for

Alvirah's pulse. His answer was low enough that Willy Meehan could not hear him. "Not necessarily. But it sure is a good sign. Whatever prayers you know, start saying them now."

Alvirah's lids fluttered open. She was looking straight ahead, and as her eyes focused, they rested on Scott. A look of urgency came over her face. "Voices," she whispered. "Wasn't."

Scott bent over her. "Mrs. Meehan, I don't understand."

Alvirah felt the way she did when she used to clean old Mrs. Smythe's house. Mrs. Smythe was always telling her to push the piano out and get at the dust behind it. It was like trying to push the piano but so much more important. She wanted to tell them who had hurt her but she couldn't think of his name. She could see him plain as plain, but she couldn't remember his name. Desperately she tried to communicate with the sheriff. "Wasn't the doctor did that to me . . . wasn't his voice. . . . Someone else . . ." She closed her eyes and felt herself slipping into sleep.

"She's getting better," Willy Meehan whispered exultantly. "She's trying to tell you something."

"Wasn't the doctor . . . wasn't his voice. . . ." What the hell did she *mean*? Scott asked himself.

He rushed to the room where Ted was waiting. Ted was sitting up now in the small plastic armchair, his hands folded in front of him. "I opened the door," he said tonelessly. "Hands were holding

Leila over the railing. I could just see the white satin billowing; her arms were flailing. . . ."

"You couldn't see who was holding her?"

"It was so fast. I think I tried to call out, and then she was gone and whoever it was just disappeared. He must have run along the terrace."

"Have you any idea of his size?"

"No, it was as if I was watching my father when he did that to my mother. I even saw my father's face." He looked up at Scott. "And I haven't helped you, or myself, have I?"

"No, you haven't," Scott said bluntly. "I want a free association from you. 'Voices.' Say the first thing that comes into your mind."

"Identification."

"Go on."

"Unique. Personal."

"Go on."

Ted shrugged. "Mrs. Meehan. She brought up the subject repeatedly. She apparently had some idea of taking elocution lessons and she got everyone into a discussion about accents and voices."

Scott thought of Alvirah's broken whisper. "Wasn't the doctor . . . wasn't his voice. . . ." Mentally he reviewed the dinner-conversation tapes Alvirah had recorded. Identification. Unique. Personal.

The Baron's voice on that last tape. He drew in his breath sharply. "Ted, do you remember what else Mrs. Meehan said about voices? Something about Craig imitating yours?"

Ted frowned. "She asked me about a story she'd read years ago in *People*—that Craig used to field my phone calls at the fraternity house and the girls couldn't tell the difference between our voices. I told her it was true. In school Craig used to bring down the house with his imitations."

"And she tried to make him demonstrate it for her, but he refused." Scott saw Ted's look of surprise and shook his head impatiently. "Never mind how I know. That's what Elizabeth wanted me to catch when I listened to those tapes."

"I don't know what you're talking about."

"Mrs. Meehan kept pestering Craig to imitate your voice. Don't you see? He didn't want anyone to think about his being a good mimic. *Elizabeth's testimony against you is based solely on hearing your voice.* Elizabeth suspects him, but if she's tipped her hand he'll go after her."

A wild sense of urgency made him grab Ted's arm. "Come on!" he shouted. "We've got to get to the Spa." On the way out, he yelled instructions at the deputy: "Call Elizabeth Lange at the Cypress Point Spa. Tell her to stay in her room with her door locked. Send another car over there."

He ran through the lobby, Ted at his heels. In his car, Scott turned on the siren. It's too late for you, he thought as his mind filled with the image of the murderer. Killing Elizabeth won't help you anymore. . . .

The car raced along the highway between Salinas and Pebble Beach. Scott fired instructions into the two-way radio. As Ted listened, the full impact of what he was hearing penetrated his consciousness; the hands that had held Leila over the terrace became arms, a shoulder, as familiar as his own, and the realization of Elizabeth's danger made him jam his feet on the floor of the car in a futile effort to make contact with an imaginary accelerator.

*Had she been toying with him? Of course she had. But like the others, she had underestimated him. And like the others, she would pay for it.*

*With methodical calm he stripped off his clothes and unlocked his suitcase. The mask was on top of the wet suit and tank. It amused him to remember how at the last moment Sammy had seen his eyes through the mask and known. When he'd called to her in Ted's voice, she had run to him. All the evidence hadn't in the end turned her against Ted. And all the overwhelming evidence he had so carefully laid out, even the new eyewitness he had planted, hadn't convinced Elizabeth.*

*The wet suit was cumbersome. When this was over, he'd get rid of all this equipment. Just in case anyone questioned Elizabeth's death, it wouldn't be wise to have any visible reminder that he was an expert scuba diver. Ted, of course, should remember. But in all these months it hadn't crossed Ted's mind that he had the special ability to mimic him. Ted— so stupid, so naive. "I tried to phone you; I remember that distinctly." And so Ted had become his impeccable alibi. Until that nosy bitch Alvirah*

*Meehan kept after him. "Let me hear you imitate Ted's voice. Just once. Please. Say anything at all." He'd wanted to throttle her, but then had had to wait until yesterday when he went ahead of her to treatment room C, waited in the closet for her, the hypodermic needle in his hand. Too bad she didn't know she'd sampled his gift for mimicry when she thought she was listening to the Baron.*

*The wet suit was on. He strapped the tank to his back, turned off the lights and waited. It still chilled him to realize that last night he'd been within seconds of opening the door and confronting Ted. Ted had wanted to talk everything through. "I'm beginning to think you're my only real friend," he'd said.*

*He opened the door a crack and listened. There was no one in sight, no sound of footsteps. The fog was gathering, and it would be easy to slip behind the trees until he reached the pool. He had to get there before her, be waiting and when she swam past, grab the whistle before she could get it to her lips.*

*He slipped out, his footsteps noiseless as he cut across the path, avoiding the areas where the lanterns sent out beams of light. If only he'd been able to finish this on Monday night . . . but Ted had been standing near the pool watching Elizabeth.*

*Ted always in the way. Always the one with money and looks, always the one the girls flocked around. He'd forced himself to accept it, to make himself useful to Ted, first in college, then in the*

*office: the go-fer, the tenacious assistant. He'd had
to fight his way up until the executive-plane accident had instantly made him Ted's right hand, and
then when Ted lost Kathy and Teddy, he'd been
able to take over the reins of the company. . . .*

*Until Leila.*

*His loins ached remembering Leila. How it had
felt to make love to her. Until he'd brought her here
and she'd met Ted. And discarded him, like garbage
tossed into a bin.*

*He had watched those slim arms slide around
Ted's neck, that wanton body snuggling against
Ted, had helplessly walked away not able to bear
the sight of them together, planning revenge, waiting for the time.*

*And he'd found it with the play. He'd had to
prove investing in the play was a mistake. It was
already clear that Ted was beginning to ease him
out. And it was his chance to destroy Leila. The
exquisite pleasure of sending those letters, of watching her fall apart. She'd even shown them to him as
she received them. He'd warned her to burn them, to
hide them from Ted and Elizabeth. "Ted's getting
awfully sick of your jealousy, and if you tell Elizabeth how upset you are, she'll quit her play to be
with you. That could ruin her career."*

*Grateful for his advice, Leila had agreed. "But
tell me," she'd begged. "Is it true, Bulldog? Is there
someone else?" His elaborate protests had had the
effect he wanted. She'd believed the letters.*

*He hadn't worried about those last two. He'd*

*thought all that unopened mail had been thrown out. But it hadn't mattered. Cheryl burned one, and he had taken the other one from Sammy. Everything was at last working for him. On Saturday he would become chairman and president of Winters Enterprises.*

*He was at the pool.*

*He slipped into the dark water and swam to the shallow end. Elizabeth always dived into the deepest area. That night in Elaine's he'd known the time had come to kill Leila. Everyone would believe it was a suicide. He'd let himself in through one of the guest suites on the upper floor of the duplex and listened to them quarrel, listened when Ted stormed out, and then the idea had come to mimic Ted's voice to make Elizabeth think Ted was with Leila just before she died.*

*He heard the sound of footsteps on the path. She was coming. Soon he would be safe. In those weeks after Leila's death, he'd thought he had lost. Ted hadn't fallen apart. He'd turned to Elizabeth. The death had been considered an accident. Until that unbelievable stroke of luck when that crazy woman had come forward and said she had seen Ted struggling with Leila. And Elizabeth had become the chief witness.*

*It was destined to be this way. Now the Baron and Syd had become material witnesses against Ted. The Baron wouldn't be able to deny that he had heard Ted struggling with Leila. Syd had seen Ted on the street. Even Ted himself must have glimpsed them on the terrace and because he was drunk and it was dark, relived that episode with his father.*

*The footsteps were getting closer. He allowed himself to sink to the bottom of the pool. She was so sure of herself, so clever. Waiting for him to come, anxious for him to attack her, ready to outswim him while she blew the whistle and called for help. She wouldn't get the chance.*

It was ten o'clock, and there was a difference in the atmosphere of the Spa. Many of the bungalows were already dark, and Elizabeth wondered how many people had actually checked out. The talk-show host was gone; the Countess and her friends must have left before dinner; the tennis player and his girlfriend had not been in the dining room.

Evening fog had settled in, heavy, penetrating, enveloping. Even the Japanese lanterns along the path seemed hooded.

She dropped her robe by the side of the pool and looked carefully into the water. It was absolutely still. There was no one here yet.

She felt for the whistle around her neck. All she would need was to be able to put her lips to it. A blast from this whistle would bring help.

She dived in. The water felt clammy tonight. Or was it because she was afraid? I can outswim anyone, she reassured herself. I had to take this chance. It's the only way. Would the bait be taken?

*Voices.* Alvirah Meehan had been persistent on

that subject. That persistence might have cost her her life. That was what she had been trying to tell them. She'd known it wasn't Helmut's voice.

She'd reached the north end of the pool; she flipped over and began to backstroke. *Voices.* It was her identification of Ted's voice that had placed him in that room with Leila a few minutes before her death.

The night Leila died, Craig had claimed to be in his apartment watching a television show when Ted tried to call him. No one had questioned that *Craig* was home. Ted had been *his* alibi.

*Voices.*

Craig wanted Ted to be convicted. Ted was about to turn over the running of Winters Enterprises to him.

When she asked Craig about changing the message on his recorder, had she frightened him enough to force him into an overt attack?

Elizabeth began a freestyle breaststroke. From beneath her, arms encircled her, pinning her own arms to her sides. Her startled gasp caused her to swallow a mouthful of water. Choking furiously, she felt herself being dragged to the bottom of the pool. She began to beat with her heels, but they slipped off the heavy rubber wet suit of her assailant. With a desperate burst of strength, she dug her elbows deep into the ribs of her captor. For an instant the grip relaxed, and she began to rise to the surface. Just as her face emerged, as she managed to gulp one breath of air and fumble for the whistle, the arms enclosed her again, and she slipped downward, through the dark waters of the pool.

# 11

"After Kathy and Teddy died, I went to pieces." It was as if Ted were talking to himself, not Scott. The car raced past the gate to Pebble Beach without stopping. The roaring siren shattered the peace of the surroundings; the headlights opened only a few feet of visibility in the deepening fog.

"Craig took over running the whole business. He liked it. There were times when he'd answer and say he was me. Imitate my voice. I finally told him to cut it out. Then he met Leila first. I took her away. The reason I was so busy those months before Leila died, I was starting to reorganize. I intended to deemphasize his job; split his responsibilities with two other men. He knew what was happening.

"And he's the one who hired the detective to follow that first witness; the detective who was so conveniently there to make sure the new witness didn't get away."

They were on the grounds of the Spa. Scott drove the car across the lawn and stopped in front of Elizabeth's bungalow. The maid rushed from her station. Ted was banging on the door. "Where is Elizabeth?"

"I don't know," the maid said, her voice faltering. "She gave me a letter. She didn't say she was going out."

"Let me see the letter."

"I don't think—"

"Give me the letter."

Scott read the note to Vicky, ripped open the letter addressed to him and began to read.

" Vhere is she?" Ted demanded.

"Uh, God, that crazy kid . . . The pool," Scott snapped, "the pool."

The car smashed through hedges and flower beds and roared toward the north end of the property. Inside the bungalows, lights began to go on.

They reached the patio. The fender of the car caught the edge of an umbrella table, knocking it over. The car stopped at the edge of the pool. Scott left the headlights on, and they shone over the water. Waves of the gathering fog shimmered in the lights.

They peered down into the pool. "There's no one here," Scott said. A terrible fear grabbed at him. Were they too late?

Ted was pointing at bubbles floating to the surface. "She's down there." Kicking off his shoes, he dived into the pool. He touched bottom and came up. "Get help," he yelled. He went down again and again.

Scott scrabbled in the glove compartment for his flashlight, grabbed it and saw a figure in a scuba-diving outfit begin to climb the ladder out of the pool. Drawing his pistol, he rushed toward the ladder. In a swift, violent gesture, the scuba diver lunged forward and butted him. The gun fell from Scott's hand as he slammed backward onto the patio.

Ted resurfaced. He was holding a limp figure in his arms. He began to swim toward the ladder, and as Scott dazedly pulled himself to a sitting position, the scuba diver fell backward onto Ted, dragging him and Elizabeth under the surface.

Gasping for breath, Scott reached out a groping hand. His numbed fingers closed around his gun. Pointing it upward, he fired two shots, and was rewarded by the insistent sound of sirens racing toward him.


Ted desperately tried to hold on to Elizabeth with one arm as he pummeled his attacker with the other. His lungs were bursting; he was still groggy from the effects of the sodium pentothal; he felt himself losing consciousness. Futilely he tried to punch the thick rubber suit. His blows fell harmlessly on the solid, massive chest.

The oxygen mask. He had to pull it off. He let go of Elizabeth, trying with all his strength to push her toward the surface. For a moment, the grip on him relaxed. A hand stretched past him, reaching to drag Elizabeth back. It gave him the chance to grab at the face mask. But before he could pull it off, a vicious shove sent him reeling backward.

She had held her breath, forcing herself to resist inhaling. She made herself go limp. There was no way she could get away from him. Her only hope was that he would think she was unconscious and leave her. Even from the feel of the arms that pinned her she knew it was Craig. She had forced him into the open—but now he would get away again.

She was slipping into unconsciousness. Hold on, she thought. No, it was *Leila* telling her to hold on. *Sparrow, this is what I've been trying to tell you. Don't let me down now. He thinks he's safe. You can do it, Sparrow.*

She felt the arms begin to release her. She was drifting down, trying to resist the impulse to fight her way to the surface. *Wait, Sparrow, wait. Don't let him see you're still conscious.*

And then she had felt someone grabbing her, pulling her up; other arms, arms that held her to him, cradled her. Ted.

She felt the night air on her face; gasped in one shuddering breath as, his arm around her neck, he dragged her along the top of the pool; heard his own breath, straining, choking, drowning out the sounds she was making.

And then she felt before she saw the heavy figure bear down on them and managed to pull in one great gulp of air before the water again covered her face.

Ted's arm tightened. She felt him flailing out. Craig was trying to kill both of them. Nothing mattered to Craig except to destroy them now. The water pressed against her eardrums. She could not fight Ted's grip. She felt the push as he tried to shove her toward the surface, felt Craig's grasp on her ankle and managed to kick it away.

On the surface she could see the cars pulling up, hear the shouts. Elizabeth gulped in air, once, twice, filled her lungs and then dived down, down to where Ted was fighting for his life. She knew where Craig was; the arc of her descent was directly over his head. He was squeezing Ted's neck. She reached both hands down. Lights were beaming over the water. She could see the silhouette of Craig's arms, the desperate struggle of Ted's body. She would have only one chance.

Now. She kicked—a sharp, cutting movement of her legs. She was directly over Craig. In a savage thrust, she managed to get her fingers under his face mask. He reached up, and she recoiled from the shove that made her head snap backward, but held on to the mask, held on until she had wrenched it away from his face.

She held it while he groped for it, while his arms grabbed her body, while he tried to pull it from her, held it until she felt him being pulled away from her, held it until, lungs bursting, she found herself being hauled to the surface, still in his grasp.

She could breathe at last. She choked in great gulping sobs as Ted finally relinquished his grip on Craig to the policemen who surrounded them in the water. Then, like two figures drawn by an irresistible magnetic force, she and Ted drifted to each other, and clinging together made their way to the ladder at the end of the pool. . . .

# Friday,
## September 4

Dear Spa guests,

Some of you will be leaving us today. Remember, our only concern has been you, your well-being, your health, your beauty. Go into the world knowing that you have been loved and cared for here at Cypress Point Spa, that we are longing for your return. Soon our magnificent Roman bathhouse will be completed. It will be the unparalleled and consummate experience. There will be separate hours for the women and men except between four and six, when we shall enjoy mixed bathing in the European fashion, a very special delight indeed.

Hurry back for another retreat into pampering and health-awareness in the serene atmosphere of Cypress Point Spa.

Baron and Baroness Helmut von Schreiber

# 1

The morning dawned clear and bright. The early-morning fog evaporated with the bright warmth of a glowing sun. Sea gulls and blackbirds swept high over the surf and returned to perch on the rocky dunes.

At Cypress Point Spa, the remaining guests followed their schedules. Water classes were held in the Olympic pool; masseurs kneaded muscles and pounded layers of fat; pampered bodies were wrapped in herbal-scented sheets; the business of beauty and luxury continued to function.

Scott had asked Min and Helmut, Syd and Cheryl, Elizabeth and Ted to meet him at eleven. They gathered in the music salon, the door closed, removed from the eyes and ears of the curious guests and staff.

Elizabeth remembered the rest of the night as a blur: Ted holding her . . . someone wrapping the robe around her . . . Dr. Whitley ordering her to bed.

Ted knocked at the door of her bungalow at ten of

eleven. They walked up the path together, hands entwined, not needing to say what was between them.

Min and the Baron sat side by side. Min's face was weary but somehow more at peace, Elizabeth thought. There was something of the old Min in the steely determination in her eyes. The Baron, still so absolutely perfect in every hair on his head, his sport shirt resting on him with the ease of an ermine robe, his posture aloof, his assurance regained. For him too, the night had exorcised demons.

Cheryl's eyes moved restlessly toward Ted, narrowed when they found his face. With her sharp-tipped tongue she licked her lips like a cat about to pounce on a forbidden dish of cream.

Next to her, Syd lounged. There was something about him that had been missing: the casual confidence of success.

Ted sat beside her, his arm thrown over the back of her chair, his manner protective and watchful as though he feared she would slip away from him.

"I think we've come to the end of the road." The fatigue in Scott's voice suggested that he had not spent the long hours of the night in bed. "Craig has retained Henry Bartlett, who urged him not to make a statement. However, when I read Elizabeth's letter to him, he admitted everything.

"Let me read that letter to you now." Scott pulled it from his pocket.

Dear Scott,
   There is only one way I can prove what I sus-

pect, and I'm about to do that now. It may not work, but if anything happens to me, I think it will be because Craig has decided I'm coming too close to the truth.

Tonight I practically accused Syd and the Baron of causing Leila's death. I hope that will be sufficient bait to make Craig feel secure in attempting to harm me. I believe it will happen at the pool. I think he was there the other night. I can only rely on the fact that I can outswim anyone, and if he tries to attack me, he will have exposed himself. If he succeeds, go after him—for me and for Leila.

By now you will have heard the tapes. Have you caught how upset he sounded when Alvirah Meehan was asking so many questions? He tried to cut Ted off when Ted said that Craig could fool people by imitating him.

I thought I heard Ted shout at Leila to put the phone down. I thought I heard her say, *"You're not a falcon."* But Leila was sobbing. That's why I misunderstood. Helmut was nearby. He heard her say, *"You're not Falcon."* He heard accurately. I did not.

That tape of Alvirah Meehan in the treatment room. Listen carefully. That first voice. It sounds like the Baron, but there's something wrong. I think it was Craig imitating the Baron's voice.

Scott, there's no proof of any of this. The only proof will be obtained if Craig has found me too dangerous.

We'll see what happens. There is one thing I know and probably have always known in my heart. Ted is incapable of murder, and I don't care how many witnesses come forward to claim they saw him kill Leila.

Elizabeth

Scott put down the letter and looked sternly at Elizabeth. "I wish you had trusted me to help you. You almost lost your life."

"It was the only way," Elizabeth said. "But what did he do to Mrs. Meehan?"

"An insulin injection. As you know, during college he worked summers at the hospital in Hanover. He picked up a lot of medical knowledge those years. But initially the insulin wasn't meant for Alvirah Meehan." Scott looked at Elizabeth. "He had become convinced you were dangerous. He had planned to find a way to do away with you in New York this week, before the trial. But when Ted decided to come here, Craig persuaded Min to invite you too. He persuaded her that you might back off from testifying against Ted once you saw him. What he wanted was a chance to arrange an accident. Alvirah Meehan became a threat. He already had the means to get rid of her." Scott stood up. "And now I'm going home."

At the door he paused. "Just one last observation I'd like to make. You, Baron, and you, Syd, were willing to obstruct justice when you thought Ted was guilty. By taking the law into your own hands, you did him no favors and may indirectly have been responsible for Sammy's death and Mrs. Meehan's attack."

Min jumped up. "If they had come forward last year, Ted might very well have been persuaded to plead guilty. Ted should be grateful to them."

"Are *you* grateful, Min?" Cheryl asked. "I gather the Baron *did* write the play. You not only married nobility, a doctor, an interior designer, but also an author. You must be thrilled—and broke."

"I married a Renaissance man," Min told her. "The Baron will resume a full schedule of operations at the clinic. Ted has promised us a loan. All will be well."

Helmut kissed her hand. Again Elizabeth was reminded of a little boy smiling up at his mother. Min sees him now for what he is, she thought. He'd be lost without her. It cost her a million dollars to find that out, but maybe she'll decide it was worth it.

"Incidentally," Scott added, "Mrs. Meehan is going to make it. We can thank Dr. von Schreiber's emergency treatment for that." Ted and Elizabeth followed him out. "Try to put it behind you," Scott told them. "I have a hunch things are going to be a lot better for you two from now on."

"They already are." Ted's voice was firm.

# 2

The noon sun was high overhead. The breeze was coming gently from the Pacific, bringing the scent of the sea. Even the azaleas that had been crushed by the patrol cars seemed to be trying to struggle back. The cypress trees, grotesque in the night, seemed familiar and comforting under the splendid sunshine.

Together Elizabeth and Ted watched Scott drive away, then turned to face each other. "It really is over," Ted said. "Elizabeth, I'm just starting to realize it. I can breathe again. I'm not going to wake up in the middle of the night and wonder about living in a cell, about losing everything in life I value. I want to get to work again. I want . . ." His arms went around her. "I want you."

*Go ahead, Sparrow. This time it's right. No dilly-dallying. Do as I tell you. You're perfect for each other.*

Elizabeth smiled up at Ted. She put her hands on his face and brought his lips to hers.

She could almost hear Leila singing again, as she had so long ago, "Weep no more, my lady. . . ."

POCKET
BOOKS

## Mary Higgins Clark
# I Heard That Song Before

Kay Lansing grew up the daughter of the landscape gardener to the wealthy and powerful Carrington family. One morning, six-year-old Kay sneaks into a hidden chapel in the grounds of the Carringtons' estate. There, she overhears a quarrel. A woman is blackmailing a man for money. When she says that this will be the last time, his caustic response is: 'I heard that song before.' That same evening, after a dinner dance, Susan Althorp is driven home by Peter Carrington. Susan is never seen or heard from again.

A cloud of suspicion hangs over Peter throughout the years. Not only has Susan disappeared, but Peter's pregnant wife drowned in their swimming pool. At 42, he is head of the family business empire when he meets Kay again at a cocktail party. Seeing him as much maligned and misunderstood, Kay falls in love and they marry. To her dismay, she soon finds that he is a sleepwalker whose nocturnal wanderings draw him to the very spot at the pool where his wife met her end.

Trying to quell her own doubts, Kay believes that the key to the truth lies in the scene she witnessed as a child in the chapel. She plunges into a pursuit to clear her husband's name. What Kay does not even remotely suspect is that uncovering what lies behind these memories may cost her own life.

ISBN-13: 978-0-7432-6857-8
PRICE £17.99

POCKET
BOOKS

## Mary Higgins Clark
# Two Little Girls in Blue

Returning home from a black-tie dinner in New York, Margaret
and Steve Frawley find the police in their house and their twin
daughters gone. The kidnapper, who calls himself the 'Pied Piper',
soon makes his terms known: on delivery of a ransom, a phone call
will reveal the girls' whereabouts. The ransom is delivered but,
when the call comes, only Kelly is in the car parked behind a
deserted restaurant. The driver is dead from a gunshot wound and
has left a suicide note, confessing to killing Kathy and dumping her
body in the ocean.

When strange occurrences begin to suggest that Kathy may still
be alive, and communicating with Kelly, Margaret finds herself
alone in wanting to continue the search for her daughter. But as
Kelly's warnings become increasingly specific and alarming, the
FBI agents set out to search for Kathy. As they close in on the
Pied Piper and his accomplices, Kathy's life hangs by a thread . . .

**ISBN-13: 978-1-4165-0260-9**
**PRICE £6.99**

**POCKET
BOOKS**

## Mary Higgins Clark
# No Place Like Home

*I cannot believe I am standing in the exact spot where I was standing
when I killed my mother . . .*

When she was ten Liza Barton shot her mother dead, trying to
protect her from her violent stepfather. The court ruled the death
a tragic accident. Many believed it to be deliberate murder.

Twenty-four years later, Liza is known as Celia. Now a successful
interior designer, living in Manhattan, she is happily married for
the second time, with a young son, Jack, by her first marriage.
Nothing can disturb their peace. But when her new husband
surprises her with a gift, her world is suddenly shattered – for it
is the very same house where her mother met her death. It soon
becomes clear that someone in the community knows Celia's true
identity. And when the estate agent who sold the house is
brutally murdered, Celia instantly becomes a suspect.

As Celia fights to prove her innocence, she has no idea that she
and Jack could be the next targets of a ruthless killer.

**ISBN-13: 978-1-4165-0221-0**
**PRICE £6.99**

POCKET
BOOKS

This book and other Mary Higgins Clark titles are available from
your local bookshop or can be ordered direct from the publisher.

| 978-0-7432-6857-8 | I Heard That Song Before | £17.99 |
| 978-1-4165-0260-9 | Two Little Girls in Blue | £6.99 |
| 978-1-4165-0221-0 | No Place Like Home | £6.99 |
| 978-0-7434-8959-1 | Night-time is My Time | £6.99 |
| 978-0-7434-6773-5 | Second Time Around | £6.99 |
| 978-0-7434-4937-3 | Daddy's Little Girl | £6.99 |
| 978-0-7434-1499-9 | On the Street Where you Live | £6.99 |
| 978-0-6710-1039-3 | Before I Say Good-bye | £6.99 |
| 978-0-7434-8431-2 | We'll Meet Again | £6.99 |
| 978-0-7434-5029-4 | All Through the Night | £6.99 |
| 978-0-7434-8432-9 | You Belong To Me | £6.99 |
| 978-0-7434-8433-6 | Pretend You Don't See Her | £6.99 |
| 978-0-7434-8430-5 | Moonlight Becomes You | £6.99 |
| 978-0-7434-8429-9 | Let Me Call You Sweetheart | £6.99 |
| 978-0-7434-8436-7 | Remember Me | £6.99 |
| 978-0-7434-8434-3 | Weep No More, My Lady | £6.99 |
| 978-0-7434-8428-2 | Stillwatch | £6.99 |
| 978-0-7434-8435-0 | A Cry in the Night | £6.99 |
| 978-0-7434-8427-5 | The Cradle Will Fall | £6.99 |
| 978-0-7434-8437-4 | A Stranger Is Watching | £6.99 |
| 978-0-7434-8438-1 | Where Are the Children? | £6.99 |

Please send cheque or postal order for the value of the book,
free postage and packing within the UK, to
SIMON & SCHUSTER CASH SALES
PO Box 29, Douglas Isle of Man, IM99 1BQ
Tel: 01624 677237, Fax: 01624 670923
Email: bookshop@enterprise.net
www.bookpost.co.uk

Please allow 14 days for delivery. Prices and availability
subject to change without notice